If I am, then death is not; if death is, then I am not.

—Epicurus

Books by Mary Lawrence

THE ALCHEMIST'S DAUGHTER

DEATH OF AN ALCHEMIST

Published by Kensington Publishing Corporation

Death of an Alchemist

MARY LAWRENCE

KENSINGTON BOOKS

www.kensingtonbooks.com

In fond remembrance of Claire McNeely and Hobbes

CHAPTER 1

London, summer of 1543

It was not the plague. The neighbor had been wrong.

The physician wiped his lancet on the bedding and returned the instrument to a leather wallet, folding the hide along familiar creases worn from use. He had bled the man, cutting the median cubital vein in his right arm to entice the bloodworms and hasten their attachment. Now they wallowed in a shallow dish, their thirst sated.

Given the condition in which he'd found the fellow, he doubted the leeches would be of benefit. But the physician suffered from a plague of convention. He rarely strayed from accepted protocol.

The effort was futile. The man died anyway.

Moments before, the victim's delirium, his tortured struggle, filled the room with life. Now life was diminished to the buzz of lowly flies settling on eyes that no longer blinked.

In his desire to help, the doctor had concentrated solely on his patient. He was alone with his medical satchel and his wits. Children's voices, a door slamming, the shrill whistle of a vendor—

the world he had left behind—now demanded his attention, as if shaking him from a dream.

His duty unfinished, he went to the door and found the neighbor waiting outside, turning his worn cap between grubby fingers.

"Summon the coroner," said the physician. He spat a wad of masticated angelica root into the road. The herb left his mouth tingling with warmth, but he no longer needed its protection. Retreating inside, he closed the door with a definitive click.

He leaned against the flimsy slats of wood, ignoring the titters of meddlesome neighbors trying to peek through the chamber's high window. Let them gawk, thought the doctor. They shall see an old man supine on sodden linens, his body withered from age. An individual no longer seeking his nightly rest, but, unwillingly, committed to the eternal one.

With the emotional charge of need over, the physician saw the rent in all its sad detail. It was almost completely empty of furniture and possessions, but for one wooden bowl and cup on a table. A moldering loaf of bread and a candle lay nearby. The walls showed lines of cracks and missing chunks of plaster; a dirt floor made the room dank and cheerless. Underfoot, the rushes reeked of mildew and cat urine.

The effect was a tedious room, void of color and stimulation. No spark of life warmed the austere interior. How might anyone endure living in circumstances so dismal? As the physician pondered, a sound, most like a raven, issued from a corner. He spied movement in its shadowy recess and moved closer for a better look.

What had first escaped his notice now caught his eye like the last rose of October. A tree branch rested in the corner, and sidestepping along its length was a magnificent macaw. Its breast was a brilliant red, the wings a rainbow of scarlet, yellow, verdant green and wodebroun blue. Where had this pauper acquired such a creature? He was penniless, yet he possessed this exotical bird.

The doctor went to the macaw, which was extending its line of tether to pluck a walnut from a small dish. The bird maneuvered the nut with its talon and cracked it with an intimidating beak. A black tongue separated the meat from the shell, working the seed toward its mouth. Having accomplished this, the bird turned its head—and a pale eye—upon him.

Intrigued, the physician studied the bird's behavior. The fowl bobbed and squawked as if to entertain. When its clattering grew tiresome, the doctor returned to a stool next to the corpse and sat.

Neighbors speculated loudly outside the rent, prompting him to reflect upon his findings. Was this the sweating sickness making an unwelcome return? Murmurings of sudden deaths spread as noxiously as the disease itself. Fevers and headaches, the unexpected onset, the inability to catch air, all were hallmarks of *sudor anglicus*. But he had seen other maladies with similar symptoms. Even a few souls dying of fever, which the physician knew was not unique to the sweat, set tongues to wagging. Perhaps fear contributed to the spread of disease—the distress producing a self-fulfilling prophecy.

Merry at supper, dead before dawn. He had seen it happen.

Sweating sickness was aptly named. The afflicted suffered a great perspiration and stinking, their faces and bodies flushed. The humours were unbalanced from too much blood, causing a mantling of the skin. Heads ached. Victims went mad as their hearts became passionate with rapid beat. The heat of fever caused an unquenchable thirst, and perspiration bounced on their skin like beads of oil on a hot griddle. If the sufferers were submerged in a bath of water, the doctor wondered, would it cool them like rain on a scorching summer day? But he never had the chance to try such a treatment. By the time he arrived, the end was too near.

However, the physician was not certain *this* patient had died of the dread disease. The man had suffered from delirium and fever but had not exhibited a tightening of the chest. His body flushed, yet there was something more. Blood seeped from the man's eyes and nose. Had the man's putrid humours sought escape by any means possible?

In his hurry to attach the bloodworms, he had not bothered to check the contents of the chamber pot. He now searched for the jordan and found it on the opposite side of the bed.

Swirling the murky urine, the doctor sniffed. Nothing extraordinary. There was neither vomit nor tarry stool. Since death had occurred, he declined a taste. He set the pot under the bed, leaving it for the landlord to dump, and returned to the bedside.

The practitioner thought about his findings. Bleeding the man had not served. By what other means might such foul humours be relieved?

With a sudden stir, the door flew open. It smacked against the wall, startling the physician from his contemplation. The parrot flapped its wings, excited. In stepped a creature amid a shower of plaster. He wore a mask with a prominent beak rivaling that of the macaw. But this creature was a coroner, an exotical bird in his own right. His long bistre robe reached the floor and the doctor imagined how disagreeably stifling such garb must feel on this warm August day.

Loath to remove the mask stuffed full of rue and bergamot, the coroner blinked behind his protection. He brushed the dust off his shoulders with a gloved hand, ignoring the powder settling on his cap.

"It is not the plague," said the physician. "You may remove your mask."

"I shall be the judge of that," remarked the coroner, his voice sounding tinny within. He turned his head this way and that, attempting to evaluate his surroundings, the mask being an obvious hindrance.

"There are no buboes marring his skin," said the doctor. He reached over and lifted a wrist, showing the coroner the dead man's hand. "No black discoloration of the digits."

The coroner crossed the room, his wool robe sweeping the floor and dragging clumps of rush behind him. He approached the body, pushed the mask against his face, and studied the corpse at close quarters, running his eyes along its entire length. He appeared something of a perversion, his long bird beak grazing the body as though sniffing it. Satisfied by the absence of swellings, the coroner removed his gloves and tucked them under his robe; however, the mask remained on his face. Apparently he had an aversion to the smell of anything except his combination of herbs.

"In your opinion," said the coroner, "of what did the man die?"

"I cannot say. I have considered the sweat, but his symptoms were not typical."

"Was there a fever and a great stinking?"

"He had a fever, aye, but I cannot say his sweat was putrid." The doctor shook his head. "Obviously the man had not the means to sweeten his skin with scented unguents. A natural odor accompanies all men of his age. But nay, it was not the expected nidorous smell of the sweat."

The coroner stared from behind his rigid white façade. The physician saw only brown eyes peering back at him. As to what opinion the official had formed, he remained ignorant. The macaw squawked, drawing the coroner's notice.

"What is that extraordinary creature?"

"I believe they are called macaws. I once saw one at market."

Fascinated, the coroner walked over to the bird. Immediately, the creature began to bob its head and flutter its wings.

"What is it doing?"

"I do not know, sir. Perhaps it thinks you are a kindred spirit."

The coroner hesitated, considering the bird and the physician's comment. After a moment he strode back to the corpse and addressed the doctor.

"I shall pronounce him dead of fever," he announced, waving his hand in dismissal. "Do not speak of the sweat. To do so might cause undue alarm. It may very well be *sudor anglicus,* but until an epidemic confirms my suspicions, I will not venture an opinion."

The coroner turned away, intending to leave, so the physician refrained from engaging him in a discussion of his findings. He reminded himself that men of authority were more concerned with signing documents and arranging the removal of bodies than with discussing academics. He had just conceded it was better to leave such men to matters of administration when a glum voice spoke from the door.

"I come for the body." A shadow fell across the floor as a collector stood in the entry, blocking the sunlight. Dirt and sweat coated his jerkin and his face, the grime an indication of his business. He held a pail of red paint in one hand and a brush in the other.

"Ah," said the coroner, motioning him inside. "I admire expeditious handling of one's office." He turned to the physician. "What was the name of the deceased? I shall fill out the register later."

Weary, the doctor stood and moved the stool away from the bed. "I do not recall the victim's name. Perhaps someone outside might know."

The coroner dipped his head in a cursory bow and strode toward the door, his gait so smooth and purposeful he seemed to float over the floor, save for the reeds gathering along his hem. Before sidling past the collector, he lifted his robe, dislodging the clump of rushes. "It is not the plague," he said, loud enough for the loitering crowd to overhear. "You will not need to mark this door with paint."

The bearer ducked his head under a low ceiling beam and lumbered into the rent. Looking about, he set the pot of paint against a wall. He straightened, his brawn seeming to fill the space, making it even smaller.

Standing aside, the physician watched the collector remove the blankets and place them in a pile next to the paint. They would be burned later. A black tiger cat emerged from under the bed to sniff the discarded wool. It lingered over the heap of blankets, opening its mouth to run the smells over its tongue. Satisfied, it slipped out of sight again.

There was no joy in carting off the dead. The bearer's expression mirrored his dull acceptance of duty. Men such as he were doomed to a short life. The risks of their chore ensured it. They slept in shacks in the graveyards, comingling with sextons and gravediggers. Feared for the possible infections they might carry, they lived lonely lives, shunned by the very people who depended on them.

"If you would shroud the body," said the physician.

The collector undertook the directive without comment. He balanced the body on its side, holding one end of the sheet against the chest, and began to roll, swaddling the deceased.

Distracted, the physician watched the bundle take on the appearance of a cocoon. He was frustrated over his inability to diagnose the disease, and the coroner's lack of concern further drained and aggravated him. He was envisioning a good night's sleep when a man cleared his throat at the door. "What is it?" he called, looking over.

"Did the coroner say what got him? He said it wasn't the Black Death," said the neighbor hugging the doorjamb, keeping his distance. "Was it the sweat?"

"It is not certain. I would not tell others that it is the disease. It may not be."

"I heard of another stricken suddenly on Distaff Lane. Took ill after his dinner prayer and was gone before the curfew bells tolled. 'Tis a cruel malady with no mercy."

"This man may not have died of sweating sickness," repeated the physician.

"Then what is it he died of?"

"I have seen much," said the physician, turning to face him, "but I cannot say I have seen symptoms such as these."

The neighbor's voice rose in distress. "Like whats?"

The doctor gathered his instruments, placing them carefully in his satchel. Engaging this philistine in a discussion of medical findings would be ludicrous. "It is you who summoned me. What first gave you pause?"

"I know Walter as well as my wife's face. He was an old man, but not so old that he didn't have more time in him. He had his habits, and every morning as the cock crew he toted his water urns to the conduits. This morning I did not see him. I came knocking. When he did not answer I grew worried and forced open the door. He was as you found him, sir, delirious and raging with fever. He must have broken his nose from thrashing. A lot of blood."

"Has he family?"

"None I know. He never spoke of any. He was a lonely man with just his cat and bird for companionship."

The feline had been circling the side table and jumped up to sniff the dish of leeches. It gingerly pawed one of the swollen *hirudos*. Spurred by its slight movement, the cat snatched it out of the dish and bit it in half.

"Have you a need for a cat? Perhaps for mice?" asked the physician, watching it chew. The cat ignored the remaining leeches in the bowl.

"Nay, sir, me wife thinks them evil. Just let it fend for itself; it seems a good hunter."

The bearer finished winding the man in the bedsheet and tucked in the ends. "I am done here, sir. If you could take the feet?"

The physician looked to the neighbor for assistance and saw the back side of him leaving. He sighed, taking up the patient's legs and lifting with the collector to remove the body. It wasn't the first time he had been left to move a corpse. Perhaps because he did not balk at such humble tasks, God saw fit to preserve him to tend another ailing wretch in the future.

As they emerged from the rent, the gathering of onlookers—with cloths pressed to their noses—stepped back, giving them room. Not everyone thought to wrap the unfortunate, and it bothered the physician to see the dead unswaddled, heaped one atop the other in the cart, some in late-stage rigor mortis and decomposition. The physician held his breath, and though blackened arms and legs were askew and seemed alive with maggots, he did not think on what he saw. They laid the body atop the others, disturbing a swarm of flies.

He crossed himself and returned to the stoop. Across the way, a few neighbors peeked from doors and windows. Pedestrians gave wide berth to the bearer, hurrying past and averting their eyes.

By now, thought the doctor, he should be used to death. Shouldn't some immunity, or rather, some sense of monotony, come with this practice?

But he was a rare doctor who always did as much as he could, with no thought to his patient's station in life. He attended the sick even if he knew he would not be paid. Even if he knew he might be placing himself in the midst of contagion. He never refused a person in need. He still possessed the one quality that other physicians eventually lost with time—compassion.

The bearer retrieved the paint pot and wedged it against the bodies. He took up the handles and the doctor watched him push the cart down the lane until he turned the corner. Another day, another dead. The doctor went back inside to collect his satchel.

Surely there must be something he could take in payment for his trouble. He worked a half-burned taper from a wall sconce and took the candle on the table. Two water urns sat against a wall, but he had no need for the bulky vessels. Looking about for any cheese or fruit, he realized that the patient, Walter, hadn't even a crumb to eat. As he took up the bowl of leeches to throw into the lane, the rustling of wings reminded him of the bird in the corner. Perhaps the landlord might sell it for profit. He had no interest in the fowl, though he did admire its colorful plumage. With the bowl in hand, he picked up his bag and started for the door.

But his inability to save Walter bothered him. Unable to prevent his death, he had failed to deliver even a mote of comfort to his patient. Did he not owe this tormented soul some measure of rest, some compensation for his failure?

He dumped the leeches in the lane and, turning to pull the door shut, hesitated. The cat and the macaw must have been a comfort to the old man. It would be cruel to leave them to starve. At the very least they might make interesting companions.

The physician set down his medical bag and crossed the room

to the bird. He untied its tether, urging the macaw onto his shoulder. The bird flapped its wings, settling on its new perch. Pleased, the doctor wrapped the leather strap around his wrist.

Tucking the cat under his arm, the physician collected his satchel and headed home.

For the first time in his life, the physician strayed from accepted convention.

CHAPTER 2

Two weeks later . . .

In the bowels of a dank hovel off Ivy Lane, an alchemist marveled at the brilliant white elixir glowing in the bottom of a vessel. The albification marked months of work. After ten stages of chemical process, here was his reward. The white elixir brought him within grasp of projecting the philosopher's stone—a substance capable of transmuting base metals into gold.

But projecting gold was not his desire.

Ferris Stannum had spent years perfecting the process that led him to this moment. He held the flask up to the light streaming through his one window. The elixir was a most beautiful and satisfying sight. If he wanted, he could continue the sublimation and use the resultant "white stone" to transmute any base metal into silver.

But even that was not his desire.

It would be prudent to set a portion aside to pay off his debts. First he would pay his back rent to the widowed Mrs. Tenbrook, whose sour expression grew more rancid every time he saw her.

He longed for her to cease pounding upon his door every day at noon. The bells of St. Paul's called the pious to prayer, but for Mrs. Tenbrook, they reminded her to harass his door.

There were others who would appreciate his financial attention. He owed money for equipment and ingredients. He owed money at market. He owed money . . . but for the moment, Stannum basked in a rarified light of possibilities instead of the harsh beacon of responsibilities. And why not?

The elixir was the culmination of weeks of maintaining a brood warmth in the calcinatory furnace. Every night he woke at regular intervals to add a goose egg–sized lump of charcoal to the fire and adjust the air vents. Eventually, the black head of the crow, the *caput corvi*, yielded to the changing colors of the peacock's tail. Over the course of weeks, the brew grew lighter in color and more iridescent, until finally, the brilliant white elixir emerged. The elixir he now held in his hand.

Incredibly, he had avoided a mishap in the early stages with the philosophical egg, a propitious event in itself. The bulbous glass vessel possessed a belly for giving birth and a tapered neck that he carefully sealed to prevent escape of precious volatiles— the sighs of angels. If a heat was too intense, the vessel would shatter or, worse, explode. The pile of broken glass in the corner attested to years of failed attempts. Now his technique was at its most perfect.

If he wanted, he could incubate this elixir until it turned yellow, then darkened to scarlet. At that point he could break open the flask and ferment the stone with a speck of real gold, priming it for the final projection. While many alchemists strove to project the philosopher's stone, Ferris Stannum stopped shy of projecting even the lesser white one.

Besides, the tenth and eleventh gates were fraught with obstacles. And now in his feeble health and old age, he hadn't the patience for endless days of watching a stone sublimate over and over. Especially when so much could go wrong.

If silver were a noble metal, then should it not possess gifts of its own? He thought of silver as the queen, the feminine counterpart to her masculine partner, gold. Besides, a woman's nature is to bestow life. Within her womb grew the secrets of the cosmos. It seemed natural to conclude that within her realm lay the desire for life and creation. Why, then, did alchemists believe "king gold" held ultimate power?

"Because gold is the father of perfection," he said aloud. "Nay, I am not so convinced," he told the parrot watching him from its roost near the still warm furnace. "Gold is masculine and with male comes submission. Destruction. Tell me where I fault," said Stannum, shaking his head. "It is faith in the perfection of gold that has thwarted others. They have forgotten what kindness there is in noble silver." He swirled the flask of liquid, its color luminous like the mantle of a polished shell.

The parrot ticked its head as if it, too, pondered such differences. Ferris Stannum withdrew a sweetmeat from his pocket and held the morsel out for the bird. "I would want a woman; however, animals are a better lenitive for an old man's broken heart." Stannum looked fondly on his bird and ailing cat. He'd already grown too attached to them. It grieved him to see the black tiger in failing health.

At first, the cat had been full of life and mischief, investigating every crevice in the alchemist's room, knocking bowls of minerals off the shelves. However, the cat had earned its keep in the number of mice it killed and in the affection it had shown the old man. Ferris Stannum had never thought to keep animals, but when Barnabas Hughes suggested they might amuse him, he agreed to take them until the physician could find them a suitable home. Now he was as dependent on them as they were on him.

"Aw, fellow," he said, gently stroking the cat. The sick creature barely lifted its head. "Our time grows short." He set the flask down and drew a stool next to it. "Blessed be," he whispered in its ear. "I shall not watch you suffer." Lifting the cat into his lap, he cradled it close to his heart. "Blessed be. Blessed be."

The old alchemist took the flask of elixir and, holding the cat's mouth open, poured the fluid down its throat. He whispered and kissed its ear.

The cat did not struggle. It hadn't the strength to fight. It accepted its master's will. It would not question.

Across the river Thames, an experiment of a different kind had reached a disappointing end.

"I'll not stay a moment longer." John gathered his wheaten hair into a tail that lay between his shoulder blades. He whisked his hose off a chair. "Appalling is far too soft a word," he said, balancing on one foot as he stepped into a leg.

"It should come as no surprise," said Bianca, searching for a pair of tongs. She moved purposely, mindful not to escalate John's temper. She, too, had reached *her* limit.

"All this and to no purpose. It has been an epic waste of time. A stinking failure worse than a bucket of rotten eggs." John stalked to the door and threw it open.

"It is no worse than living in a barrel behind the Tern's Tempest. Remember your humble beginnings?" Bianca gripped the flask's neck with the tongs and pushed past her husband, who was standing on the threshold. She walked to the drainage ditch and poured out the contents.

"You will kill every carp in the Thames if it makes it there."

"All the better," said Bianca. "I've never liked carp."

"But others do," said John, trying to snatch her by the waist. Bianca skirted past.

"Why are you so resistant?" John followed her back inside, unable to let the matter drop. "It would be better for both of us if we moved to a place that had more windows. Even one more window would be an improvement. You could crack it open and let some of these vapors escape so it wouldn't be so overwhelming."

"The air is not as foul as you say." Bianca removed the bain-marie from the furnace and closed the damper.

"You're immune to it," said John. "Between your father's alchemy and your mother's herbal remedies, your sense of smell is ruined. You don't seem to notice how rank it is."

On the contrary, Bianca's sense of smell was so acute, she could pick out individual scents and name them from nearly any combination of herbs. Her ability extended even to the strange amalgamations alchemists conjured. What she was able to do, and what John could not, was ignore less than pleasing odors—for the most part.

John buttoned his shirt, still standing near the door. "Besides, we hardly get a breeze in here. What little we get either smells of chicken manure or the river. There is a reason this area is called Gull Hole."

"We can afford living here. Until you finish your apprenticeship it makes little sense to move."

"We could move into London," said John. "It would be closer to Boisvert's and . . . your parents."

Bianca tossed the iron tongs onto the table, rattling the crockery. "Thank you, but I shall keep my distance."

More than a year had passed and Bianca still had not mended her relationship with her father. At sixteen, she had uncovered his dangerous liaison with Sir George Howard, member of King Henry's privy chamber and older brother of the now beheaded Catherine Howard. Sir George had witnessed Albern Goddard's humiliation and expulsion as a favored alchemist to the king. Granted, Goddard's favored status was short-lived, but when a younger, more cunning alchemist replaced him and he lost his royal stipend, Albern Goddard grew indignant. Sir George capitalized on her father's bruised ego and easily enlisted his help to prevent Catherine's ruin. The whole convoluted imbroglio resulted in his being accused of trying to poison the king, which resulted in Bianca risking her life to prove his innocence. For that not so small gesture, Albern Goddard had dismissed her bravery as simply a daughter's duty. He had resumed his life with nary another thought about it. Furthermore, Bianca's marriage to John had met with an icy reception.

A few months ago, John and Bianca had signed a marriage bond, swearing that there were no precontracts preventing them from matrimony. John had no living relatives that he knew of, except a brother he rarely saw. Because she was the daughter of an alchemist, there was no money for a dowry and, in Bianca's mind, no reason for her parents to have a say in the matter one way or the other.

The two had waited for a warm spring day when the field beyond the Paris Garden Manor was blooming with white clover. Bianca had washed her finest, a pale blue linen kirtle with a rust stain she could not remove. Meddybemps, their streetseller friend, had given her a new apron embroidered with flowers that acceptably covered the blotch. The morning of, she had picked violets and tucked them into her wavy hair, which hung loose, as was the tradition and a sign of purity.

John had worn a thin wool jerkin the color of a baked biscuit, with deep cream hose and a dashing flat cap of scarlet damask. Bianca wondered from where he'd gotten the hat, but decided that was a discussion to have another day. His hair was pulled into a tail and he had shaved and slapped his cheeks with rose water.

Meddybemps arrived outside her door and emptied his pushcart of talismans and salves, affording Bianca and John room to sit. He steered them through the streets of Southwark, to the occasional shouts of well wishes from passersby. Indeed they were a peculiar sight, all of them grinning as if they'd lost their good sense.

At the field, John leapt from the cart and lifted Bianca into the air over his head, whirling around twice before setting her down. When they had all stopped teasing one another, Meddybemps held up the blue satin ribbon that would bind their hands and their promise.

Bianca vowed her love solemnly, as did John. They had come to an agreement, while perhaps unconventional, that she would not be considered his property. She would give his opinion the respect of an equal and she expected due consideration in return. They were friends first, and as such, John saw her as his partner, cherishing and promising to preserve her happiness no more and no less than his own.

There would be times of discord; Bianca expected that. John conceded to let her work her chemistries unfettered, though he couldn't resist complaining when she completely ignored him.

But John could not imagine life without her. They had come to depend on each other. True, she was the daughter of a man consumed with the dark art. And she had inherited his single-minded focus. It was John's hope that in time, she might lose some of her passion for medicinals and learn, instead, to cook a decent meal.

John knew her history and circumstances, but he never shied from needling Bianca about her parents. He'd never known his own father, and he thought anyone with the good fortune to have one should do what they could to reconcile their differences. In that regard, Bianca thought John naïve.

On his urging, Bianca had visited her parents afterward and told them of her marriage to John. Her mother had been surprised but embraced Bianca in a rare show of affection.

"You could have done worse," she said, when she heard it was John. "He's a good enough lad." She leaned in close. "I suppose you married for love?" She pulled back to look in Bianca's eyes, then whispered in her ear, "Be careful, that."

Her father had said not a word. Bianca had expected a sharp rebuke, a comment to the effect that she had displeased him by not waiting for an arrangement that could have benefited the family. But she had risked much to save him and because of this, he realized, though he would never admit it openly, that he must forfeit that claim on her.

Bianca took apart the alembic and peered into the beak-shaped head. Perhaps some sort of debris or leftover precipitate had contaminated her sample. She wrapped a strip of linen around a rod and swabbed out the inside. It had not been the first time her experiment had failed.

This was her fifteenth attempt at sublimation. Her father used sublimation to purify dross. All alchemists knew the process was a vital step in projecting the philosopher's stone. "Raise up the Son of God from the earth into the air and ascend thee upon the cross in purity," her father would often say. "A body must be made spiritual. Its soul must be separated from its filthy original. Then it shall become clean."

While Bianca did not embrace all of alchemy's theories, she did find some usefulness in its methods. If sublimation worked correctly, she could place ground material in the base of a cucurbit, place an alembic on top, and seal the juncture. When the device was heated, a purified sediment would collect in the upper vessel, which she could scrape off after it cooled. The sediment often took the form of crystals that she used in her medicinals, the most recent of which she hoped would cure the sweat.

Perhaps there had been too little heat, or perhaps contamination had prevented the growth of crystals. She simply could not get the material to sublimate. Several times she opened the vessel and found either a slimy residue or nothing at all. She had adjusted the heat, tried different retorts, obtained her base material from a different source. All to no avail. And this last attempt had resulted in a noxious smell of rotten eggs, to which John was now reacting.

"If we moved for no other reason than to escape the possibility of contracting the sweating sickness, then we should do it."

"John, there is no proof that living near the river makes us more susceptible."

"Except I have heard that it has taken three on Bermondsey Street in the last week."

"Unless you know by your own eyes, then do not trust a rumor."

"Usually there is a hint of truth in these stories." John ladled a cup of steaming rainwater from the top of a furnace and sprinkled in mint and dried orange rind. He prepared a second cup for Bianca. "If I should pay no mind to hearsay, then why are you intent on making a palliative for the disease?"

Bianca accepted the cup and blew on it before taking a sip. "Because it is that time of year. And Meddybemps has asked me to work on one."

"Ha! So you see he must have had inquiries." John arched an eyebrow at Bianca. "And so you chide me for giving an ear to chatter on the street."

"Meddybemps sees more than you do pent up at Boisvert's forge all day. He moves from market to market and covers more ground in a day than either of us do in a week."

John finished his tea and set the cup on the table crowded with bowls of ground minerals and minced herbs. He wondered how much of Bianca's medicinals he inadvertently ingested since their dinner plates and bowls sat on the same table as her ingredients. Organization was not Bianca's strong point.

"I need to be on my way," he announced, "before my clothes become saturated with stink. Boisvert will have something to say about the smell. He never fails to remind me that we Anglais are an uncivil, malodorous lot."

John cleared a space on the bench to put on his shoes. Pulling one on, he looked around for its mate. It couldn't be far. It could not walk on its own. Besides, he never removed one, then walked around before taking the other off. "Have you seen my shoe?"

Bianca gazed at the interior of their rent. The rush was in need of replacing with fresh, sweet-smelling reed. Broken crockery piled in a corner and a disarray of pans and spilled ingredients covered the board. A calcinatory furnace awkwardly sat in the center of the room, consuming a large portion of floor space. She had recently vented its belching smoke outside—but not very effectively. Apart from herbs dangling from the rafters, her room looked discouragingly like her father's room of alchemy. Perhaps his fixation had now become hers.

"Bianca, have you seen my shoe?"

Bianca startled from this disconcerting realization. "Shoe?" she repeated, as if remembering what one was. Bianca thought a moment. She brushed her tangle of wavy hair away from her eyes. Next to the calcinating furnace she found its remnants.

"What did you do?" exclaimed John, staring at what used to be his left shoe. Only the heel remained.

"I needed some leather to wrap around the juncture of my alembic. It was releasing volatiles."

"So you sliced up my shoe?"

"I can stitch it back together."

"Nay, I don't believe you can." John snatched away the pitiful remnant and strip of burned leather.

"Am I interrupting?" said Meddybemps, ducking under the door lintel and parting the curtain of hanging herbs. The dried stems often caught on his cap and pulled it off.

"Not soon enough," grumbled John. He pushed past the street-seller, who noted his single bare foot. Meddybemps looked at Bianca, puzzled.

"Shall I tell him he is wearing only one shoe?"

"He's well aware." Bianca finished her cup of tea.

Meddybemps caught a whiff of the unpleasant remainder of a failed concoction. He considered mentioning the odor, then thought she probably knew. Likely it was the source of John's irritability. Cautiously, he took a few more steps into the room, worried the smell might make him retch.

"I've sold a number of your dried poultices and balms for the itch of fleas and rash. The heat suits insects and oily plants. No one needs expectorants for phlegmatic illness right now." Meddybemps deposited a sack of coins in Bianca's palm.

"I'd better put this in a safe place," said Bianca.

Meddybemps glanced around, wondering where that might be. The appearance of her room always gave him the impression of danger. He never knew whether a fire in her furnace might flare out of control and burn the place down, or whether he would show up one day to find Bianca and John dead from inhaling so much smoke.

But Bianca was a gifted chemiste and her burgeoning reputation had benefited him well. He sold her balms and medicines at market and they split the profit. In fact, her medicinals sold better than his talismans and trinkets. He didn't mind because he was becoming known for carrying her remedies and people sought him out. If he could convince a fretful wife to part with another penny to buy an amulet for added assurance, then all the better.

Meddybemps removed his red cap and smoothed back his thinning hair. "So what, pray tell, is John in a tiff about now?"

"He wants us to move. He says it is too stifling here and too close to the Thames."

"I agree it *is* warm in here. And, well, the smell . . ."

"I just finished a process; I had a fire going." Bianca nodded toward the furnace and its dying embers. "John worries the sweat has returned and he believes the sickness occurs more frequently near water."

"He may be right. There is a growing demand for a remedy or preventative for the disease."

"Have you heard of the sweat's return?"

"I have, but I know how you dislike rumors." Meddybemps sat on her bench and his eyes started to burn, probably from a caustic ingredient on the table. He stood and moved closer to the open door.

"So have you seen evidence of an outbreak?"

"A few instances have sprung up. The disease seems to appear during the warming days of summer. Odd thing, that."

Bianca turned a retort upside down, emptying a bluish powder on the floor.

"Any progress creating the next miracle?" Meddybemps's errant eye quivered with anticipation. His eyes never moved in a coordinated effort. This was a disconcerting if not alarming quirk to those used to meeting a focused gaze.

"Phht. I am stalled. I cannot sublimate this dross. Volatiles escape the junctures."

"Flummoxed by flux?" Meddybemps's eye skipped with delight.

"For cert. Nothing I try is of any use. I am at a loss."

"Perhaps I might offer a suggestion. Why not seek the advice of an alchemist?"

Bianca bristled at the thought. "I can find my own answers." In her mind, asking an alchemist was tantamount to asking a

Frenchman to explain the meaning of life. One was sure to hear lots of flowery language amounting to nothing of purpose.

Meddybemps held up his hand, hoping to prevent her from launching into a well-practiced rant. "Spare your breath, my prodigy. I've heard your arguments before. I am speaking of an alchemist I know who is as old as the earth and keeps his quackery to a minimum. He is a kindly yet irascible puffer, practiced and often willing to share his techniques with those he deems worthy. Of course, no alchemist fully divulges all his secrets."

"How do you know him?"

"My dear, one cannot live as long as I have and tread these streets through every ward without hearing or seeing something of what goes on behind closed doors." Meddybemps helped himself to a fig, being careful to wipe it on his thin linen shirt first. "I can tell you where to find Ferris Stannum. I'm sure you can charm some answers out of him."

CHAPTER 3

Bianca had no difficulty finding the alchemist off Ivy Lane. She simply followed her nose past the smell of freshly baked bread to an aroma far less comforting. All alchemists were secretive, and that extended to where they worked their science. No puffer ever hung a sign announcing his vocation; to do so was inviting mischief. An alchemist's goal was to project gold. What thief could ignore such a lure? Even destitute puffers kept stores of silver or crystals of value for their projections.

The odor beckoned. Bianca followed it past wood-frame buildings with upper stories leaning over the street, threatening to topple onto the road below. A lack of sunlight cast the neighborhood into a shadowed assembly, unable to cheer anyone strolling down the lane and certainly incapable of lifting the hearts of the unfortunate few who lived there.

On this day, Mrs. Tenbrook spied her tenant rattling open his door and caught him before he could close it in her face. She hunted him like a ferret after a rat. She hounded his every step, dispensed threats, and cast a disparaging eye on the ruined interior of his quarters—her property.

"You owe me more than four months' rent. I've not the patience to wait a day longer. A woman's got to eat and pay her way if she has no one to do it for her. I've a mind to call the ward and have ye thrown in debtors' prison."

"Goodwife Tenbrook, save your wind for another battle. I have made a great discovery. Better you give me a little more time because once I reap boundless rewards, I shall repay you tenfold."

"Spoken like the charlatan ye are. By troth I never should have allowed ye here if I'd known. The smells I can barely abide, the excuses every month. It is only this talisman that has prevented the entire place from burning to the ground." The landlady held up a cross with a center stone as red as her face and waggled it.

"Mrs. Tenbrook," said the alchemist, procuring his journal and displaying it proudly. "I will be sending my work for validation, and once it is found solid, neither you nor I shall ever have reason for unkind words again. I do not forget those who have given me their trust."

"Trust? Ha! Ye mistake my tolerance for favor. I assure you that is not my intent."

Bianca arrived in time to hear every word. She hovered, unnoticed, just outside the door. Indeed, this was a room of alchemy. Whether it was Ferris Stannum's room, she was not sure. Always curious to know a person's particular circumstance before they should know hers, she was careful to avoid their notice.

"Leave me, woman," said the alchemist, his temper flaring. "I've matters to attend. You are wasting my time. I swear you shall have your money soon enough."

From her vantage point, Bianca could see the old man trembling with rage. He looked as old as Methuselah and seemed not to have trimmed his beard in about as long. It nearly touched his knees. Perhaps if he were less stooped his whiskers might just reach his stomach. Bianca wondered how he had managed to avoid catching the monstrosity on fire. Perhaps he was as expert as Meddybemps said.

"Thunder on, old man. But I shall not cease pestering ye until I have every last coin. And I shall have it. Do not doubt." For her part, Mrs. Tenbrook looked equally distressed. A shower of spittle rained from her mouth and the midday heat did not favor her complexion. The two adversaries flushed like currants near to bursting.

"By your standards, half of England would be in debtors' prison."

A sudden piercing squawk followed by a scream startled Bianca. She had never heard such a noise. The screech was somewhat human in quality and alarmingly strange. She peeked around the door.

"Leave off my bird!" said the alchemist, rushing to stand between the woman and a crimson-colored parrot. "Trouble me all you want, but give my poor creature its peace. You have no reason to bother it."

"It bit me, ye fool!" said the landlady, holding her finger. A trickle of blood coursed down the crooked appendage. "If you do not get rid of it, I'll wring its neck and have it for dinner." She raised a hand to strike the bird, but the alchemist seized her wrist.

"Fie, ye vulgar old man!" she shouted, delivering an elbow to his ribs. "Remove your filthy self from my person! And silence that confounded bird!" She found a jar and cocked her arm to hurl it at the flapping parrot but was stopped by Bianca's shout.

The alchemist and landlady started. Mrs. Tenbrook squinted at Bianca standing inside the door. She lowered her arm. "And who might you be?"

Bianca dipped in a brief curtsy. "My name is Bianca Goddard. I am looking for Ferris Stannum."

Mrs. Tenbrook raked her eyes over Bianca and, once she'd sufficiently conveyed her disapproval at being interrupted, pointed her chin toward the alchemist. "You've found 'im. Lucky ye came today." She set the jar on the table with a thud. "Because he may not be here tomorrow."

Ferris Stannum massaged his sore ribs. "It will take you longer than a day to find a ward who will even care. They've no interest in a mewling landlady." He dug into his pocket for a treat to feed his parrot.

"Mock me not, old man," said Mrs. Tenbrook. She stormed past, shouldering Bianca aside, and stomped up the stairs to her quarters. A door creaked open, then slammed, rattling the walls of Stannum's rent.

Indifferent to his landlady's threat, the alchemist lavished attention on his bird. In soothing tones, he reassured the parrot until it calmed. He leaned toward the bird and it rubbed its head on his cheek. A moment passed before the old man turned to face her.

"Do I know you?" he asked.

"You do not. I create salves and medicinals in Southwark."

"Did you say your name was Goddard?" A look of suspicion clouded his face. "It is a name of shady reputation." He took a step in her direction and looked into her eyes. "Are you related to Albern Goddard?"

Bianca hesitated admitting it. However, it was better to be honest than mimic her father's example by lying. "I am his daughter."

"You resemble him."

"Only in appearance," said Bianca, defensively.

Ferris Stannum did not respond. He stroked his parrot and fed it another sweetmeat. "Tell me, what brings Albern Goddard's daughter to my room of alchemy?"

"I have been told you are one of the finest alchemists in London."

Stannum snorted. "You are mistaken."

Puzzled, Bianca looked around at the obvious accoutrements of the noble art.

"I am *the* finest alchemist in all of *England*."

A black tiger cat appeared from behind a congelating furnace and brushed against Ferris Stannum's calves. It stretched, reaching its front paws up the old man's leg, snagging his hose. Ferris Stannum patted its head.

"Are you here on behalf of your father?"

"My father and I have not spoken in a while. Meddybemps, a streetseller, my streetseller and friend," she added, "told me of your accomplishments. He suggested I seek your help."

"Help? What can an old man offer a young woman?"

"As I said, I make physickes and medicinals. I combine what I know of herbs with methods used in alchemy."

Ferris Stannum picked up the cat and scratched behind its ears. "To whose philosophy do you ascribe? Galen or Paracelsus?"

"There is some truth to both. However, I am less inclined to Galen's philosophy."

"Why?" asked Stannum.

"Because it reflects my father's belief in alchemy, and I have seen nothing come from his following Galen's principles." Bianca sensed she had gotten Stannum's ear, so she continued. "Supposedly creation is composed of varying proportions of the four elements—air, water, earth, and fire. If one succeeds in altering the balance of a particular substance, then one shall succeed in projecting the philosopher's stone. Which, in a word, is perfection, is it not? By that argument, if people are composed of four humours mimicking the four elements, what happens if we alter *their* balance?" Bianca paused for effect. "They become ill, and illness is not perfection."

"However, illness is a natural process that brings man to his ultimate perfection."

"Meaning death?" Bianca shook her head. "Perhaps some might believe that is true. But I believe perfection in man is health, not death."

"But some argue that human perfection can only be achieved by dying," said Stannum, dabbing the corners of his eyes with a rag.

"Galen believes a physician must restore the balance of humours by applying proper medicines. I do believe illness is the result of an imbalance. But a human body is more than four arbitrarily assigned humours. It is bone and flesh and heart and lungs. Separate organs that must work together. Galen has no explanation for how the humours become unbalanced, only that they do. I believe there are forces that cause an imbalance and the imbalance can occur differently in each person. However, certain illnesses occur with similar symptoms. Ultimately, I want to learn why."

"Your ambitions are honorable." Ferris Stannum stuffed the cloth into his pocket. "Why bother with medicines if you seek answers in physiology?"

"What woman can enter that dark brotherhood and not be burned as a heretic?"

The old man set his cat on the floor so Bianca could not see him smile. The girl had certainly inherited the contrived arguments of her father.

"I want to change those forces of illness with my medicine." Bianca was not sure she had sufficiently explained herself. "I learned about plants from my mother. Granted, much is old-world knowledge, but it is in her blood. She is not always successful. In fact, much of her advice is folly. But she makes do with the plants she collects from the banks of the Thames. Plants have a secret language, and I seek to learn all that I can about them."

"But why use alchemy to concoct your medicinals?" asked Ferris Stannum.

"I use its methods to distill and purify my tinctures. I've found the purged extracts stronger and more effective."

"So you rely solely on plants."

"Nay, I have used cinnabar and salt. A few other minerals."

"And do you believe poisons can be made pure?" It was a basic question, but one that revealed much about an alchemist's belief system. Some alchemists believed that poisons could be separated into three primordial parts—mercury, sulfur, and salt. The residue that remained was worthless. But the newly acquired beneficial constituents could be purified and recombined to create a more powerful medicine, free from its previous toxic quality.

"I believe impurities can be removed and a tincture made stronger. But poison shall always remain so. Poisons cannot be undone. Their nature cannot be altered."

Bianca knew Stannum was testing her, but she refused to argue with an alchemist about alchemy. Instead, she remained firm in her beliefs, her knowledge based on observation.

"Then you do not subscribe to every idea Paracelsus has put forth."

"I do not. Poisons cannot be made harmless. But I've observed they can sometimes ameliorate a malady, if they are given in small doses. But their dosage must be carefully controlled."

Ferris Stannum knew her father's reputation and did not care to learn more about the unscrupulous character, but he was still a fount of knowledge. Stannum puzzled over why Bianca rejected his help. Perhaps it was, in part, due to a difference in opinion. Though Stannum carried a low opinion of the man, he *was* interested in the ignoble alchemist's line of investigation. He wondered if Albern Goddard, like most alchemists, believed the stone could be wrought only from minerals. So he asked.

"My father believes the stone can be made from anything. Vegetable, animal, mineral—familiar ingredients. Worthless to some, yet precious to others. Vile but beautiful," answered Bianca.

The old alchemist smiled at Albern Goddard's flawed premise. Stannum had invested years in his art and he thought of himself as having reached the pinnacle of his craft. His success was proof that his intentions were pure and his heart was honorable. Indeed, more honorable than that of any other alchemist in the realm. He straightened a little. He alone was worthy.

Ferris Stannum took a breath of this rarified air and considered the young woman standing before him. She was perceptive and thoughtful, if not a bit strange—what young woman bothers to think about Galen's theory? His own daughter would never do that.

"Tell me, Bianca Goddard," said Stannum, watching her intently. "What is it you wish to learn from me?"

Bianca explained her failed attempts. "The precipitate remains moist. It will not crystallize. Sometimes it may never collect at all."

"You must sublime through violent heat wherein your child will cling to the top of the alembic waiting to be made spiritual through heat both moist and temperate. It is not a process for an impatient young heart, for the spirit takes forty days to be reborn. And in those forty days, it is like a child in a womb. You must attend to it, without distraction, keeping the heat steady. If you falter, all is lost. But I have methods to accomplish this and in less time."

"Will you show me?"

Ferris Stannum's reticence softened. Bianca's humble quest was not a threat and, in fact, endeared her to him. His altruism bloomed and he did not mind dispensing some of his knowledge to this earnest young woman. He would not live forever—but he could.

Bianca and Ferris Stannum sat next to a congelating furnace waiting for the charcoal to glow orange. She had learned much from the experienced alchemist in a short time. She had observed his setups and technique, committing the details to memory. At one point, they had stopped to sip aqua vitae, as he called it (more like burning water, thought Bianca), distilled from tangleberries.

Once the embers glowed and blue waves rolled in the cucurbit, Stannum showed Bianca how to maintain the needed warmth for sublimation. Perspiration trickled down her back as the ambient temperature climbed from the heat of the stove. She wished she had worn a thinner kirtle rather than the one she had on. She unlaced her bodice as much as was proper, but the heat sapped her enthusiasm.

It came as a welcome interruption when a friend of Ferris Stannum's rapped on the doorjamb.

"I have been hoping I would see you," said the alchemist, motioning his friend inside. "I have someone for you to meet."

The man entered, doffing his flat cap but leaving a black silk coif to cover his hair. Dressed entirely in black, from his head to his boots, he removed a satin gown that fell just below his knees and set it by. His neck was adorned with a neck chain ending in a pomander box that gave off a pleasing floral scent. He had a quiet, dignified manner that immediately impressed Bianca. She would have almost thought him beautiful if not for the unfortunate pox scars on his cheeks above a neatly trimmed beard. He nodded to her.

"Barnabas Hughes, this is Bianca Goddard, a young chemiste."

He looked at her with curiosity. "I have never met a female alchemist."

"Nor have I," said Bianca.

Ferris Stannum rummaged through a shelf and found an empty cup. "Barnabas, she is not interested in alchemy. Bianca creates physickes and medicinals. My methods are of some interest to her." He uncorked a bottle of wine and offered some to Barnabas.

"Nay, Ferris. I am returning home from Newgate Market. A butcher sliced his finger and it would not have healed. I amputated the digit and wrapped the wound." He looked at the furnace bellowing smoke and heat. "The weather is not ideal for testing a chimney draft."

Stannum smiled, his face creasing like parchment. "Hughes is a well-respected physician, Bianca. He does see men of station, but not exclusively. I would say he is the rarest of healers, with the education to practice his art in court. But he prefers to understand all aspects of his science. You might say he is the most learned barber surgeon in London. Perhaps the two of you might confer someday. You might benefit from each other's findings." Stannum poured himself a measure of drink and took a sip. "Barnabas, I would not bother starting the furnace in this heat if I didn't have a reason for doing so. I am showing Bianca how to maintain a constant brooding heat."

"She need only observe an alchemist's nature to learn that."

Stannum raised his cup, acknowledging his friend's barb, and polished off the contents.

"Ferris, I would not encourage you to drink wine on this warm day. The excessive heat may melt your good sense and leave you light in the head."

"I am already feeling light in the head," quipped the old alchemist. "But I have reason to enjoy my drink."

At that moment, another voice called from the street and a second man appeared at the door, apparently known to the others.

"Thomas, my good man," said Stannum. "Come in, come in. Join our gathering."

The man entered, wearing a faded doublet of fulvous yellow taffeta. It was carefully mended near a front pleat to still look presentable. He swept off his cap and bowed overly far, appraising Bianca with a salacious eye.

"Ferris, you old goat," said he, from the side of his mouth. He kept his gaze on Bianca. "Where did you find this trinket?"

"This is Thomas Plumbum, Bianca, a fellow alchemist." Stannum looked over his shoulder at her. "Could you not tell?"

Indeed, Bianca knew an alchemist when she saw one. The stained and well-worn clothes, the attempt to seem greater than one was, both in demeanor and in dress. Thomas Plumbum wore his occupation like a placard.

"No other sort would call me a trinket without first knowing me," she said.

Thomas Plumbum took no offense. He thought himself clever and ignored the derision of those who found him annoying. He slung insults and abuse with no forethought. "And from where might you hail?" he asked.

"Across the bridge."

The younger alchemist tucked his chin, considering. "Southwark?" He glanced at Stannum for confirmation.

"She lives in Gull Hole," said Stannum. "No one notices her strange chemistries in a borough just as strange."

Plumbum nodded in sage agreement. Like his accomplished mentor, Thomas Plumbum had taken an assumed name to set him apart from other, less devoted alchemists. And like Ferris Stannum, he thought his choice auspicious.

"Ferris, I thought I would find you alone. Instead, I seem to have interrupted some festivity."

"This is no planned occasion," said Stannum, brightening. "But I admit I feel celebratory."

Barnabas Hughes looked both surprised and a bit worried.

"Ferris, I propose you cork that bottle of wine and stash it on a high shelf." He moved to do just that, but Ferris hid the bottle behind his back.

"Barnabas, do not deny an old man his merriment," warned Stannum, pointing his finger in the physician's face. "I wish to share my news. My friends are here, and while I have you, I must trumpet my achievement."

Plumbum snatched the bottle away from Stannum and took a whiff of its contents. "I am always willing to help celebrate good news." He looked about for a cup, but when that proved fruitless, Plumbum satisfied himself with a swig from the bottle and handed it back. "Do tell all," he said, pulling up a stool and sitting on it.

Bianca moved to the other side of Barnabas Hughes, keeping the august physician between her and Plumbum. She had sensed that Ferris Stannum's willingness to tutor her had come at the end of some momentous discovery. If he had been occupied with an experiment, he probably would not have been so gracious.

Once his audience had settled, Ferris Stannum launched into a long explanation of alchemical theory. Thomas Plumbum sat rapt, listening to his old friend deftly discount accepted alchemical convention. When Bianca and the physician started yawning and their eyes began to glaze over, Stannum rushed through his lengthy discourse. Finally he spurted, "I've discovered the elixir of immortality!"

Bianca's and the physician's eyes flew open. Thomas Plumbum stood and applauded. "Of all the alchemists I know, including myself, none deserves success more than you, my friend." He slapped the old man on the back, which would later leave a purple bruise.

Barnabas Hughes blinked in astonishment and looked at Bianca. Bewildered, he said, "I do not understand. Why do you make this claim?"

Ferris Stannum pointed to the black tiger cat curled on his pallet. "Do you recall how ill this creature was at your last visit? Do you remember my heartbreak that I would soon bury him?"

Stannum picked up the cat and faced it toward his friends. "He lives." He looked round at their puzzled faces. "He lives because I discovered the elixir of life."

Thomas Plumbum could hardly contain his enthusiasm. "When last I visited, this cat was at death's door. I was sorry for you to have grown so fond of the creature. If you lost him I worried your grief would consume you."

"But could it not have been a disease that your cat survived?" asked Bianca.

"Barnabas, you saw how weak he was. You barely heard a heartbeat—remember?"

"True, I do not deny the feline was in a bad way."

"Then do not doubt this elixir is as I say. With imperfect metals alchemy's quest is to balance the four elements into perfect proportions. The perfection of metals is gold. Likewise, alchemy's other great quest is to banish imperfections of the body, the imbalances that result in illness. The perfection being immortality—life without death."

Barnabas Hughes considered this without comment.

Bianca listened respectfully. If what Stannum said was true, then the possibilities were astounding. An elixir such as this could change the course of humanity. It could change the course of history. Bianca tried to envision the ramifications of such a discovery. She could not begin to fathom the implications of such a sauce. Was this even a triumph worth celebrating?

"Have you tested it on yourself?" she asked. Bianca had learned one must thoroughly vet a discovery before claiming success. In fact, she had employed the unorthodox practice of spreading her balms and extractions on rats to test them. It was another one of John's pet peeves. He disliked trying to sleep with rats rasping and chewing at their cages.

"I have not sampled my elixir," replied Stannum. "I do not choose to live forever. Nor do I choose to die before I am prepared. But I am sending my results to Madu Salib in Cairo, a colleague whom I trust."

Thomas Plumbum threw back his shoulders and puffed out his chest. "I can review your results," he offered.

"Thomas, this is not your specialty. Madu is a descendant of al-Rāzī." Stannum didn't chide Thomas for his less than stellar reputation but astutely tried to avoid mentioning it. "Al-Rāzī wrote the *Book of Secrets*, a revered tome in alchemy."

Thomas grew insistent. "One learns the science through years of sacrifice and toil. You aren't born an alchemist. Why is he better suited to validate your findings?"

"Because Madu is a well-known scholar on the matter."

"It will take weeks for the journal to get there. Then it must be validated and returned. You are not a young man."

"I am not a young man, but it is the course I am taking. Madu will deal earnestly with me and will give my findings an honest judgment."

Thomas started in again, but Stannum spoke over him. "My decision is final. The arrangements for delivery have been made. It is no longer open for debate, my friend."

Thomas Plumbum gaped and looked at Barnabas Hughes, hoping he would take up the cause. But Hughes, being a man of measured thoughts, answered in a measured voice.

"Thomas, it is not your discovery. If Ferris deems it necessary to have his findings validated, then we must accept his decision." The physician looked pointedly at the old alchemist. "However, think of how many lives might be lost while you wait. Lives that could be saved."

Thomas heard only the second half of Hughes's statement. "The door of opportunity is open," said Thomas. "If you wait too long, it will slam in your face."

The old alchemist remained firm. "Thomas, I can open the door whenever I choose."

Thomas Plumbum stared at Hughes and Stannum in disbelief. "Gentlemen, you disappoint me. This is the single most important discovery in all of history, and you are prepared to let a Moor do with it as he pleases? Ferris, it may never reach your intended destination. Have you considered that? Have you considered what you might lose if the journal is intercepted—or lost?"

"Thomas, why torment yourself with my decision? Protest all you want, my dear friend, but your words are wasted. I will not change my mind."

Plumbum had worked himself into a rage. His sallow skin bloomed to an almost bronze shade of health. He could no longer abide his friends' stupidity and was dismayed they could be so dull of wit. "You are wrong in delaying," he said, seizing the last word. "Neither of you recognize the possibility of what I am saying." Plumbum stumped to the door, fury the fire under his feet. "There is no use in trying to reason with either of you." He pulled on his faded silk hat so that it covered his ears and forehead in a dispirited fashion.

Barnabas and Ferris watched Plumbum disappear out the door. They glanced at each other, then at Bianca. "You have remained tactfully silent," said the old alchemist.

Bianca had learned a healthy sense of skepticism watching her father and his dealings. She had not been surprised to see Plumbum try to dissuade Stannum from delaying his findings and insinuate himself into the discovery. However, she wondered if Plumbum could stay silent until Stannum's claims were verified. But Ferris Stannum was neither troubled nor distrustful of the younger alchemist. Bianca decided Stannum must have thought Plumbum a trustworthy friend to have told him the news.

"It is not for me to give you my opinion," she said. "We have only just met and you have known Plumbum far longer."

"It does not matter how long I know a person. I have a sense of a person's character within minutes of meeting them. Plumbum is arrogant, but really he is inconsequential. He is one of the finer charlatans in our field," said Stannum.

"Then why did you tell him about your discovery?" asked Bianca.

"Do you worry what he might do with the knowledge?" Stannum

scoffed at the suggestion of it. "He cannot replicate my findings. He has no clue to the meaning of my scribbles. Only Madu knows my particular *Decknamens*."

Bianca had never heard the term. "*Decknamens?* What are they?"

Stannum opened his alchemy journal, which was sitting on a lectern, and pointed to a line of text. "I may substitute the term 'king's crown,' meaning gold," he said, "with 'Apollo,' here." He glanced up at Barnabas and Bianca. "Apollo is king of the sun."

"And the sun represents gold," said Bianca.

"Aye." Ferris Stannum showed an accompanying illustration of a king ascending to the sky. "If you know and understand some basic references, you should be able to interpret my methods. But only Madu has the same knowledge base to figure it out exactly." With effort, Stannum closed the bulky journal.

"Ferris, you must rest, my friend," said Hughes, taking note. "You have overextended yourself." He took Stannum by the elbow and led him to a chair. "I fear that the next time I see you it will not be for pleasure."

Bianca filled Stannum's empty cup with ale and Barnabas handed the old man the drink. "There," he said, encouraged that Stannum accepted the cup. "Now I must be on my way. And you must heed my advice and rest."

Bianca found a round of brown bread and shared it with the old alchemist. The two ate in silence, enjoying a slight breeze wafting through the door. Bianca gazed at her surroundings, admiring the variety of equipment lining the shelves. Stannum had an enviable supply of cucurbits and alembics in various sizes, some of copper, some of clay and even glass. There were three different furnaces, one for calcination, a fusory furnace for melting metals, and a solutory furnace with a water bath for dissolving ingredients that must not be scorched. His shelves appeared to be well stocked with cinnabar, lead, sal ammoniac—all the necessary ingredients to perform the noble art. Her eyes settled on a long cylindrical vessel with a glass dome.

She went over to it. "What is this?" she asked.

Ferris Stannum swallowed the last of his bread. "You've never seen a kerotakis before?"

"May I look at it?"

"Of course. It has finished its work for the time being." Stannum stood and put his hand on the table to steady himself. He waited for his head to clear.

Bianca examined the kerotakis, turned it over, and looked through its glass top.

"Remove that piece," said Stannum, showing her how. Reaching a finger inside, he picked out a round plate punched with holes. "You start a fire at the bottom of the vessel." He turned the cylinder upside down and shook out a mesh sieve and concave receptacle.

Bianca looked into the cylinder.

"The receptacle is where you place a liquid, say, mercury. Above that," he said, holding up the plate with holes, "is where you place the body to be acted upon. The body reacts with the heated vapors and is changed by them. The vapors rise and condense in the dome, then trickle down the sides." He pointed out the openings surrounding the vessel near the bottom. "It would not do to have the system closed off. This allows ether to feed the fire."

"Clever apparatus," said Bianca, putting it back together.

She had just handed the instrument back when a man called from the stoop of Ferris's room of alchemy. "Stannum?" The caller clutched a leather portfolio with papers jutting from the edges. His attire was one of a man of money, or at least the outward show of some. He wore a fine damask doublet of ladie blushe pink with gold cording trimming the collar and armholes. A white rosebud was pinned over his heart. But what caught Bianca's eye was his codpiece, elaborately beaded and ridiculously large. "You have company?"

Ferris Stannum groaned under his breath. "I have more now," he muttered.

The man stepped into the alchemy room, the feathers on his

perky cap snagging on the rough lintel and lifting it off his head. He irritably retrieved his hat and pressed it down on his crown. "I have come to collect my due."

His eyes were small, reminding Bianca of a weasel's as they darted about, taking in his surroundings. A manicured beard suggested an attention to detail and appearance. His codpiece, decorated with pearls and stuffed with bombast, confirmed it.

Ferris Stannum dabbed his forehead before answering. "I haven't got it, Tait."

The usurer considered the two of them with a long, measured stare. "You disappoint me again, Stannum." He looked about for a place to set his portfolio. Not finding one, he untied its binding and balanced the folder on his raised knee until he found the paper he wanted. He removed it and held it in front of Stannum's face. "At the bottom of this list of loans is your signature and a date of February, the twelfth day, in the year 1543. It is now the twelfth day of the month of August, in the said year—the year in which we now live." Tait showed the paper to Bianca for her perusal, then whipped it away. "I had your assurance a month ago, Stannum. You said you were on the cusp of greatness."

"Greatness is delayed and so am I," said Stannum in a soft voice.

"How so?" Tait's manner was brusque but not callous.

"I have achieved that which I sought. But there is one last assurance I must take before I can announce my discovery."

"That being?" Tait struggled to control his dwindling patience. His small eyes bored into the doddering alchemist.

"A colleague must verify my findings."

"Pray tell, how long will that take?"

Stannum shrugged and blotted his neck. All the excitement had tired him. "Not long," he said. "Once the results are found reliable, I shall be making more profit than I will know what to do with. And then I shall pay you back in full, Tait, including interest."

The usurer glanced at Bianca. "Are you the one to verify these findings?" he asked condescendingly.

"Nay, sir, I am here to learn."

The macaw, which had been mostly silent, let loose an ear-piercing screech.

Startled, Tait spied the magnificent bird perched on its roost. "I would have hoped, Ferris," he said, walking over to it, "that my funding would go to your experiments—not wildlife." He bent his head to make eye contact with the creature. "I've never seen such a creature. Certainly not one with such flamboyant plumage." He reached out to touch the bird.

"He bites, Tait."

The usurer quickly withdrew his hand and stepped back.

"My dear," said Ferris Stannum, looking apologetically at Bianca. "Come back tomorrow if you wish. The day is late and I have much to finish."

Bianca hesitated, feeling protective of her gentle mentor. She felt as though she should stay and defend him against the cross lender. But Stannum nudged her toward the door, reassuring her.

"Tait shall soon leave. Do not worry yourself with my troubles. They shall soon be in the past."

CHAPTER 4

Thomas Plumbum should have known better than to take his meal at the ordinary within spitting distance of the Crooked Cork. He had wrongly assumed Jack Blade and his rascals had moved their game south of Knightrider Street. Rumors circulated that a younger man, more nimble and clever, had found the district to his liking. His cozening crew had driven out the old rakehell and Thomas Plumbum dined in the belief that he would never cross paths with Jack Blade again. He could easily avoid the area where Blade now presumably worked. But he would be sorely mistaken.

He had his fill of peas porridge with its bits of brown bone that he spat upon the floor. Its blandness could not be improved with the addition of salt, which he always carried on his person. With enough turbid beer to make him truculent, he rose from the board and squeezed past tables, crunching enough bone underfoot to make him wonder if an entire carcass had been tossed in the day's stew. He was surly enough not to notice that he was being watched as he moved to the door.

Plumbum had been in a foul mood long before his meal. His

disappointment with the fare heightened his irritation. He had sat shoveling stew in his mouth and ruminating over his friend's obstinacy at sending his alchemy journal to some currish Moor across the sea. How could he be such a fool? Ferris Stannum was no longer blessed with youth. It could take weeks to verify his findings. It could take months. Plumbum had slammed the tankard of beer on the board before him. "Years!" he had exclaimed, to no one in particular.

If Barnabas Hughes and that girl hadn't been milling about he could have easily convinced Stannum to let him take the journal. He could have run the necessary projection in half the time of anyone else. After all, hadn't he been the king's most favored alchemist? He frowned, remembering that the honor had been years ago and excruciatingly short-lived.

At least he still possessed a license to practice the noble art.

He turned onto Maidenhead and passed St. Margaret Moses, wondering when the bells would toll the time. It was getting darker sooner, an unfortunate reminder that autumn and the dreary months of winter lay ahead.

Thomas Plumbum returned his thoughts to the injustice he had once incurred, mulling it over, bringing its sting and humiliation freshly to mind. He had lost his stipend when another, more promising, alchemist caught the king's fancy. Hadn't the same situation happened to the girl's father? What was his name? Plumbum scowled, trying to remember. Oh, how could he forget? Albern Goddard. Papist reveler and presumed poisoner.

Well, at least *he* had not stooped that far.

Thomas sniffed at this inconstant king's whims. What number wife was he on? He snorted at his private joke. Aye, indeed what wife did he lay his bloated, petulant self upon now? Catherine Parr? Well, no matter to him. It took a woman made of stronger stuff than he to submit to being docked by that scary beast.

Plumbum thought about Ferris Stannum's journal. Had he really discovered the elixir of immortality? He wished he had been able to look over the recipe.

Part of Plumbum's desire came from his painful inability to

dazzle the court with anything of merit. He'd performed his buf-
foonery one too many times, and his last attempt had gotten him
a chorus of unrestrained jeers from the entire court and a boot out
the door. How was he to know another alchemist had shown the
king how the trick was done? He would get even with that
scalawag someday, indeed he would. He would make the usurper
sorry he ever stepped foot in an alchemy room.

But if Plumbum were honest—which he allowed on rare occa-
sions—he would admit that he had run out of tricks. "There, I've
admitted it," he said, looking up at the heavens dotted with stars.
He tripped over the sad corpse of a dog, then circled back to kick
it out of the way. He, Thomas Plumbum, once esteemed alchemist to the king, had run out of ideas.

As he clumped along Carter Lane in the direction of St. Paul's,
he decided to pay one last visit to Ferris Stannum and see if he
could convince the old man of his folly. He hoped with all his
being that Stannum had not yet sent the journal on its voyage
across the sea. At the very least Plumbum hoped Stannum might
entrust him to deliver the journal to the courier. If he did, Thomas
could delay the delivery long enough to sneak a look.

All was not lost. Thomas Plumbum brightened and a little hop
found a way into his step. Didn't Ferris Stannum love him like a
son? Thomas smelled redemption in the air. He would have a
new trick to show the king. He thrilled at the thought. And it
wasn't even a trick.

After all, who better to reap the reward of years spent in selfless devotion than he? He had promoted the noble art, had wor-
shiped it, had championed its sublime and worthy pursuit. Ferris
Stannum had always said one must have the right destiny to pursue the stone. And though he might be remiss, Thomas Plumbum
believed he had earned that destiny.

As is often the case when a man's worries subside, ideas came
flooding in. Thomas Plumbum stopped walking while one particular thought rushed over him. It had to do with changing silver
into gold and it required a measure of piss obtained from a youth.
A fresh start on a new projection was just what he needed. His

optimism convinced him he would succeed. He glanced around for a young boy, but none were about. Was that movement farther down the lane? A dog barked and a door slammed. Probably some cuffin returning home for the night, which he should be doing, but first he had to procure some piss and visit Ferris Stannum.

He jogged up a lane that cut through toward St. Paul's, where legions of orphans huddled against the stone bulwark at night and begged for alms in the morning. He stopped to check his purse. A penny for some piss was extremely generous. Why, he'd have a bevy of young boys wagging their little pricks for such a price.

Imagining the sight got the attention of his own member, and he rearranged his codpiece to give it a little room. He reached into his doublet and dumped out the salt in his stoppered jar. It would not be difficult to fill it with the requisite golden pee.

Approaching one of the waifs might take some tact. As he turned onto the churchyard he concluded he should find a boy on the perimeter. The orphans operated with their own social code, and often there were one or two boys ostracized from the rest for whatever reason. Plumbum stopped shy of the hulking cathedral and scanned its length.

At the opposite end, Plumbum spied a number of boys playing cards. A small lantern illuminated their youthful faces in the gathered circle. Cheats had to learn somewhere, and where better to practice their cozenage than in the shadow of St. Paul's? As he watched the boys hunkered round and listened to their boisterous gibes, he turned his sights to a few boys propped against the cathedral's stone wall. They slept, snatching what patchy relief they could find in dreams away from their nightmare existence during the day. He could remember doing the same.

Glancing about, Thomas Plumbum approached a dozing urchin apart from the others. He stood before him and nudged the boy's foot with his boot. The boy startled and looked up.

"I've a penny for your piss," said Plumbum, deciding that the best approach was simply the truth. He held the coin between his thumb and finger so the Queen Moon could smile upon it.

The boy scowled and rubbed the sleep from his eyes. He looked around and saw he was alone, apart from the boys farther down. It was a queer request, and maybe the old bugger meant something else altogether. Either way, he needed the money. The boy shrugged and got to his feet, noting the dagger tucked in the man's belt.

He followed the man along the wall of St. Paul's to its darkest corner. He could barely make out the man's silhouette as it folded into the inky black.

"Here," said Thomas Plumbum, shoving a small jar at the boy. "Take your relief in this."

The boy took the jar. "Ye want me to take a leak in it?"

"That's right. The penny for your effort."

The boy could make out the man's eager eyes glinting in the dim light. Again he shrugged, turning away to do his business but keeping the man in his sight. He pulled out his wanger, tickled it to get the stream flowing. He gave over to the relief that comes with emptying one's bladder and filled the jar to the brim, spilling some on his fingers. He handed it over his shoulder, sprinkling the last drops on the cobblestones at his feet.

The man took the jar, and the boy heard him sigh as he took his turn spraying St. Paul. Well, thought the boy, that was the strangest penny he'd ever earned. He started to tuck his young member into his pants when he felt a helping hand.

"Now, boy," said the man, his breath hot on his ear. "Let me feel what you've got." And he stroked the boy's pizzle.

The boy jabbed an elbow at the man's ribs but struck air instead and was slammed forward against the cathedral. The man's ragged breathing blew down the back of his neck and he was warned not to shout, for a blade would cut the words from his throat if he bothered. Another strike sent him against the wall again, smashing the lad's nose against the stone, convincing him of the man's sincerity.

He felt his pants yanked, and they pooled at his ankles, exposing his tender cheeks to the horrors of a monstrous sin.

The searing pain and blood filling his mouth were nothing

compared to the pain of corruption that filled his body and soul. His fingers dug into the stone of St. Paul's as he wished the man done. Wished God would smite the bugger dead and cut off his wally.

The boy almost got his wish.

Thomas Plumbum was in the throes of pleasure when he was tackled from behind, seemingly out of nowhere. The weight of his attacker pulled Plumbum off his feet, and he toppled to the ground. A pain from his head hitting the cobbles coursed down his spine. He had barely registered the sting when he was sprung upon by a man who insisted on choking him. His eyes bulged from the pressure and he tried pushing the attacker off. Without air and the strength that came with it, Thomas Plumbum flailed to no use.

He saw only a glimpse of the man's face.

Jack Blade was back.

The man's visage disappeared behind a sea of red, blinding Thomas from a final look. It was just as well. He wouldn't want to see the beating that followed.

"You foul blasphemer," said Jack Blade. He released his grip on Thomas Plumbum's throat and stood, looking down at where Plumbum lay coughing. "Your blood runs black with unnatural desire. Can you not find a whore who would take you?" He kicked Plumbum in the bollocks. "Or are you too niggardly to pay?" As Plumbum curled into a ball like a pill bug, Blade pummeled his exposed back side, concentrating on a kidney.

Meanwhile, the boy skittered away, far enough to take some pleasure in the man's beating while keeping a safe distance.

Thomas Plumbum coughed blood upon the cobbles. There he lay, gasping for air, his arms crossed, holding his ribs. It was a desperate situation, being unable to breathe, much less fight. Surely Blade's leg must be getting tired from kicking him. He fought to remain conscious as he wallowed in blood and spit, the hard ground the pillow beneath his cheek. Eventually, the battering ceased. The only sound was his coughing. He vomited.

"Get up, you vile traitor. I should save the executioner the trouble and hang you myself."

Plumbum slowly got to his knees, every muscle screaming, and was promptly booted in the rear, returning him face first onto the cobbles.

"I've not forgotten the debt you owe. And let this be a reminder that I always collect my due." Blade paused for Plumbum to stagger to his feet but grew restless waiting. He hauled Plumbum up by the collar of his dismal yellow doublet, waited for the alchemist to focus on him, and spat in his face. "Now I know your filthy heart." He pushed Thomas away in disgust. The force of it sent Plumbum sprawling backward.

If that were not enough trouncing, Blade took one last pleasure in humiliating the alchemist.

Thomas Plumbum was gifted all the piss he ever wanted.

CHAPTER 5

If all men slept soundly, think on what tranquility their souls might enjoy. But this night, one restless soul could not sleep and sought peace through other means.

Those looking for ill-gotten gains benefit from stifling summer heat combined with the dark of night. Denizens with the luxury of windows open them wide, hoping for a breeze to find their beds. Others worry their open door might invite thieves or even rapists, and while some gamble they might be spared such crimes for a decent night's rest, others are not so complacent and lock their doors and windows. Ferris Stannum, the alchemist, was of the trusting kind.

What could befall a man who had discovered the secret to immortality? He alone had been granted that destiny. Most alchemists espoused their virtues and single-minded purpose trying to convince God (as well as themselves) that they deserved success. But Ferris Stannum had been blessed beyond all others.

Hope filled a puffer's heart but not his purse. Alchemists spent money that should have bought food for their families. They squandered their last coin; they squandered their future in a desperate pursuit to project the stone. Ferris Stannum smiled in his sleep. Yes, he, too, had squandered, but soon he would recoup every loss he had ever incurred.

All but one.

Though he was hopeful he might turn that around.

His mind was soothed by the knowledge that he had been blessed with a great destiny. However, there was one who crept into Ferris Stannum's rent who did not think about matters of destiny.

Stannum turned over on his pallet and faced the wall, the damp plaster spotted with mildew. Soon he might live where the sun could find him as he worked to make vial after vial of elixir. His journal of alchemy sufficed as a pillow, providing some comfort for his mind, but not particularly so for his head. His ear pressed hard against its cover. Still, exhaustion pulled him under, and in his repose, he kicked off a thin sheet. Even that was too much weight this hot night.

The black tiger returned from its nocturnal prowling carrying a limp shrew in its mouth. A dog alerted the entire neighborhood of its arrival and successful hunt. This proved a noisy and unnecessary announcement, requiring the feline to deftly skirt the dog's snapping jaws. Relaxing upon entry to its master's home, the cat found a suitable place to dismember the creature and set about doing so. Shrews were delectable except for their long, bony snouts.

Ferris Stannum began to snore, and his steady breathing filled the rent.

When he rustled, the footsteps stopped. When he settled, the footsteps started.

The cat abandoned its shrew.

All was at peace until a most unnatural sound disturbed the red parrot and set it squawking.

Across the river, Bianca and John left the door and their one window open. What little breeze they enjoyed was suffused with the smell of chicken manure from across the way. John thrashed, pulling a sheet over his nose to filter the awful stink. This lasted half a minute, until he grew too warm and threw it off.

Beside him, Bianca slept soundly. She was bothered by neither the smells nor the oppressive heat. Her dreams were soft, filled with visions of herbs and flowers, the combinations stoking her subconscious with ideas for remedies she would pursue later, when she woke.

John propped himself on one elbow and stared at her—willing her to wake and hear his complaints. But she turned away from him, a serene smile on her lips.

Restless, John sat on the side of the bed. He twisted his hair into a bun and stabbed it in place with a metal stirring rod from Bianca's wares. The room had not cooled. No breeze found their door. He went to open it wider, catching sight of the crescent moon hanging in the sky like a silver hook. Even the trill of a nightingale did not soothe his foul temper. John leaned against the jamb. They had been married for a few months now, and still he had not convinced Bianca to move. Nor had he convinced her to take his surname. She would rather stay a Goddard than be called a Grunt. Though, John had to admit, Grunt was an appalling last name.

What would it take to get her to leave this dreary hovel? John shook his head, thinking how stubborn she could be.

He remembered back to when it was rumored the king's fourth wife, Anne of Cleves, was to process through Bishopsgate, and even though it was a cold day in January, Bianca positioned herself within sight of the expected entourage and waited hours in the wind. It wasn't even certain, but a rumor passed from eager tongue to ear. She endured without complaint the sharp pelts of sleet on her face, hoping for a glimpse of the new queen. John had told her no woman was worth waiting for, especially if one must suffer physical pain in the process. But Bianca had shown remarkable tenacity, and even though her feet were numb and would take hours to thaw, she got her glimpse and was pleased.

* * *

In another year or so he would be done with his apprenticeship. His mentor, the French metallurgist Boisvert, would suggest where John might set up smithing. John wished to stay in London, with its ample supply of merchants and courtiers with deep purses. He could do a fine business catering to those with the means to pay him. But he would not be so brash as to compete directly with Boisvert. He owed his livelihood to the petulant Frenchman.

Boisvert *had* rescued him from living in a barrel behind the Tern's Tempest tavern. He had been nothing but an abandoned waif living off his wits and kitchen scraps. If Boisvert hadn't taken him in, he might have ended with one less finger, or hand, for all of his thieving.

But the smells of Bianca's room of Medicinals and Physickes were not the only reason that John wished to move. There was hardly room to sit, and the board was always littered with the bowls and equipment from her experiments. The shelves were lined not with staples of food, but with jars of herbs and powders for her salves. And in the corner was the constant hiss of rats in cages stacked one atop the other.

Still, he could not convince Bianca to find a larger, better-ventilated rent in which to live and work.

John sighed as he headed back to the bed. *"La nuit porte conseil,"* he mused, sitting on the edge and listening to Bianca's relaxed breathing. "And a pillow is my best advisor."

CHAPTER 6

The next day, Bianca expected to find Ferris Stannum busy at work. Instead, she found Ferris Stannum busy being dead. She had hoped to spend more time with the brilliant alchemist, learning more about his methods, tapping his store of knowledge. Instead, she arrived to find him stiff on his pallet, surrounded by an ineffectual clutch of onlookers discussing his demise.

"Well nows," said Constable Patch, surprised to see the young woman at yet another scene of death. "Bianca Goddard, strange to see ye here."

"I might say the same of you," said Bianca, unruffled. The sight of him conjured bad memories of when he had accused her of poisoning her friend. It had been only a few months since that ugly charge, and the thought of their paths crossing again so soon and for yet another death filled Bianca with apprehension, which she was careful to hide.

The constable straightened and tugged on his new suit of popingay blue, the shine not yet off his brass buttons. "Since last we mets, I was promoted. Southwark is in my past. Is it in yours?"

"I still live in Gull Hole."

" 'Tis a shame you have not improved your station." Constable Patch picked at his goatish wisp of beard. "Methinks if I was you I would stay away from dead bodies."

Bianca stood next to Barnabas Hughes, the physician she had met the day before. "It is not that I purposely seek them out." She looked disconsolately at her lifeless mentor. "What happened?"

"Is it not obvious?" said Constable Patch. "He died."

"He was quite alive yesterday," said Bianca.

"Yesterday, you say?" said Patch, lifting an eyebrow. "You were here yesterday?"

Bianca did not answer. It took a concerted effort to remain silent and not comment on what he was insinuating.

"Oh, aye," said the landlady, sidling up to Bianca. "She was here. And I never seen her before. It was like she came out of nowheres."

"Indeed," commented Constable Patch. An interested expression flickered across his face. "Mrs. Tenbrook, I am familiar with this maid and I agree. She is quite peculiar. However, if ye would be so kind as to repeat your story?" He watched her begin to speak, shifting his eyes to Bianca.

A flushed Mrs. Tenbrook looked round at the small gathering. The district coroner wore a bored expression and continued his examination, unbuttoning Stannum's nightshirt, exposing the alchemist's thin chest. Barnabas Hughes watched without comment.

"It was a warm night, it was," started Mrs. Tenbrook. "Most everyone on the lane had thrown open their windows and doors for some night air. Ye would think, bein' as it was so steamy, that most cozens would respect a man's right to slumber and not go prowlin' about murderin' old men in their sleep."

The coroner leaned over Ferris Stannum's neck, sniffing the skin. "I have not yet determined this is murder," he said without looking up.

"Mrs. Tenbrook, it is not our place to jump to inclusions." Constable Patch felt the need to demonstrate a newfound objectivity, as if it came with his newly acquired position.

The goodwife blinked at the constable, momentarily confused. Bianca understood what Patch meant, having dealt with him before. She thought the suggestion was more of a reminder to himself than to the landlady to remain impartial.

"Aw. I just think it is low for anyone to murder another in their sleep, especially an old man."

"You had harsh words for your tenant yesterday," said Bianca.

Mrs. Tenbrook took exception. "What you saw yesterday was just our daily dealings. I never mean nothing by words. I just wanted him to pay his back rent." She looked anxiously at Constable Patch, who nodded for her to continue.

"As I said, last night, every window and door was open on the lane. He probably left his open, too. 'Cause that's how I found it this morning—wide open." She appealed to Hughes and Bianca. "And he had it open all day. Both of you was here. Is it not true he had his door opened wide?"

Barnabas Hughes and Bianca agreed.

"It was a fitful night for most, but I slept like the dead." Mrs. Tenbrook looked round at them, glanced at Stannum, and crossed herself. "I didn't hear a cricket until morning, until that bird started squawkin' and carryin' on."

The coroner pulled Ferris Stannum's nightshirt below his shoulders and down his arms. He stood back for a full view. No bruising or ligatures marked Stannum's skin. "And you attended him yesterday?" asked the coroner of Barnabas Hughes.

"I visited him," said the physician. "I found him overtired. From lack of sleep. I encouraged him to rest."

"As I was saying," said Mrs. Tenbrook importantly, "that bird was screeching like it was being beat. Bobbin' its head . . ." She imitated the parrot's gesture, which garnered everyone's attention.

"Usually the old man could get it settled and I wouldn't hear but a few shrieks every once in a while. But it kept up its shrieking. After a time, I came down to see why he couldn't get it to shut its beak. I don't want the neighbors complaining. It sounded like Stannum was trying to kill the thing."

The attention went to the parrot, which was sitting passively on a limb that served as its perch. The macaw appeared untroubled by the roomful of strangers and cocked its head, peering at them through one eye.

"And that's when I saw him," said Mrs. Tenbrook. "Frozen stiff in his bed. Like a winter gale had blown through."

The coroner pulled up Ferris Stannum's nightshirt, leaving it open at the neck. "He died of natural cause."

Bianca was stunned by his quick pronouncement. "How can you be certain?" she asked.

"There are no signs of strangulation or poisoning." The coroner was assured of his office. "I see no stab wounds. What has happened internally, I know not. However, it appears he died in his sleep."

"Look how white his lips and nose are."

"I would not expect rosy lips on the dead," said Constable Patch.

"He lived his life in this alchemy room. He rarely saw the sun," said Hughes.

"But white?" said Bianca. "And his face. It has a bluish cast. Don't you see?"

Everyone peered down at Ferris Stannum.

"Nay, I do not see," said the coroner after a moment. He looked at Hughes, who shrugged and shook his head. "Sometimes we see what we imagine," said the coroner.

"I do not imagine," said Bianca. She bent over the alchemist's face and studied his glazed expression. "His eyes are bloodshot."

"The man worked in dim conditions. My eyes would be bloodshot, too, if I worked in this cave." The coroner stepped away and sat before a folio at the table. "He was an old man." The coroner opened the folder, ran a hand over a page to smooth it down. Missing a requisite pen, he looked around. "Constable, hand me that quill." He pointed to an inkwell and pen beside it.

Bianca stared at her mentor. How could the coroner be so sure Stannum had died of natural cause? He had been full of life the day before. True, his hands had shaken, but he had been excited about his discovery. Though perhaps, she thought, he could have been fatigued and his trembling could have been from lack of food and sleep.

The coroner began writing and Constable Patch hovered near his shoulder. Bianca bore a healthy distaste for public officials. They thought more about collecting their pay and where they might spend it than about performing their duty. The only thing that saved the common man from officials was their inefficiency.

As Bianca thought of this and watched the two functionaries, she noticed that Ferris Stannum's journal of alchemy was not on the lectern.

She walked over to the writing desk. She looked around, searching the floor and bench beside it. "I do not see Stannum's alchemy journal."

Neither Mrs. Tenbrook nor Barnabas Hughes answered. Constable Patch had no interest in her comment and continued to attend the coroner.

"Perhaps he sent it off to Madu in Cairo," said Hughes. "That was his wish."

"But it was late when I left and he was tired. I would have thought he would have waited until today." Bianca checked the shelves and tables. Puzzled, Bianca addressed Mrs. Tenbrook. "Do you know if Ferris Stannum left yesterday evening?"

"I do not watch his comings and goings," said she. "I am his landlady, not his wife."

As Bianca continued her hunt for the missing journal, she came across a square of linen. She picked it up off the floor. It was speckled with dots and smears of blood. Yesterday she had noticed Stannum occasionally wiping his eyes. Glancing up to see Mrs. Tenbrook and Hughes watching the coroner and Constable Patch, she stuffed it in her pocket.

Unable to find the journal, Bianca concluded that Stannum had probably sent it off. But, she thought, it was also possible someone had taken it. Unfortunately, she had no proof either way.

The coroner laid down the quill and blotted the wet ink. "I'm finished here," he said, handing the paper to Constable Patch. "I would not delay in the body's removal. The height of summer is an unfortunate time to die."

The coroner left, dismissing Bianca's further questions. Mrs. Tenbrook wandered around the room, lifting jars and sniffing them, peering into tubes and retorts. Hughes stood silently next to his friend, reticent in his grief. Bianca looked askance at Constable Patch, who was surreptitiously studying her. She wished the ineffectual plod gone.

As Mrs. Tenbrook shamelessly picked through Ferris Stannum's belongings, it seemed to Bianca that her nonchalant curiosity was more of a determined search. Though she stood next to Stannum and appeared to be thinking of her mentor's untimely departure, she kept an eye on the impertinent landlady.

"So, Bianca Goddard," said Constable Patch. "What brings you to Ferris Stannum's?"

"I sought him for advice," she answered, avoiding his gaze. She imagined his mouth twisted in an obnoxious smirk. A glance at him confirmed the sneer. "Meddybemps recommended I ask Stannum for help."

"Meddybemps, you say? How is the knave? Is he still vending his talismans and your medicinals?" He said "medicinals" as if it had as much credibility as a rumor.

"Aye, he does well by his business."

"So's ye came to Stannum for help? What sort of help?"

A familiar pang of unease settled in Bianca's gut. Only a few months earlier, Constable Patch had accused her of murdering her friend Jolyn, and her quest to prove him wrong had been a difficult and deadly undertaking. Patch had had her thrown in the Clink, where she had been beaten. Bianca had recovered from the ordeal, but losing Jolyn was a loss with which she still struggled.

"Constable, you know I endeavor to help the sick. Sometimes I concoct my medicinals using methods I've learned from observing alchemists. Ferris Stannum taught me how to sublimate my tinctures." She hoped her directness would prevent his suspecting her of rascally intents.

But Constable Patch had a tendency to provoke before backing off. "I just finds it peculiar how ye show up when there's a death in an alchemy room." He raised an eyebrow, anticipating her response.

Mrs. Tenbrook found a bowl of something that suited her and dumped its contents in her apron pocket. She set it back on a ledge and looked up to see Bianca steadily watching her.

"Ferris Stannum was old," repeated Bianca, facing Constable Patch. "He died of natural cause." She repeated the coroner's findings as if she had finally accepted them.

Patch stroked his beard.

"Did you find what you needed?" Bianca called to Mrs. Tenbrook, who was shaking a vessel and listening to its contents. The landlady quickly returned it to a shelf. She wiped her hands on her skirt as though she was trying to remove evidence of her snooping.

However, Mrs. Tenbrook's embarrassment was soon forgotten when a mournful cry cut through the prickly silence. A young woman stood at the door, her hands covering her mouth. She was about Bianca's age, around eighteen, with copper hair poking out from beneath a cap. She wore a tavern maid's greasy apron and looked as though she had just left her workplace. Her apron reeked from spilled ale and her blouse clung to her damp torso. She was of small bone structure but blessed with curves in the right places. The maid dropped her hands. Her mouth agape, she ran to Ferris Stannum's side.

"Your father's dead," said Mrs. Tenbrook, abandoning her search and quickly coming round to stand next to the alchemist. She sounded as if she had coveted the chance to tell the girl for a long time.

The girl's face registered dismay. She stood over the body, staring in disbelief. "When did this happen?"

Constable Patch began to explain the circumstances, but Mrs. Tenbrook spoke over him. "I found him, I did," she said proudly. "That bird of his was louder than the parish bells this morning. I came down and there he be. Dead as wood."

The young woman looked up at Constable Patch. "Who are you?" she asked in alarm.

"I am the constable of this ward. Patch is my name." He swept off his cap and bowed. "And ye are . . . ?"

The girl's stare darted from one face to another. "Amice. His daughter."

"Ah," said Constable Patch, "then his death comes as a surprise?"

Amice did not answer. Her reticence visibly annoyed the constable. His eyes narrowed and he wondered whether all alchemists' daughters were chary. Perhaps they were taught from an early age to disrespect authority.

"Your father was unwell," said Barnabas Hughes. He said this gently, but Bianca heard a slightly accusatory tone.

"He was an old man," Amice said, glancing at Hughes. She returned her attention to her father.

"And he owes me four months' back rent," piped up Mrs. Tenbrook.

Amice ignored the landlady, riling Mrs. Tenbrook. The landlady's fists went to her hips. "I expect full payment of his arrears." Then, adding more venom, she spouted, "This room is brimming with heathen equipment. It needs to be got rid of."

"What am I to do with all of this?"

"Sell it!" said Mrs. Tenbrook. "This mess must be cleared straightaway."

"You want it gone because you have another tenant ready to move in." Amice possessed a quick temper and a formidable manner. "I wouldn't be surprised if you murdered him to get him out."

The two began slinging barbs at such a fevered pitch, neighbors paused outside to peer through the door. If the dead could wake, Ferris Stannum would have roused.

Instead of trying to mitigate their rancor, Constable Patch threw another dung patty on their fire. "It needs to be determined where burial should be."

"A pauper's grave," blurted Mrs. Tenbrook.

"I'll not have him buried and forgotten." Amice could not abide another insult and shoved the landlady, sending Mrs. Tenbrook stumbling into Constable Patch. He caught her and set her firmly back on her feet.

"Me ladies," he said, stepping between them. Mrs. Tenbrook tried reaching past to swat Amice. "Please take a breath and calm yourselves."

The landlady stood on her toes to address Amice over Patch's shoulder. "Death does not end his debt with me. If you can sell this ungodly equipment and repay me, then whatever is left you can have and ye can do with as ye likes." She quipped, "Bury him at Whitehall; I do not care."

"I'm afraids circumstances will not allow you the time to manage that," said Constable Patch. "I mean the heat. Bodies dissolve."

While they argued about burial and such, Bianca took the opportunity to look around again. She returned to Ferris Stannum's body and studied his face, though it saddened her to do so. Perhaps the old alchemist *had* died of natural cause. She remembered his trembling hands and how he kept mopping his forehead. Perhaps the heat had caused a strain on his feeble body. No doubt, his health had been in decline.

As she considered his vigor, she thought it odd that he slept with no pillow. She remembered seeing one on his pallet the day before. Why would he choose to go without a bolster last night? Even if one were uncomfortable from the heat, one would throw off a coverlet but not toss away one's pillow. She began to search around his pallet.

Barnabas Hughes disengaged himself from the bickering and walked over to Bianca. "You seem to be searching for something?"

"Aye, his pillow."

"I don't believe he used one," said Barnabas Hughes.

"I'm certain I saw one on his pallet yesterday."

"Perhaps it may have been his rolled nightshirt."

The arguing between Mrs. Tenbrook and Ferris Stannum's daughter pitched ever louder. Constable Patch looked on, smirking, enjoying the histrionics and doing his part to escalate them.

"I've no use for any of ye," bellowed the landlady. She pointed a finger at Amice. "I expect this cleared away in two days' time. If not, I'll sell it meself." Her face flushed to near purple, Tenbrook defiantly looked round at them. She spied Ferris Stannum's bottle of wine and snatched it off the table. Dramatically tromping to the door, she stopped just shy of exiting. "I'll write that alchemist friend of his and see if he will buy any of this," she said. "But the money goes to me first. For all me troubles."

An uncomfortable silence followed in her wake. A door slammed from above, punctuating the end of her tirade.

Barnabas Hughes was the first to speak. "I believe my duty here is done," he said. He went to his friend's body, paused to cross himself. Turning to Amice, he said, "I am sorry for your loss, Amice. Your father loved you so." He bowed his head and bid farewell to Constable Patch and Bianca.

"I shall summon the bearer post hates," said Constable Patch, waving the flies off Stannum's body. "Ye must say yer good-byes." He turned to Bianca. "I hope it is not a president, finding ye here at the rent of a dead alchemist," he said. He straightened his doublet and gave a curt bow.

The two alchemists' daughters watched him leave, then looked at each other. Amice did not ask, but Bianca felt compelled to explain herself.

"I only met your father yesterday. He helped me with my chemistries."

"What do you mean—your chemistries? Are you an alchemist?"

"I make balms and remedies for the sick. Transmuting lead into gold is not important to me."

"I don't see why not. I should think it would earn your fortune faster than selling cures."

"My father has spent his life working the noble art and he has never made gold."

Amice listened distractedly as she wandered through her father's belongings. Her manner reminded Bianca of Mrs. Tenbrook before Amice had arrived. "It's gone!" the girl suddenly exclaimed.

"What is gone?"

"My father's bag of silver." Amice felt behind a shelf, then turned an accusatory eye on Bianca.

"That is not the only thing missing. Your father had an alchemy journal. He believed he had discovered how to create the elixir of life."

A look of puzzlement came over Amice's face. "What is this elixir? Of what do you speak?"

Bianca explained. "His intention was to send the book to a colleague in Cairo for confirmation. Perhaps he managed to send it off last night. I was here yesterday, and the last time I saw the journal, it was on his writing desk."

"So his journal and a bag of silver are missing," said Amice. "It sounds like thievery."

"I am not certain the journal was stolen," said Bianca. "But I know nothing about his missing bag of silver."

Amice went over to the parrot pruning its feathers. "I think Mrs. Tenbrook probably took the silver." She stroked the parrot's head. "She took advantage of my father's passing and stole his silver before summoning the physician and constable."

"It is possible," said Bianca. "But we don't know that for sure."

"If my father had discovered the elixir of life, why didn't he partake of it?"

"He said he did not want to live forever." Bianca looked up from searching around the writing desk. "Nor did he want to die before he was ready."

Amice gazed around her father's room of alchemy, then sighed. "What shall I do with all of this? I am not surprised he should leave me with this muddle." She picked up an alembic resembling the head of a bird with an overly long beak. "Do you want any of this?"

"I could use a few retorts."

"How much would you give me for them?"

Bianca suggested an amount that seemed fair to both of them.

Amice set down the alembic, then found a sheet and shook it out over her father. It floated down, covering his body, and she carelessly tucked in its edges. "I can't bear to see his eyes staring up at me." The parrot clacked its beak, and she looked over. "Now I have a bird and a cat to feed."

"I can take the cat," offered Bianca. "A bird of this kind should fetch a good amount." Bianca found the black tiger sleeping in a dark corner behind a stash of still heads. It had curled into a tight ball and looked up at her. After some urging, it stood, then stretched, and wound its way through the maze of crockery to rub against her legs. "What is this?" Bianca reached behind the pile and pulled out a pillow. "Why was this in the corner?"

She carried the pillow into the light for a better look. The beige linen was dingy from use, but there was little mistaking the stains. Two red stains, probably blood.

"May I keep this?" asked Bianca. "The cat seems to like sleeping on it."

"Take it. It is one less thing I must clear away."

Bianca tucked the pillow under her arm and set aside the retorts. "I'll have to leave these for now. I'll return tomorrow."

"That is fine," said Amice, glancing up from a stack of papers she was going through. "None of this is going anywhere soon."

CHAPTER 7

The black tiger climbed up Bianca's back and balanced with its front paws draped over her shoulder, digging into her bodice. The cat didn't scare during the walk back to Southwark, and it rode with its face next to her cheek, both of them focused on the road ahead. Bianca stopped at the market, buying milk and oats, and then headed home.

She had just enough time to start a new experiment before John returned from Boisvert's. The cat settled in with a bowl of milk and Bianca began to mince dried mullein leaves. She thought about the stains on Ferris Stannum's pillow and, after setting up a pot of water to boil, sat on a stool next to the open door, where she could study the spots in better light.

In life as in death, Ferris Stannum's eyes had been bloodshot. Bianca thought it unusual and didn't know what to make of the condition. Perhaps he, more than most alchemists, could not tolerate the fumes from his science. She remembered the square of linen and pulled it out of her pocket. Comparing its stains to the pillow's, she noted that they were of equal intensity, both tinged with blood. The difference being that the pillow had only two stains, while the linen was dotted with them.

Bianca scrutinized the cushion more closely. An idea dawned on her. She pressed the pillow against her face. The stains were separated by the width of a nose.

"Is there a reason you have your face buried in an old pillow?"

Bianca jumped and dropped the bolster. "John, why must you startle me?"

"Why are you sitting by the door sniffing pillows?" He picked it up and took a whiff. "It is not because you miss the scent of me. This smells worse than a dead fish. I never find you behaving like a normal wife." He handed it back.

"If I behaved like a normal wife, you would grow bored."

John kissed her forehead. "True, that." He looked past her into their rent and saw the interior in the same disarray as when he had left. Unfortunately, the room did not smell of roast goose or of a hearty beef stew. Instead, he caught a whiff of musty leaves, reminiscent of hay.

"I didn't expect you for a while. You are early."

"It is too hot to do anything of purpose. Boisvert didn't want to start the forge, and I'm grateful. This heat has stolen my ambition." He walked over to the pan. "So what is this?"

"I am infusing mullein leaves for my next salve."

John knew better than to ask about dinner. If Bianca was in the middle of her chemistries, then meals and sleep—the circadian clock by which most humans danced—were ignored, even derided as intrusive. He pulled off a pair of shoes and laid them aside.

"Where did you get those?" asked Bianca.

"I carried a woman's water jugs to the conduit and back and she gave me her husband's shoes."

"He won't be happy about that."

"He won't care. He's dead." John removed his damp shirt and hung it on a nail, then went outside to the cistern to splash water on his face. "Hello. What is this?" he asked when he returned.

The black tiger had finished its bowl of milk and was grooming its face when John spotted him.

"It was Ferris Stannum's." Bianca picked up the cat and introduced it to John.

"Stannum didn't want it?" He looked into the cat's green eyes and rubbed its cheek.

"Stannum is dead."

"You just met the man."

"I returned today, with more questions, and found him surrounded by his landlady, his friend Barnabas Hughes, Constable Patch, and a coroner."

"Constable Patch." John whistled. "I was hoping never to see the little squit again. You must have been surprised."

"He was just as surprised to see me."

"He didn't accuse you of murder, did he? I don't think I can take the excitement of rescuing you from the Clink again."

"I can't begin to fathom what he thinks in that funny skull of his. But the coroner pronounced Stannum's death of natural cause. He died in his sleep."

John looked at Bianca, sensing the doubt in her voice. "You don't believe Stannum died in his sleep, do you?"

"Stannum had just discovered the elixir of life. After decades of work, he had finally reached the brink of greatness."

"He was an old man," said John. "Old men die in their sleep. If they are lucky."

Bianca stirred the leaves in her pot of boiling water. "Granted, he was not in the best of health. I just think his death was rather sudden. I find it sad that he would die so soon after achieving success."

"Perhaps it is God's will," said John. "If the elixir of life is as you say, then having such a potion could bollocks up the whole works." John searched for a clean pan. Bianca might not be interested in eating, but he was.

"And there God saw the infidel alchemist asleep in his bedchamber and He smote ruin upon his blasphemous heart."

John held up a pot. "Aye, something like that. Can I use this?"

Bianca took the pot and wiped it out with the hem of her dress. "I believe there is more to this than an old man dying in his sleep." She handed it back.

John searched through a cupboard, finding jars of dried herbs and crockery. "Have we any food? Usually this is where most people put edibles."

Bianca held up a sack of oats. While not the capon of which John dreamed, it would suffice.

"Dare I ask—are you pondering that someone murdered your alchemist?"

Bianca snatched away the pot to ladle in some water from their cistern. When she returned she found her pan of boiling mullein leaves sitting on the table.

"That can wait," said John, reading her irritated expression. "I need to eat." He took the pot from Bianca and set it on the tripod.

"I've discovered a few peculiarities. The thought has occurred to me." She didn't wait for John to ask what those peculiarities were. "For one, his alchemy journal is missing."

"You said last evening he was sending it to an alchemist in Cairo. Perhaps it is on its way, sailing across the Mediterranean."

"It was late when I left, and he looked weary. I thought he would have waited until today to send it."

"So you admit he was tired."

Bianca sat on a bench and pulled the cat onto her lap. "John." She gave him a look and he knew to keep quiet. "Amice, his daughter, said a bag of silver was missing."

"He may have used it to send the alchemy journal on its voyage."

"Possibly." Bianca scratched under the black tiger's chin. The cat closed its eyes and lifted its head, purring roughly. "It seems Stannum had a lot of debt. Mrs. Tenbrook, his landlady, claims he owes back rent. And before I left yesterday, a lender named Tait came by to collect. I didn't linger to hear the outcome of that, but the man was not pleased that his payment would be delayed, yet again."

"All perfectly legitimate reasons for bitter disappointment. It sounds as if Stannum was frittering away people's money."

"I suppose when one is on the verge of discovery, obligations, even one's own health, suffer." Bianca bent her head and the cat gave her a smeary rub on her cheek. "I also met an alchemist by the name of Thomas Plumbum. He was friends with Stannum, but he became furious when Stannum said he preferred to send the results to a colleague in Cairo."

"Why should that anger him?"

"He wanted to verify the results himself. He thought it a waste of time to send the journal to Cairo."

John dumped the oats into the boiling water and wiped a wooden spoon on his hose. He hoped whatever was clinging to it wouldn't eat through the fabric. "I hope you are not thinking of involving yourself in this."

Bianca ignored his warning. "One more thing troubles me."

John shook his head. Bianca was beginning to obsess over Ferris Stannum's death. It did not bode well for a calm, lazy end to the summer.

"I discovered his pillow." She shooed the cat off her lap to retrieve the dingy bolster, pointing to the two stains.

John glanced over to humor her. "Lots of people sleep with pillows."

"Nay, look!" Bianca thrust it under his eyes. "Look on these two stains."

John irritably pushed the sour-smelling cushion away. "Aye. Two stains."

"Two stains separated by the width of a nose." Bianca brought the pillow up to her face to demonstrate.

"Are you saying he slept on his stomach?"

"I am saying he could have been smothered!"

"Well, he could have slept on his stomach."

"The pillow was nowhere near his bed."

John shrugged and searched for some spice to add to the porridge.

"I found it later behind a stack of still heads. The cat was sleeping on it."

"He may have given it to the cat to sleep on."

Bianca plopped onto the bench. "I think someone tossed it there to hide it."

"Perhaps, but it is just as likely that he gave the old pillow to his cat." John found a jar of a sweet-smelling herb. He wasn't sure what it was, but if it didn't burn his nose, then it was probably edible. Just to make sure, he held it up for Bianca's approval.

"He gave the elixir to the cat."

John sprinkled in the spice and eyed the black tiger. "So, is this cat going to live forever?"

"I won't live long enough to know."

"Well, if it plans on staying here, I'm glad it likes me. Eternity is a long time to spend with a cat that despises you."

John knew Bianca wasn't listening. His warnings to stay out of Ferris Stannum's death turned into pleas, but he stopped shy of arguing and threatening to leave if she ignored him. They both knew he would never do that. So he abandoned his cause for a new one.

He would not mention the subject of moving before he had had his pleasure that night. He convinced Bianca to abandon the mullein leaf physicke for a bath scented with rose petals and lemon balm. The evening was warm and he did not have to heat much water to make her comfortable. John sipped wine as she dropped her kirtle and smock to the floor in a heap around her ankles. Boisvert had gifted him the French vintage in gratitude for slicing a footpad lurking in an alcove one night. The sight of his wife naked, combined with the spirits, successfully lifted his.

She stepped into their tub, a barrel sawed in half and caulked with waxed twine, and sat with her knees drawn up, obscuring her breasts from view. But the curve of her shoulders, the curve of her neck and knees, hinted at more. John wished they had a tub long enough for her to stretch out, but he did not lack imagination and enjoyed filling in what he could not overtly see.

He even helped her wash that unruly head of black hair, pouring buckets full of softened water to rinse away the peppermint mash she used to scrub her scalp. It always surprised him to see her hair wet and clinging against her skull. He thought the shape of her head was lovely. When dry, her hair obscured that delicate feature; its heavy, thick waves seemed to double the size of her head. Bianca finished bathing and beckoned John to join her. But the tiny tub was no place for their exuberant passion. He held out his hand for her, and when she stood, he smoothed melted wool grease and beeswax over her skin.

He kissed her neck, so fragrant and soft that he fancied his nose would disappear into her bone. She responded in kind and twined around his body like ivy. Lifting her in his arms, he navigated the stacks of crockery and carried her to their bed. It wasn't until after St. Mary Overie's midnight tolling that their sighs gave way to deep puffs of blissful slumber.

But John's peaceful respite was short-lived. The question that pestered him awake, that compelled him to win her affections that night, begged to be asked.

John looked over at his sleeping love descending into a private sea of dreams. She twitched and murmured. Whispers of content floated from her lips. He rustled, punched his pillow, and resettled. If he could not sleep, then why should she? He asked so little of her; why could she not obey his wishes?

Still, when he gazed over at her, he could not bear to disturb her sleep. Instead, he whispered in her ear his desire to move from Gull Hole. And she smiled.

CHAPTER 8

Barnabas Hughes reluctantly made his way back to Ferris Stannum's, his leather satchel by his side. The satchel bulged with an apothecary's balms and tinctures. He had been summoned to attend Goodwife Tenbrook, for she had taken ill. It was not for him to judge who should receive care. He was undoubtedly the most virtuous physician in London. Known for his selfless attendance in even the dourest of circumstances, Hughes could not in good conscience ignore a dying man's needs. Or, in this case, a dying woman's needs, though he was not certain how ill Mrs. Tenbrook actually could be.

Yesterday the landlady had been fuming and full of bluster. He objected to her callous treatment of Amice; the girl had just arrived and was shocked from her father's sudden death. How sacrilegious to speak ill of the dead when in the same room as the corpse. To Hughes, it did not come as a surprise that she should take ill soon after. The dead find a way to exact retribution.

A shame Amice and Stannum had not reconciled before he died. A daughter was a treasure for any widower and should be appreciated as such. Could Stannum not see her mother in those eyes? The mother's chin, the mother's brow—did he not remember? How could his heart not flutter recalling a time in his youth? Barnabas Hughes shook his head. His old friend's intransigence would remain a mystery.

As he turned down the short lane off Ivy, the shadows from the overhanging rents fell across his path and his heart. His mood grew more somber from the cheerless character of the neighborhood. He resented being called upon to return to his old friend's home. He was not ready to face the unsettled emotions that would surely surface when he was faced with the alchemist's locked door and no Ferris Stannum beckoning him to enter.

Hughes paused in front of the familiar residence and sighed. Controlling his emotions, he entered from the street, barely glancing at Stannum's closed door. He climbed the stairs leading to Mrs. Tenbrook's and knocked.

Her muffled call bade him enter. A single candle flickered near her bed, and he remained in the doorway until his eyes adjusted to the dim interior. The landlady peeked out from under a sheet that was as pale as her skin. Her robust complexion appeared ashen in contrast to the day before.

"My head feels stuffed with bombast," she said, drawing down the cover from her mouth so he could hear her weak voice. "I can't think two thoughts straight."

Barnabas Hughes stepped inside and immediately opened the shutters to a small window. She pulled the sheet back over her head. "The light hurts me eyes," she cried. "You'll blind me."

"I cannot see to treat you. And we must have some air. I cannot breathe in here." He stepped through piles of rubbish, the collected leavings of a lonely life. Chairs with broken or missing legs, blankets and bowls—no doubt pilfered from previous tenants. They littered the floor, taking up valuable space. He stood over Tenbrook, then sat on the edge of her bed and addressed her through the sheet. "Tell me when you first had your symptoms."

"I was fine until the middle of last night." She clenched the edge of her cover, preventing him from drawing it down. "I tell ye, I can't bear the light! Then I woke short of breath and fought to get air."

"You have no issue breathing now—with your sheet over your nose?"

"I am improved, I believe."

Hughes rose from the bed and closed the shutter halfway. He stumbled over something and bent to pick it up. Ferris Stannum's empty bottle of wine. Assuming the cause of her discomfort, he said, "Mrs. Tenbrook, you are wasting my time. You suffer from too much drink."

The frailty in Tenbrook's voice fell away, replaced with her characteristic spleen. "Nay, it is not that. I know what a hangover feels like, ye fool."

"If you are improved, then why summon me?"

Mrs. Tenbrook threw down the cover. "Because me eyes ache and me head pounds and I have no one to look after me."

It was an oft-heard complaint. If Barnabas Hughes had a groat for every time an old woman sought him for attention . . .

"Mrs. Tenbrook, it does little good to worry over your circumstances. You have shelter and some coin, which is more than most. Be glad you are not living under a tree." His patience thin, he grabbed her under the armpits. Ignoring her moaning and attempt to beat him about the head, he pulled her to an upright, sitting position. "I must listen to your heart and lungs." Instead of laying his ear against her chest and leaving himself vulnerable to further clubbing, he laid his ear against her back.

"I hear no congestion." He looked around for her chamber pot. "I must ask for your waters."

"I'm too weak to stand," she whined.

So Barnabas Hughes found her slop bucket and helped her onto it.

Ignoring John's warnings, Bianca waited until he had left for Boisvert's before setting out for Ferris Stannum's room of alchemy. If John asked later, she would tell him she was collecting the retorts Amice had set aside for her. Which was partly the truth, but Bianca did not accept that her mentor's sudden death was from natural cause. She had a few questions for Mrs. Tenbrook. Her first priority was satisfying her curiosity.

She walked down Bankside toward the bear-baiting venues in Southwark and waited at Molestrand Dock for a wherry. The day promised to be another steamy one; the sky had a gray, lifeless hue. A few swans dabbled in the reeds, their white feathers dingy from the muck. A ferrier poled his skiff to the landing and Bianca climbed in.

The sun bore down as they angled across the river to Paul's Wharf. Bianca almost wished she had taken a ferry closer to London Bridge, where she could have ridden across in its shadows even though it would have made for a more rolling ride. The shallows on the other side harbored biting flies when she disembarked, and she hurried up the steps to escape them.

Taking the narrow Paul's Chain, Bianca walked toward St. Paul's parish. Along the way, it seemed every door of every rent was thrown open for air, allowing her a rare peek inside as she walked past. Bianca was privy to wailing babes and shouts of domestic life, reminding her she had not seen her parents in several months. They lived one street over, but she had not forgiven them from her last visit. News of her marriage to John should have been met with joy. True, her mother had responded with cheer, but her father's pale eyes had shown as cold as quartz in January. She should not have expected more from her father, but his disinterest had burned her worse than any caustic remark. Since then she had stayed away. Hadn't her father once told her to be cautious of fire?

Nearing the lane where Ferris Stannum lived, Bianca attempted to shake off her feelings of disappointment with her father. Instead, she thought of her tutor and his untimely demise, but the dreary lane and its despondent inhabitants further added to her gloom.

At Tenbrook's building, Bianca pushed open the outer door, leaving it unlatched for light. Ahead, the door to Ferris Stannum's room was closed. She rapped on it, tried pushing it open, but found it locked. A faint sound of conversation ranged from the second floor, so Bianca abandoned Ferris Stannum's to climb the stairs. Ahead, Goodwife Tenbrook's door was ajar.

Bianca called through the gap and was answered by Barnabas Hughes.

Inside, Bianca was surprised to find the interior only slightly brighter than the stairwell. She paused, noting the maze of hoarded possessions. On the other side of the room, the physician stood next to Mrs. Tenbrook. The goodwife sat on the edge of her bed wearing a shabby night shift. Her hair hung loose and uncombed, a wild gray nest. Her whole demeanor surprised Bianca, who had just seen the woman vindictive and full of rancor the day before.

"Goodwife Tenbrook, you are not well."

The landlady's rheumy eyes found Bianca. "Ye state the obvious," she said in a raspy voice.

"She woke in the night unable to fill her lungs," said Hughes. He placed a pillow against the wall and eased her back against it. "You must stay upright until your strength returns. It will keep the phlegm from pooling." He searched in his medical satchel and removed a vial of tincture. "This will help clear your lungs. Tell me where to find a cup." He glanced around at the cluttered interior.

Mrs. Tenbrook waved her arm at a cupboard. "Over there," she croaked, resuming her previous pathetic voice. She squinted at Bianca. "So what are ye about?"

Bianca took a few steps but took care to stay back from the disagreeable old bit. "I came for the retorts Amice said I could have. The door to Ferris Stannum's room is locked."

"Pay me and I'll unlock it for ye."

Barnabas Hughes searched for a cup in the dark corner and lit a candle to better see.

"I promised the money to Amice."

"Well, Amice isn't here, is she? Ye came over from Southwark for nothing."

Hughes pinched his mouth in distaste as he picked through

the old woman's cupboard. He found mouse droppings in abundance and moldy bread that should have been tossed out the window weeks ago. It was bad enough helping her onto her jordan and tasting her urine, but the squalor in which Mrs. Tenbrook lived was more than he could stomach. He found a cup and dumped out a desiccated moth, and just as he turned, his eye caught something of interest. He blinked and held the candle for a closer look.

"Perhaps you might tell me where to find Amice," said Bianca.

"I might, but I won't." Undeterred by illness, Mrs. Tenbrook still generated enough strength to remain ornery.

Barnabas Hughes turned on the landlady. "Mrs. Tenbrook, tell the girl where to find Amice or I won't give you the medicine." His voice had enough edge that Mrs. Tenbrook momentarily shut her mouth, taken aback.

"No needs getting your willy in a dither," she said. "Amice lives above the Royal Poke boozing ken. She lives there with her thieving husband." She glared at Hughes.

"She is married?" asked Bianca.

"Much to her old man's displeasure. Though it matters little now."

"They did not end on happy terms," added Hughes. He poured the tincture into the cup and added a few drops from a second vial. He handed the cup to Mrs. Tenbrook.

"Ye isn't trying to poison me, is ye?" She sniffed the mixture and winced.

"I would not be so obvious." Hughes packed his satchel as she downed her medicine.

"Meeting her yesterday, I would not have guessed she was married," said Bianca.

"A girl her age should be settled and chasing after babies," said Mrs. Tenbrook. "Instead, she is a tavern wench supporting her lazy baboon of a husband."

"You should feel better by tomorrow," said Hughes. "I shall return to check on your condition." He bowed from his neck to Bianca, who pulled a stool next to Mrs. Tenbrook and sat.

Once the physician started down the stairs, Bianca pressed the landlady for specifics. "Tell me, Mrs. Tenbrook," she said. "How long had Ferris Stannum and Amice been estranged?"

"I'd say a year. She rarely came round anymore. It was shocking to see her suddenly show up yesterday. Peculiar in that she picks the day her father dies to finally come calling."

"Do you know why they were at odds?" Bianca asked.

Mrs. Tenbrook placed a fist on the bed and pushed herself into a more comfortable position. Her voice lost its raspy quality as she continued. "Amice took up with some rascal. Her father didn't like him. Stannum wanted her to take a position in a home of gentry. But Amice fell for the rake the first she clapped eyes on him." Mrs. Tenbrook smacked her parched lips and held out her cup to Bianca. "Would ye fetch me a drink?"

Bianca took the cup used for Mrs. Tenbrook's tincture, noticing the strong scent of mint and the remains of the yellow syrup pooled on the bottom.

"I'll have what's in that cask," said Mrs. Tenbrook, pointing.

"It is not the first time a daughter should marry against her father's wishes," said Bianca, setting aside the cup and ladling the brew into a bowl next to a small cask.

Mrs. Tenbrook took a sip of the flat ale. "Sometimes it matters more to a father when the daughter is his only child."

Bianca supposed that might be true, but she had experienced little proof of it in her own life. Her father was too involved in his alchemy to concern himself with what she chose to do. She wondered if it would have been different if her brother had lived. Would he have garnered any interest from her father? Philip had been her twin, and while she had grown and thrived, he had died within a month of their birth. If her mother hadn't told her, she never would have known she had a sibling. Perhaps Albern Goddard's disinterest was just his nature. Maybe it was better he didn't interfere with her affairs.

"So Amice did not visit often?"

"Bah, I never seen her."

"But perhaps you were occupied and didn't know when she came."

"Oh, I knows all right," said Mrs. Tenbrook. "Once she married, the two could never have a civil discourse between them." Mrs. Tenbrook finished the ale and handed the empty bowl back to Bianca.

Bianca thought it a harsh judgment coming from the combative old biddy. "You heard arguing?"

"Enough to set the dogs barkin' up and down the lane. I had to come down and tell them to pipes down for fear the neighbors would call the ward." She rubbed her eyes with balled-up fists. "I don't need any wards poking around my place."

"Could you hear what they were arguing about?"

"Oh, sures. Mostly Stannum was displeased with Amice's husband. And Amice said who was he to choose who she could love? The girl has her point. But then, when it comes to choosing lovers, we get the kind of love we think we deserve. Seems to me, the girl didn't have a particularly high opinion of herself." Mrs. Tenbrook tipped her chin to drink. "I'll have another go of that."

"There is no more," said Bianca. The small barrel was not empty, but Bianca decided the woman had had enough.

Mrs. Tenbrook groused, trying to convince Bianca to fetch a fresh cask from the neighborhood ken. Eventually, the landlady relented and continued with her story. "There was the subject of a dowry," she said.

Bianca listened with interest. Her own father had never bothered with a dowry. He spent every coin he had on alchemy and ingredients. She wondered what alchemist could provide for a daughter's dowry. None, she thought.

"The stingy alchemist refused to pay a penny for her hand."

"That does not surprise me. And if her betrothed was a spendthrift, then all the more reason to deny her a dowry."

"Not done that way." Mrs. Tenbrook yawned and snuggled back against her pillow. "Ye just don't decide to ignore the old ways. Even if ye have nothin', ye try to help in some way."

"Even if the father should object to the betrothed?"

"She's still his daughter." Mrs. Tenbrook closed her eyes and waved her away. "Take your leave. I want to rest."

Bianca thought it odd that Mrs. Tenbrook should come to Amice's defense. After all the sniping yesterday, she would have thought the old woman would rile at the mention of Amice. Instead, she seemed to empathize with Stannum's daughter. Perhaps Tenbrook saw herself in the girl.

Bianca stood motionless, studying her surroundings while Mrs. Tenbrook's eyes were shut. Pails filled with kitchen waste needed to be emptied. Filthy bowls crowded her table. The floor rush was trampled and dusty, needing to be changed—Bianca would later trace the origin of several red welts on her legs to the flea-infested reeds. Mrs. Tenbrook had no desire to tend to her own accumulation of objects, only those of others.

As Bianca made her way down the stairs to the floor below, she heard a sound from Ferris Stannum's room. Perhaps it was Amice clearing the room, but what if it wasn't? She crept down the remaining steps to the landing, cautiously tiptoed toward the door, and placed an ear against it.

The clatter of glassware and sudden shatter caused Bianca to try the door for a second time. It opened with no effort.

"Sir!" she exclaimed, catching the usurer fumbling with several alembics.

Tait straightened, reflexively hiding something behind his back.

"How did you get in here?"

"I walked in," said Tait, defensively.

"The door was locked when I tried it."

Tait's eyes drifted away from Bianca's. "Perhaps you were mistaken."

"Sir, I know how to open a door. I am not mistaken."

"I do not know what you are implying."

"Have you a key to this room?"

"I do not," said Tait. He gave Bianca an appraising once-over but did not offer an explanation.

"Why are you here?"

The lender studied Bianca's face before answering. "I learned that Stannum died and I came to see if it was true."

"Who told you he died?"

"His daughter."

"You spoke with her?"

Tait stared at Bianca. "Are you a lawyer? Because I feel as if I am in court. Unless I am mistaken, I am standing in the home of a man who owes me a good deal of money." The usurer stepped up to Bianca, purposely standing close enough to intimidate. But Bianca stood firm.

He continued, "Perhaps you are unaware of the service I provided Ferris Stannum." Tait removed his blush velvet hat and wiped his brow with the inside of his sleeve. He returned the cap to his thinning pate, all the while studying Bianca carefully. "I have made it my life to lend money to men I deem worthy. Over the years, I have had some success in sniffing out talent." His lips flicked in a brief grin. "Ferris Stannum had such potential. Perhaps he was the most gifted alchemist I ever met. So many are nothing more than pretenders. They surround themselves with gimcrack embellishments, like these strange . . ." Tait picked up an alembic and his brow furrowed as he looked at it.

"It's an alembic," said Bianca.

"Alembic," repeated Tait as if he were trying out the word for the first time. "These men try to convince others that they are special. That they alone are imbued with a unique destiny. Only they have been kissed by angels." He set the still head on the table.

"I have learned, unfortunately, that there are more charlatans than true alchemists." Tait stepped away and wandered the room, running his hand over the equipment. "But Ferris Stannum was a true alchemist. He stood on the brink of glory. His miracle was the great elixir." He stopped and turned toward Bianca. "The mythical potion of immortality. And I invested heavily to ensure his success. We were to share those rewards." Tait paused to savor the thought of his unfathomable wealth. "But suddenly, he is dead."

Tait scanned the room. "I have lost every coin I ever invested in him. It has all been for naught."

"You have managed to avoid telling me why you are here," said Bianca.

"I need not explain myself to you. Who are you but some trug who came calling the day before Stannum died. What is it *you* wanted from him?" He took a few menacing steps toward her. "I will not stand here and be interrogated when I have every reason to be concerned with Ferris Stannum's demise. What have *you* lost? How dare you treat me like a murderer?"

Tait shouldered past Bianca, striding to the door. He turned, and his ostentatious codpiece struck a bizarre profile. "Do not suppose to accuse me," he said. "I am undeserving of your recriminations."

CHAPTER 9

Thomas Plumbum sat naked at his board, slumped and sipping Spanish sack, nursing his bruised kidney and ego. He had shed his ripped doublet and soiled clothing and they lay in a pile before him. They reeked of Jack Blade's piss.

Thomas no longer fit in his old doublet from three years before. A paunch cushioned his once svelte stomach and the buttons were already set against the edge, making it impossible to close the cumbersome fashion. His nose twitched from the odor, and with a pair of tongs he lifted the besmirched clothing and carried it out to his rain barrel. There he dropped it in and poked it under the surface. He would be without water until the next rain, but he did not care.

The sun was high in the sky, and in spite of his pounding head, Thomas Plumbum thought about alchemy. Mostly he thought of what a mess it had made of his life, but then he reminded himself—if not this, then what? What else could he do? He had invested too many years in its pursuit. He knew the players. He knew the tricks. His whole existence was about alchemy.

Forced to rethink his bungled plan, he hatched a new one.

He knew a process by which he could turn copper into gold. Thomas grinned. Well, not actual gold, but a nugget that could look convincingly similar. This he could sell to the gullible who frequented the Royal Poke and other such boozing kens where he was not a regular. At least it could supplement his dwindling funds for the time being.

Thomas finished the last of his drink and rose from the table. His head still throbbed, but the sack had dulled the pain of his sore kidney. Searching his shelves, he found a clean flask and bottle containing the remains of a wine that had soured months ago. He poured the wine into the vesicle, the vinegar stinging his eyes, and dropped in several small lumps of copper. He swirled the flask, ensuring the nuggets were evenly coated.

If anyone passed his open window, they would have seen Thomas Plumbum perform his experiments in the nude. The alchemist was too preoccupied to care; the day was already uncomfortably warm. It did not matter to him that he might be considered lewd or even mad in God's eyes or his fellow man's. He found a measure of lye and cadmia and heated the two in a shallow dish. The noxious fumes stung his nose and he threw open the door for a breeze.

It was a process he had discovered years ago. A process used on rare occasion. It would not result in the windfall that the elixir of life would ensure, but at least he would be able to pay Jack Blade, which for now took precedence.

Fishing the lumps of copper out of the flask, he dried them thoroughly with a piece of chamois. He then plunked the lumps into the boiling solution in the shallow dish. He sat back and waited.

Thomas Plumbum had never been interested in pursuing the elixir of life like Ferris Stannum. His was a more venal pursuit. The fame and riches that would come from transmuting base metal into gold seduced him like the sirens of Faiakes. He was drawn by alchemy's seductive song into an impassable reef that could ultimately destroy him. But still, he could do nothing to free himself of the enchantment of his dark science.

The solution boiled off, changing the copper to a matte silver. To those satisfied with the lesser metal, unpolished and somewhat plain in appearance, he might have been able to pass it off as unpolished silver. In fact, he had seen lackadaisical alchemists do just that. But Thomas Plumbum was not lazy. He knew that added effort resulted in a better profit and he dropped the lumps into a pan of water and stoked his stove.

As much as he hated adding heat to his already suffocating workplace, he pumped on the bellows like a madman. The little fire he had in his stove began to catch. Soon it roared and the flames worked their magic. The plebeian gray copper changed to a shiny gold.

Had he successfully transmuted the base metal into gold? Of course not, but to the undiscerning eye—and Thomas Plumbum knew where to find them—it would appear that the alchemist had succeeded where others had failed. He would be able to sell the lumps for profit, and no one would know until the sheen wore off, which would be months from now.

He was holding a lump up to the light, admiring it, when he heard the sound of someone clearing his throat. He looked over to the door.

"Thomas Plumbum?" inquired a young lad, averting his eyes.

"What is it?" answered the alchemist. He had learned his lesson, and the sight of the fresh-faced boy did not so much as register even a rill of interest in him.

The boy remained outside the room of alchemy and held up a letter. "I've a missive for you."

Thomas Plumbum frowned with suspicion. He walked over to the boy and whipped it out of his hand. The boy took a step back and watched the man break the seal and read. In a moment, the alchemist's face relaxed. "Aye, indeed. The answer is yes," he said.

CHAPTER 10

Bianca sat in a corner at the Royal Poke waiting for Ferris Stannum's daughter to finish serving a pair of laborers. From the splats of daub dried on their jerkins and bits of straw stuck in their hair, they appeared to be plasterers. The boozing ken was relatively quiet, allowing her to sit in peace. She always hesitated before entering such establishments, bracing for an onslaught of rude remarks and, if it was crowded, the sly groping that came as she squeezed past bodies and tables.

She had left Ferris Stannum's with an uneasy feeling after her confrontation with Tait, the lender. Perhaps Tait *was* truly disappointed about Stannum's death. If he had invested a large sum of money in the alchemist's efforts, then it would be discouraging to have the man die and never collect any of it back. What puzzled her was his sudden defensiveness. He assumed she had accused him of murder. But she had never even mentioned the word. He had.

Bianca scratched her legs and glanced under the table. The floor was littered with bits of fallen food and mice dashing off with crumbs. She straightened, waving away the flies that pestered her as she sat in thought.

The lender's impertinent treatment of Stannum two days before was not what she would have expected from a man who said he believed in the old alchemist. Though, she reasoned, perhaps after years of investment, Tait was impatient to reap the rewards and unwilling to wait any longer.

Amice finished serving the men and came over to Bianca. "Odd to see you here," she said. "An ale for you?"

Bianca shook her head. "Nay, just a little of your time."

Amice looked over her shoulder at the mostly empty benches and settled in opposite Bianca. "How did you find me?"

"I asked Mrs. Tenbrook. She told me you work here and live in a room above with your husband."

"She's free with tellin' folks about my life." Amice removed her muffin cap and rewound her hair, coiling it in a bun to keep it off her neck. She replaced the cap and wiped her brow with her wrist. "It's warmer in here than it is outside. What else did Goodwife Tenbrook tell you?"

"She told me you married a man against your father's wishes."

Amice looked away. "What a meddlesome old hag. She'd do better worryin' about herself. Have you ever seen a more tiresome prattler?"

Bianca reached into her pocket and pushed several coins across the table. "This is for the retorts."

The girl counted the coins. "Have you collected them?"

"I have not." Bianca had been so troubled over Tait's break-in that she had left without the retorts. "Did you tell Tait that your father died?"

"Who is Tait?" asked Amice, biting at a nail.

"You don't know who he is?"

"I wouldn't ask if I knew, would I?"

Bianca disregarded her impertinence. "He's a usurer. He lent your father money."

"A usurer? I know nothing about any lender."

"He said you told him your father died. That is how he found out."

"Did he, now? I don't even know who he is. Nor have I told anyone about my father's death, except my husband."

"Could your husband have mentioned it to Tait? Perhaps he knows him?"

"You can ask him yourself. He's upstairs."

A patron called to Amice, waving an empty tankard in the air.

"Keep your wits—I'll be there in a minute," said Amice.

"It doesn't make for an easy life, being the daughter of an alchemist."

"I agree with that. And so would my mother," said Amice. "If she were alive. Once she died, I was left to my own. My father was too distracted to properly think about me. He expected me to cook for us but hardly gave me any money for market. After a couple of years, I got tired of pottage made from a turnip and a stolen carrot. At least when I came here, I was able to eat. Imagine a father giving me grief for wanting to eat solid meals. And now he has left me with a mountain of debt."

"If you haven't the means, they cannot collect. It is his debt, not yours."

"I wish life were as reasonable as that. Certainly Tenbrook will hound me to my grave."

Bianca did not mention the landlady taking ill. Instead she reminded Amice that her father's equipment should make her some money.

"And when do I have time to sell it? My hours are spent fetching men ale and plates of mash." Amice rose from the table and put her hand against the small of her back to stretch backward. "Well," she said, straightening. "Is your father still alive?"

Bianca nodded.

"Be glad he hasn't left you with his mess . . . yet."

Bianca watched Amice snatch the empty tankard from the patron's hand and disappear into the back. After a minute, Bianca ventured into the kitchen, which was hazy with smoke. Amice was busy filling several mugs from a barrel.

"What is your husband's name?" asked Bianca.

Amice secured the stopcock and gathered the brews. "Gilley," she said. "Just Gilley." She motioned to a back stairwell.

No one had bothered to light a lantern, so Bianca pressed her hand against the wall as she made her way up the stairs in near darkness. The treads creaked as she consciously placed her foot in the center, mindful not to trip on their bowed surface. At the top, a shaft of light from a small window lit a short hallway. She had a choice of two doors opposite each other. After a few steps, she listened for voices.

An outburst of boisterous gibes and swearing came from the room to her left.

The banter briefly quieted at the sound of her knock but was quickly followed by a hearty welcome summoning her from within. Bianca opened the door. In front of an open window, a gaggle of men sat around a table, apparently having just finished a round of cards. Bianca scanned the room and the men's faces.

Two of the men were clearly disappointed Bianca had not brought four mugs of fresh ale. "Where is Amice?" said one, whose face lacked a definitive chin. Another rose from the table, excusing himself to go water some roses. He brushed by Bianca on his way out the door. A third man shuffled the deck of cards, taking his measure of her, and the last, most likely Gilley, swept up the pool of stakes. He was younger than the rest and somewhat dashing in a roguish sort of way. Clearly, he was the source of the vociferous good cheer. He looked up and, seeing Bianca, his enthusiasm faded.

"I might ask who you might be, but suppose you just tell me," he said.

"Amice said I would find Gilley here."

"How might you know Amice?"

"I knew her father."

The man sat back in his chair. "And how would you know the old man?"

"I only recently met him. I asked his advice to solve a problem I was having with my chemistries."

The corner of his mouth turned up in a cynical smile. "You a puffer?"

"Certainly not," said Bianca, taking his question as an insult. "I do not dabble in the dark art like your father-in-law did."

The man did not deny that he was Gilley. "If you don't send metals through their paces, then what do you do?"

"I create medicinals."

Gilley rolled his eyes at his mate sitting next to him. The two burst out laughing.

Bianca waited for their hysteria to subside, watching them with a level stare. She noticed Stannum's great parrot sitting on a perch, lifting one foot and stretching it.

Gilley gestured toward the bird. "You want a bird? I'll sell him for a good price."

"I'm not interested," said Bianca.

The parrot began to squawk. Its piercing call took precedence until finally, Gilley rose from the table and moved the creature to a back room.

The fourth man returned from his "gardening," carrying four tankards of ale past Bianca. He distributed one to each player, then dropped into his vacant chair.

"So why are you here?" asked Gilley, returning to the table.

"Do you know a lender named Tait?"

Amice's husband sat and began stacking his winnings. "The name is not familiar. Why?" He continued counting his money without looking up.

"He told me he learned of Stannum's death from you."

"Did he, now?"

Bianca went on to describe the usurer. "The man is of medium build and favors the subdued colors of a delicate palette. He has smallish black eyes and a neatly trimmed beard." She refrained from mentioning his codpiece. "So you can say that you know him not?"

Gilley shook his head and straightened the stacks of coins.

"The man you describe is none I know." He watched Bianca as he chuckled meanly. "Was the old dog on the books? For how much?"

"I do not know, nor is it my purpose."

The parrot kept up its cackling and shrieks from the back room. Bianca raised her voice over its loud screeching. "Ferris Stannum was a kind man. Most husbands would be thankful to have a talented and generous father-in-law."

"Phaa!" said Gilley, spewing out his sip of ale. "Generous? Ferris Stannum didn't care a tiddle about anyone but himself. He left Amice to raise herself while he frittered away his life and money on the noble art." The last two words he weighted with unrestrained contempt. "A father should assure his daughter a proper dowry first. Afterward he can pursue his pleasure."

"And I should think a husband would ensure his wife's comfort before *his* pleasure."

Gilley's chair scraped the floor as he rose from it. "I would thank you to leave. I believe we have nothing left to discuss." Gilley's sculpted face turned ugly with ire. If the other men had not been present, he looked as though he would have tossed Bianca down the stairs, and would have enjoyed doing it.

Bianca held his stare. The man with the disappearing chin tugged on Gilley's shirt in an effort to break the menacing silence. He consoled his friend, speaking reasonably to him in a low, calm voice. The parrot's unrestrained squawking further aggravated the already tense mood. Finally, Gilley relented and eased himself into his chair. Attempting a more temperate tone, Gilley announced he had nothing more to say.

Bianca tucked her chin in a clipped gesture of respect and removed herself from the room. Here was a man who purported to love and hold Amice above all others. Yet Amice toiled long hours as a tavern wench, enduring the caviling clientele of the Royal Poke, while he gambled their money upstairs.

Bianca passed through the kitchen and nodded to Amice, who

was chatting up a pair of newly arrived patrons. Amice responded in kind. She held up a finger for Bianca to wait and crossed the tavern floor.

"Is he winning or losing?" she asked.

"It appears he is winning."

Amice's face relaxed in relief. "That's a change."

CHAPTER 11

In a profession considered an offense against the king, Joseph Tait trod lightly. The vice of usury was once left to those of a Jewish persuasion; however, Jews were scarce, having been expelled some 250 years before. Joseph Tait believed wholeheartedly in the Virgin's Immaculate Conception and considered himself a forcibly subdued papal-loving Catholic. His resentment of the king's Act of Supremacy and separation from the Roman Catholic Church simmered, but he knew better than to speak of it. To do so was treasonous. And although charging interest on a loan was a sin punishable by imprisonment, it was yet another penalty he firmly wished to avoid.

Joseph Tait had spent far too many days staring at the dank stone walls of Ludgate Prison to ever go back again. However, his desire to avoid a repeat visit did not result in his reform. What man chooses godliness if it means he must starve? Nay, incarceration only makes a man more cunning.

Before his present circumstance, Tait's facility at picking locks earned him a living—unfortunately, an illegitimate one. He was a larcenist. And while his manner of committing robbery was more sophisticated now, it was still considered ungodly and a dishonest way to enrich oneself. But, Tait would argue, destroying gentlemen by profiting on their misfortunes seemed part and parcel of the English way of life.

The usurer reasoned he was providing a valuable service to men in need of working capital. To those working in a reliable profession he wrote bonds so that his profits were modest and easily masked by the increasing cost of goods. Tait disapproved of King Harry's policy of selling the cathedrals and religious houses to line his already bloated pockets. What had Harry done for the men who had to live under his rule? Tait might be a sinner and a thief, but his crime was trivial compared to Harry's. Or so he believed.

Joseph Tait's lending was not limited to the tidy, humdrum transactions of familiar merchants. He rashly invested in more sketchy professions, hoping for a better return. Thus his interest in alchemists. Tait thought himself shrewd, but truly, he was as gullible as the next man.

And now a threat of bankruptcy loomed large. Over the past year, Tait had spent increasing sums on Ferris Stannum in the hope that the alchemist's recent discovery would shower both of them in gold sovereigns and angels. As he sat at his polished walnut table counting his remaining money, his gut gnawed at the realization of his folly. He stopped counting and studied the vase of roses centered before him. The blooms sagged from the heat and he swiped them out of their vessel and threw them in the street.

His fury with Ferris Stannum was unbounded. The old man's idea to send his recipe to some camel-eating Moor a thousand miles away was unconscionable. Not only was it irresponsible—it was absurd. Fortunately, Tait no longer had to worry about such nonsense. But his search of Stannum's room of alchemy had been futile. There was no elixir, nothing of significant worth. Only a pile of peculiar alembics and jars stuffed with pulverized boar brains and such. Frustrated, Joseph Tait dropped himself in the chair and resumed counting his silver, sliding the coins into his pouch. His investment in Ferris Stannum had been his undoing.

CHAPTER 12

Bianca skirted the area directly around St. Paul's, avoiding the gangs of boys who could surround a person and pick a pocket faster than a knife fight in a barrel. Having been versed in the finer art of cutting purses, she knew their tricks. Often there was no avoiding the occasional lost coin. The streets could be crowded and the distractions many, and even though Bianca's kirtle was torn and eaten through from her chemistries and her shoes were worn, she could still be made a victim. Sometimes, appearance had nothing to do with being swindled.

Perspiration ran down her back from the summer heat. The grit from the roads settled in her throat, so she sought the conduit near Cheapside. Plenty of others had the same thought, for the street was congested with water bearers and citizens taking their turn to drink. Even stray dogs looked for a chance to lap from the fount, which resulted in their getting slapped, which did nothing to deter them. Bianca narrowly missed getting kicked when a dog skirted his punishment and she was left in its place.

When her turn arrived, she cupped her hands and dipped them into the trough, which was lined with a thin growth of furry moss. She wished she could remove her shoes and stand in the water, but a constable stood nearby to prevent anyone from pursuing that idea. Just the cool feel of the water in her hands was enough to quench her dull exhaustion. She stepped away from the conduit, and as she did, she glimpsed the familiar red cap of Meddybemps disappearing around a corner.

Bianca pushed through handcarts and pedestrians and dodged two stray geese honking and chasing a dog. She turned down the lane after the streetseller and stood on her toes to try to catch sight of him. His red cap blazed like a flame in the night.

She caught up as he struggled to move his pushcart down the crowded narrow lane. He was so intent on maneuvering his cart that she was able to jump up and snatch the cap off his head without his notice. She put it on.

Meddybemps did notice the sudden naked feeling of his balding pate exposed. He looked up, thinking a gull had swooped down and stolen it. Bianca shoved him from behind.

"Bianca, my prodigy, my dove," said Meddybemps, looking over his shoulder. "I should have guessed it was you."

Bianca handed him his cap and he set it on his head at a rakish angle.

"Where are you going?" she asked, joining him by his side.

"I am taking my cart to Tyburn Hill, where tomorrow there shall be an execution."

"It's a bit early. Why go now?"

"So I may have a preferred place to sell my wares. It promises to be a popular spectacle. I believe twelve will be hanged. A variety of offenses. Robbery, treason, murder . . ."

"Are you going to sleep under your cart? You can't just leave it. Someone will make off with your talismans, not to mention my balms and salves."

"Unless I find a trustworthy soul to guard it, I'll be sleeping under the cart."

Bianca watched the talismans swing wildly as he avoided a particularly deep rut filled with stagnant water. Flies rose and dispersed; a few tagged along behind them. Bianca had always been fascinated by the trinkets Meddybemps sold. She had often accompanied him when she was younger.

By the time she was nine, Bianca had learned to take advantage of her mother and father's not speaking to each other. She would lie to one that she was running an errand for the other, while doing as she pleased. Rarely was she caught, and her education on the streets proved useful. She learned to cut purses and steal food off carts. There were no alleys or lanes in all of London that she had not explored, and she knew every shortcut home.

A girl wanting much and possessing little was a recipe for mischief, and the sight of Meddybemps with his cart of necklaces glinting in the sun was impossible for a young Bianca to resist. It wasn't so much that she cared to adorn her neck with his offerings; she just wanted to touch them and hold them up to the light. She studied him from afar, watching his mannerisms and learning his habits. Finally, when she had grown familiar with his every inclination, she was ready to snatch a necklace for her own.

She watched him set up his wares at Cheapside Market and waited for the busiest time of day, when the vendors were practically accosted by customers. Meddybemps relished the attention his cart brought him. Bianca noticed whenever a well-endowed woman paid his goods any mind, Meddybemps would lavish his attention on her and think up a rhyme or patter on the spot. This usually assured him a sale, or at least a repeat customer. (Of course, now she knew his ulterior motive was a romp at a future date.)

Bianca waited until Meddybemps became overrun with customers. He engaged several women, each asking questions and fingering amulets hanging from crosses of wood erected for display. Meddybemps was a masterful charmer and lavished attention on each woman without snubbing another.

A carved butterfly with a body inlaid with mother-of-pearl caught the sun as if it were the only object that existed in the entire world. Bianca could barely keep from running up and snatching it. But experience had taught her that a more measured approach was needed if she was to be successful. Bianca neared the cart, casually blending in with the crowd.

Meddybemps graciously engaged each lady in turn, breaking into rhyme to tout the benefits of buying a charm from his collection—

> "A maid doth know in day's broad light
> Comfort comes with seeing.
> But swift comes night
> And with it fright
> Be soft! The devil's keening!
>
> For sooth, what's that?
> Your chest doth thump
> And no one sees him coming.
> A missing charm,
> May bring thee harm
> Your nerves are ruckus thrumming.
>
> But had you bought my talisman
> Your fears would be for naught.
> One look would send him back to hell
> And you shall not be caught.
>
> An evil puck is he
> A clever pip is me.
> Cast him back to hell's hot steam
> And buy a charm from me."

Meddybemps doffed his cap and bowed, delighting the women, who showered him with attention. Bianca saw her opportunity.

She appeared at the front of the cart, opposite Meddybemps, and while the women were focused on the streetseller, Bianca lifted the prized bauble and turned away. But she had not anticipated a butcher hanging his sausages directly behind her.

Bianca bounced into him and landed backward, falling squat

in a puddle of blood from his slaughtering. Disgusted by the feel of it seeping through her skirt, she scrambled to get her feet under her. The butcher took her arm and helped her up.

Meddybemps heard her yelp and saw her clutching his talisman. "Hold there," he said to the butcher. "I believe you have nabbed a cutpurse!"

The butcher looked down at Bianca and gripped her arm more tightly.

The streetseller came round to the front of his cart. "I cannot let you have a trinket for nothing. I know how enchanting my amulets are, and sometimes a girl might lose her good sense desiring one." He looked at her, and one of his eyes started to roll independently of the other. "Have you a coin you've neglected to hand over?"

By then, a constable had caught sight of the commotion and moved closer. Bianca was keenly aware of what might happen if a constable intervened. No thief was ever granted mercy in this man's kingdom. Not even a young girl. Bianca gulped.

Luckily, she did have a coin in her pocket, one filched earlier from an old woman. She dug it out and held it up.

Meddybemps glanced at the constable. He picked the shilling out of the young girl's palm and deposited it in his pocket. "I knew you just momentarily forgot to pay for it." He ruffled her head as if she were a good dog and nodded to the butcher to let go of her arm.

Bianca stood in silent astonishment. She was too surprised to think of anything that might have saved her situation. Meddybemps could have made it worse and she would have been in a great deal more trouble than just a public shaming. She could have lost a finger for her trouble. She owed the streetseller some gratitude.

The next chance she had, Bianca sought him out. If he was pushing his cart to market, she walked alongside him. If he was already selling, she came by and kept him company. Theirs was an unlikely friendship, and except for a time when he had seduced her mother, causing untold havoc, their fondness for each other grew. Meddybemps was a gossip and capable streetseller, and when Bianca eventually struck out on her own, he sold her concoctions. And he proved to be a reliable ear on the street. Meddybemps kept Bianca abreast of any news worth a listen.

As for Meddybemps, not only did he profit from Bianca's expanding repertoire of remedies, but his affection for the girl grew like that of a father for his daughter. It seemed her own father cared not a whit, and she could use a voice of reason. Not that he possessed much of it, but he tried.

"So what brings you out on this sweltering day?" asked Meddybemps as they passed beneath a shady overhang. "Shouldn't you be working on a cure for the sweating sickness? Did you take my advice and seek Ferris Stannum?"

"I did," said Bianca, nabbing a plum as they squeezed by a cart going in the opposite direction. She took a bite of its sweet flesh and spoke with her mouth full. "It has ended in a bad way."

"I fear to ask."

"No need, because I was planning to tell you." They came to the end of the lane and turned onto a new one. The sun managed to find them and beat down from above. "When I first met him he was in a tiff with Goodwife Tenbrook."

"Who might Goodwife Tenbrook be?" asked Meddybemps.

"She owns the building where Ferris Stannum lives. Or rather, lived."

"On my conscience, I do not like how this is unfolding."

"Goodwife Tenbrook claimed he owed several months' back rent and was badgering him to pay it when I arrived. He promised her he would soon have the money and then some."

"Of course he did. It is the expected response from a tenant in arrears."

"She was quite spiteful. Apparently, she had heard his excuses before. Just as she was leaving, she said to me, 'Lucky ye came today, because he may not be here tomorrow.'"

Meddybemps's errant eye quivered. "A threat. Though she could have meant she was kicking him out."

Bianca continued. "There was another who took issue with Stannum."

"Wait," said Meddybemps. He stopped pushing his cart, causing those behind him to curse as they tried to pass him on the crowded street. "Is Ferris Stannum dead?"

"Aye. Of course."

"How could I hope otherwise? It seems you have a gift for finding people dead."

"It is not that I actively seek those who will soon die." Bianca finished her plum and tossed the pit in the road. "You must hear my entire story. It helps me sort it out."

Meddybemps took up the handles to his cart and leaned into it. "Carry on. I shall listen."

Bianca told Meddybemps about Stannum's belief that he'd discovered the elixir of life and about his sending the journal to Cairo. As they trundled toward Holborn Hill, she explained the chain of events and her suspicions about how the old alchemist must have been murdered. She detailed the motivations and physical descriptions of the people involved. When she had finished, Meddybemps stopped his cart next to a stone wall in front of Ely's Place. He removed his cap and sat down.

"You say Stannum believed he had discovered the elixir of life. Do you agree?"

"I have no proof one way or the other. It is a bold claim."

"Then how can he make such an assertion?"

"He says he gave it to his dying cat and the cat now lives."

Meddybemps looked askance at Bianca. "And where is this immortal feline?"

"It's with me."

"And you have not tried to strangle it?"

"Certainly not!" said Bianca, aghast. Bianca settled down on the stone wall beside Meddybemps and removed her coif to fan herself with it. "And don't you think of doing such a deed." She scooted over into the shade, glad for the small relief it afforded her.

Meddybemps leaned back on his elbows and squinted up at the sky, hazy with heat and humidity. "So what do you conclude?"

"I cannot conclude anything. I need more information."

"Is that where I come in?" Meddybemps turned his gaze on Bianca.

"Mayhap," she said. "I'm not sure what you can learn. You don't even know who any of these people are."

"I shall keep my ears and eyes open and do a little inquiring where possible." Scuttlebutt and hearsay were Meddybemps's specialty. To him, one tawdry tidbit was as coveted as a bounce with his favorite tavern wench. He plucked his wine flask off the cart, took a long pull, and offered it to Bianca.

"I must be on my way," said Bianca, taking a sip to wet her mouth and handing it back. She stood and picked her smock from her damp skin, allowing a puff of air to reach it.

"Wait," said Meddybemps. "Have you done any work on a remedy for the sweating sickness?"

"I have not had a chance to try what I learned from Ferris Stannum."

"Methinks it might be prudent to start."

"Have you seen evidence of people taking ill with the sweat?" asked Bianca.

"I've heard of a few falling victim." Meddybemps hopped off the stone wall.

"John says it is spreading."

"Perhaps near Boisvert's there has been more of it. Rumors are abundant. But it would not hurt for you to spend your efforts working on a palliative. It is summer and the sickness is never far from making an ugly return."

"John thinks it is more prevalent near the river. He wants to move from Gull Hole."

"My dove, why do you refuse to move from there? The prevailing winds carry the constant rank bloom of polluted river water right to your door."

"It masks the prevailing rank bloom from my experiments."

Meddybemps's face pinched as he imagined the competing airs. "Indeed," he agreed.

CHAPTER 13

Joseph Tait rose from his chair and looked out over his walled garden from his window on the second level. He had spent an inordinate amount of money having a trellis built for his wisteria, and osiers woven into symmetrical raised beds for his plantings. He eyed his melon plant and reminded himself he must turn the fruit to even its ripening. There was no better escape from the unpleasant chore of collecting payments than a stroll through the lavender and rosemary. Their scents soothed his troubled mind. His patch of green was a welcome respite from London's gray and muddy composition. A tanager swooped in and landed on the high wall, announcing its visit by breaking into song. Tait closed his eyes and listened to it twitter. He hoped this would not be the end of his sumptuous living.

Had he been a fool to lend Ferris Stannum such a large sum of money? He poured himself some wine and tossed it back, trying to muzzle the niggling voice inside his head. His rent was due, his taxes were due, he owed a cobbler for the new pair of intricately stitched leather boots with brass tacks accentuating his thighs. He preferred looking at his feet clad in supple leather rather than chained in iron shackles. The sweet French wine tamped the sinking feeling in Joseph Tait's gut. Perhaps all was not forsaken. There were still a number of men from whom he could collect.

Finding his ledger, he donned his ladie blushe doublet and flat cap. It was time to elicit some resentment. Admittedly, collecting his due was unpleasant, but it was necessary, and afterward Tait felt he had truly earned his money. First on his list and his mind was another alchemist to whom he had lent plenty.

When Tait arrived at Thomas Plumbum's, he found the alchemist poring over a book with such absolute concentration that Tait had to cough several times before he was noticed. Plumbum startled and slammed the book shut, draping his arms over the cover.

"I've come to collect on the bond," said the lender in a cool voice.

Plumbum rose from his stool and came around the table to speak. "Remind me, sir, the amount that is required?"

Joseph Tait flipped open his register and found the signed bond. He read, "Inventory of Thomas Plumbum, alchemist of Soper Lane, London, debt due to Joseph Tait, of London, by bond fifteen pounds, no shillings, to be paid to Joseph Tait at or upon sixth August next ensuing the date hereof. In witness whereof we have both hereunto set our hands this sixth March 1543." Tait looked at Plumbum. "Shall I continue?"

Thomas Plumbum responded neither yea nor nay, so Tait read on. "Inventory of Thomas Plumbum, alchemist of Soper Lane, London, debt due to Joseph Tait, of London, by bond two pounds, six shillings, thruppence, to be paid to Joseph Tait at or upon third July next ensuing the date hereof. In witness whereof we have both hereunto set our hands this third April 1543." He turned the bond around and held it in front of the alchemist's face.

Thomas Plumbum blinked at the paper.

The usurer tipped his head and peered around the edge of the note. "What say you?"

Thomas Plumbum swallowed. "I haven't got it," he said softly.

Tait drew down the note, staring hard at the alchemist. "You say you have not got it?"

The alchemist's eyes were wide with remorse. He offered not a word.

"Sir, you are in arrears *summa totalis* of seventeen pounds, six shillings, thruppence, a not so minuscule sum. It is now the twelfth day of August and you have had five months in which to secure the funds. Am I to assume you have frittered my money with no forethought as to how you might keep your honor and repay me?"

"Sir, I mean to meet your honor with my own. A spate of poor luck has but nearly trounced me, but lo, as I have come unto a most propitious bit of fortune"—Plumbum regained some of his former pluck—"it shall not be long before I have created an elixir, a rare and wondrous potion the likes of which has never been known."

Tait's eyes narrowed. He had heard such claims before. And with Ferris Stannum's demise, he questioned any alchemist touting a grandiose discovery. His patience for Thomas Plumbum was as meager as the money in his pocket. "Tell me of this discovery," he said, preparing to discredit any addlebrained scheme the problematic alchemist might espouse.

"I hope you will understand my reticence. Until it is in my hand I must not speak of my accomplishment."

Now it was Tait's turn to blink, dumbfounded. Plumbum was more pretentious than most and for him to soften his bluster was unusual. Though, thought Tait, perhaps this claim was a bluff and a ploy to stall. The usurer had always been more guarded with Plumbum, knowing better than to lend him the excessive sums of money he had lent Stannum. Simply said, he was not the same caliber alchemist. Yet despite his posturing, Plumbum had, until today, always managed to make his bond. If he got his money paid by his success in alchemy or by some other means, what did it matter? Tait was almost drawn in, then remembered how Ferris Stannum had deceived him with a similar plea.

"Your bragging does not pay your bond. And I have no time to wait for this success of which you speak." Tait sorely regretted not collecting the lesser bond when it had come due. Such a trivial sum had not been worth the bother four months ago. Four months ago, Tait had not foreseen his current financial predicament. Still, he remained determined. "If not the payment in full, then what of value can you give me now?"

Plumbum dug into the pocket in his doublet and removed two pounds and an angel. He offered the coins to Tait.

Disappointed, Tait accepted the coins, but his eyes slid past Plumbum to the table behind him. "You are certain you have nothing more of value?"

Plumbum lifted his chin, the muscles taut in his throat. "Nay," he replied.

The lender searched the alchemist's face. "I shall take these and reduce your loan, but if you do not produce the balance in a day's time, I shall have you thrown into debtors' prison."

Having dispensed his threat, Joseph Tait thought Thomas Plumbum a fool not to notice his darker intent. He had given the silly alchemist a chance to settle his debt, not with coin but with something perhaps more valuable. It was an offer Thomas Plumbum should not have refused.

CHAPTER 14

Bianca stopped on Old Fish Street to buy from her favorite fish-wife. Meg Kant was a stout woman with a delicate nose that nearly disappeared between the folds of her ample cheeks. Beneath her bountiful chest was a pair of lungs that could outbellow a bull in heat. She did a good business. Her offerings were the freshest. Because her voice carried above all others, she attracted more attention. If a customer could endure her sudden outburst of promotion, then he could come away with a catch that wouldn't make him sick later.

" 'Allo, lass," she said when Bianca approached. Her brown eyes looked like small seeds buried in a fleshy apple. "Nelson just brought me some fresh cockles."

Bianca looked over the mollusks. "I'll take thirty."

"Ye don't have your basket?"

"I'll just put them in my pockets."

Meg Kant didn't think twice. She didn't warn Bianca her kirtle would stink of fish later. Who was she to tell anyone they would smell like fish? She counted out the thirty cockles and watched Bianca stuff them in her pockets.

"My cat will like these."

"Well, save some for yourself. Cats can take care of themselves."

Bianca took a wherry to Southwark, avoiding a walk across London Bridge. Even though the sun had dropped in the sky, she preferred the cool thought of water beneath her to the oppressive heat above.

She landed at Molestrand Dock and walked the final distance to Gull Hole thinking about Amice and her husband, Gilley. Perhaps if she returned to Goodwife Tenbrook's and the old lady was recovered from her malady and in a better mood, Bianca could collect the retorts from Ferris Stannum's alchemy room. She could further question the landlady about Amice and especially Gilley. Not much escaped the meddlesome biddy, and with the right questions, Bianca might discover more.

The chickens startled when she turned the corner to the narrow lane where she lived. Her neighbor had let them run loose, and Bianca thought it was only a matter of time before a dog nabbed at least one of them. She arrived at her rent and found the door wide open. Expecting to see a couple of chickens pecking through the rush, she found, instead, John asleep with the cat curled next to him. He roused and sat up on his elbows.

"You are home early," said Bianca, clearing a space on the board to deposit the cockles.

John dropped back onto the bed. "I didn't feel well."

"How so?" Bianca went over to him.

"I am tired. I can barely muster the desire to get myself a drink."

Bianca found a mug and opened the stopcock to a barrel of ale to fill it with warm brew. She brought it to John. "How long have you been here?"

"Since noon or thereabouts. Boisvert didn't have much ambition either. This heat is the devil to deal with." John took a long drink. He looked up at her. "Where have you been? I expected to come home and find you working on your latest concoction."

"I visited the fishwife and bought cockles."

"It took you four hours?"

Bianca stroked the cat while thinking of an excuse. John had asked her not to get involved in Ferris Stannum's life—or death, as it were. "I ran into Meddybemps and we had a long talk."

"About what?"

"He was on his way to Tyburn Hill to spend the night. A goodly number will be executed tomorrow. He didn't want to miss a business opportunity." Bianca rustled about trying to find a pot to boil water.

"As long as you are finished bothering over that old alchemist dying."

Bianca didn't answer but pretended she could not hear him for all the clattering of bowls. She hurried out the back door into the alley and removed the lid off their rainwater. Tonight she would begin a new sublimation using what Ferris Stannum had taught her about the process.

The pot filled with water and she swatted an insistent wasp. It wasn't usual for John to come home early from Boisvert's two days in a row. It *was* abominably hot, but Boisvert didn't usually care how hard he drove John. The silversmith saw a young man with endless strength and stamina and used him no better than a draft horse. John tolerated the Frenchman's callous handling as a means to an end. He would soon be finished with his apprenticeship, and afterward he could set his own work habits.

Bianca returned the lid to the barrel and carried the pot back inside. Besides, John would say the benefits of being Boisvert's apprentice far outweighed the sore shoulders and long hours. He was proud of learning French. Bianca wondered why any Englishman would want to speak the flowery tongue, but she supposed it could be useful. How so? She could not say.

Bianca positioned the pot on top of a tripod that served as an easy place to cook in the summer. It sat just inside the calcinating furnace, allowing the smoke to escape through a chimney outside. Though not all the smoke escaped. Cracks in the mortar allowed fumes to snake through the gaps, often filling the rent with a haze that was worse when the doors were closed. But for a meal of cockles, it was worth the inconvenience. She laid a fire and struck a flint.

John lethargically got out of bed and relieved himself in the back alley. He dragged himself to the bench and watched Bianca chop an onion and carrot for the broth.

"You don't look well," she said. "Your face is flushed."

"It is the heat." John sat in a daze, his eyelids heavy.

"Why don't you go back to bed? I'll fix this and bring it to you."

John shoved a fist under his chin, propping up his head. He fought to keep his eyes open, but his battle was lost to exhaustion. Bianca dumped minced onions and dried parsley in the water. "Come on," she said, pulling his fist out from under him. "You need rest."

John did not argue. He rose from the board and shuffled back to their pallet, his shoulders slumped, barely lifting his feet. Bianca plumped his pillow and helped him lie back. She stood over him, watching until his breath evened out and he dropped asleep.

The cat smelled the steamed cockles and twined itself between her calves. "Come, tiger. You must eat. Even cats that live forever need food."

Bianca ladled some broth into a bowl and pried open a couple of shells to pull out the meat. She gave the dish to the cat and it sat watching the steam rise. She fixed a second bowl for herself. Like the cat, she studied the steam curling into the air and waited for it to cool.

Four people wanted money from Ferris Stannum. She counted them out on her fingers. His landlady, his usurer, his daughter, Amice, and her husband, Gilley.

One person was angry with Stannum for a different reason. Thomas Plumbum. The alchemist took exception to Ferris Stannum's sending the alchemy journal away for validation. She didn't think Plumbum was going to benefit monetarily from the old alchemist's discovery. Bianca lifted the bowl to her lips and slurped the broth. Unless he dispatched the old man and took the journal for his own glory. Bianca set the bowl on the table and fished out a cockle. She pulled the meat out and dropped it in her mouth. Tomorrow she would return to Ferris Stannum's and collect the retorts she had bought. She would ask Goodwife Tenbrook more questions about Amice. And she would also ask where Thomas Plumbum lived.

The cat chewed the flesh of a cockle, working the small piece of meat around in its mouth like a bit of gristle. "There, my friend," said Bianca. "A bit of a chore, but it is good for you." She stroked the cat affectionately. "Promise me you won't run off like the other."

Across the room John lay silent in bottomless sleep. She'd never seen him so weary. She ladled a bowl for him and set it aside to cool. Once he stirred awake, she would give it to him. But for now she would let him rest.

She collected the flasks and ingredients for a new decoction. Mindful of Ferris Stannum's advice, she would test what she had learned and see if her try at sublimation might finally work. She would be up the entire night, but she would not have slept well even if she tried.

Later, while Bianca's experiment cooked, she watched John twist in sleep. He had woken once and she had gotten some broth down him, but she worried. His exhaustion was so complete. The signs of sweating sickness would be evident, the threat becoming more possible as the night drew on. If it were the sweat, he could succumb to its horror within hours. She admonished herself for thinking the worst. John was simply tired. He worked so hard. His body was simply telling him to rest. Still, Bianca found some solace in that he had not complained of headache—yet.

The cat jumped on the table before her, groomed itself, then stretched out among the flasks and bowls. Had Stannum found the elixir of immortality? She glanced at John, unable to stop from thinking how quickly the disease could take him and change her life forever. She had known him since she was twelve. They had watched out for each other, and what started as a kind of sibling affection had grown. John was her history and her future. She sucked in her breath, trying to imagine her life without him.

What if *she* had Ferris Stannum's alchemy journal? Would she be able to decipher his *Decknamens* and secret language? It was a rhetorical question, but one she let herself contemplate. As the sun began to fall, Bianca finally dismissed her musings as wishful thinking and concentrated on the experiment before her. She sealed her alembic with the flux Stannum had taught her and settled in to attend the process. But when her mind wasn't thinking of John or the elixir of life, it flitted from one acquaintance of Ferris Stannum's to another. Unless she was dissuaded, she believed the old alchemist was the victim of murder.

CHAPTER 15

Sweltering heat makes for a terrible bedfellow. Bianca was not the only one stirring in the darkest hours of that night. On the opposite side of the river, Barnabas Hughes sat by his window staring up at the sky. A celestial river spilled across the black. A few stars winked seductively. He wished he could be so easily enticed to forget his distress.

Like Bianca, he sat in vigil over the one he loved. Her decline had come in small, almost imperceptible signs. Signs so subtle that at first he had dismissed them. He'd convinced himself his imagination was raving. Such was the fate of a man constantly asked to piece together symptoms into a named disease so that he might cure it.

Such was the fate of a man refusing to accept that his daughter might die.

It is a monstrous injustice to make a man endure the loss of his wife, then watch as his only child grows weak. Had he not suffered enough? Barnabas Hughes silently cursed his God. He could not see the purpose in being put to such trials. Was he not God's faithful servant, tending the sick in times of plague and outbreak? He was not like some who refused their duty when circumstances were uncertain or even perilous.

And for what reward? More pain and heartbreak? A merciful God should not allow his most principled disciples to be constantly cast into a hellfire of grief with no hope. Did God not want him to attend the sick and suffering?

The physician pondered the ethos of such a God and could think of no reasonable explanation. He believed himself a compassionate caregiver. An educated man. A thoughtful man. A man who worked tirelessly for the sick.

He rose from his chair and went to his daughter, asleep on his bed. Verity would be five next week. Her perfect skin appeared alabaster in the blue shadows. Every time he looked at her he saw remembrances of his lost wife. His wife was in his daughter's face, in her gait, her carriage.

His concern had begun when his daughter lost balance as she rose from the table one day. He thought she had caught her foot on a chair leg, and in the endearing logic of a young child, she scolded the chair for tripping her. A child's balance is never so assured as an adult's. Children had to grow into their sometimes awkward-fitting body. What parents didn't hold their breath and nervously watch their child navigate the top of a stone wall?

But the stumble was accompanied by dizziness, and Barnabas saw the skittering eye of one whose balance was impaired. And when her falls became more frequent and difficult to excuse, he became worried.

He left her in the care of neighbor Ann, the wife of a bread maker, who often put Verity to good use kneading dough and doing simple chores. She enjoyed the girl's sweet nature and never saw her as an inconvenience. His heart sank when he returned from tending a man with a broken leg to find Verity not at the bread maker's, where he had left her, but passed over to a second neighbor. "Verity lost her stomach a couple of times," complained Ann. "I couldn't have her in the shop like that. No customer is going to buy from a place that smells of sick."

Barnabas Hughes carried his daughter home, gave her a simple beef broth, and put her to bed. She recovered from her upset and the physician tried to remember what he had fed her. He suspiciously threw out their staples of barley flour and oats and bought new. However, he wondered, could he have unknowingly exposed her to the contagions he regularly came in contact with? Had he carried disease on his breath so that when he kissed Verity good night, he unwittingly contaminated her? He refused to give weight to these thoughts. How could he be the cause of his daughter's illness? God could not be so unmerciful. A father is a daughter's greatest protector. But Barnabas Hughes privately feared that he might have been her greatest betrayer.

However, Verity showed great strength of spirit. She improved to the point of tame routine. The falls and upset stomachs were committed to the past and to memory. All was forgotten. All was well.

When Verity took ill again, Barnabas believed that with his loving help she would again respond to his care and recover. But her strength waned. She stayed in bed, not having the strength even to sit up. Hughes bled her, covered her torso in every healing poultice he could think of. He sought syrups from the apothecary and forced them down her throat. Still, each day she grew increasingly weak.

Lamenting the death of his friend Ferris Stannum, the physician gazed at the boundless heavens and thought about the elixir Ferris claimed to have projected. Had the old alchemist truly discovered the nectar of immortality? The clop of hooves on cobblestones broke his rumination. Barnabas returned to his chair by the window. Unfortunately, no one would ever know.

Even if he had possession of the journal, how would he interpret Stannum's findings? How could anyone interpret those findings? Alchemists wrote in a convoluted language all their own. Sometimes only they understood their own scribbling.

Barnabas admonished himself for even thinking of the elusive philter. Its potential tortured him as much as the thought of his daughter dying. Still, what father could not imagine preventing his daughter's death when faced with its possibility? A silky breeze touched his cheek and its gentle nudge briefly distracted the physician from his sinking despair. But the interruption was short-lived. Barnabas Hughes buried his face in his hands and wept.

His mind in a muddle, Thomas Plumbum escaped the stifling heat of London for its more crooked counterpart to the south. Wishing to avoid Jack Blade and his coven of cheats, he headed in the opposite direction. Though Southwark teemed with decadent options and was an invitation for its own kind of trouble, Plumbum knew he could not sleep and he sought a distraction to soothe his frenetic mind.

Unwilling to part with his second most precious possession, he strapped it against his chest and buttoned his doublet. He left his rent unlocked, preferring a thief to enter without fracturing his door—doors being irksome to replace. If a clipper were to ransack his rent while he was gone, he would find nothing of value for his effort.

Thomas Plumbum's face and kidney still ached from his previous misadventure with Jack Blade, but with enough spiced ale he would sufficiently forget his discomfort. Besides, he needed to gather his wits and he could not do so at home.

He crossed the bridge, keeping to the center between the handsome homes and businesses of the wealthy. Every dark alcove harbored possible danger, so that even after he passed, he kept glancing over his shoulder, his head swiveling as if it were on a pike. He could not shake the feeling he was being followed. Relieved to be nearly halfway across, Plumbum approached the drawbridge and was glad it was level so he would not have to wait. He stepped onto its iron and timber cross members, careful not to catch his shoe in a gap. Below, the murky Thames flowed, creating the sensation that the bridge moved beneath his feet. Thomas Plumbum did not like being exposed to such height. Why had he taken the bridge? To save a mere sixpence in fare? Fool—he would take a ferry home later.

* * *

Thomas Plumbum *was* being followed. But his pursuer did not creep along behind the apprehensive alchemist as he crossed London Bridge. His stalker followed him from below.

In a cavern beneath the bridge a wherry clung to a support. For most, this would have been impossible with the water rushing by, squeezing past the constricting starlings, of which there numbered twenty. The water churned and boiled, but for this ferrier, the river's capricious nature offered no hazard. Nor did it garner even a second thought.

What caught this ferrier's attention was the unmistakable smell of alchemy.

As old as the river itself, this ferrier was not mortal. But, he *was* made from the stuff of mortal men. He was the vessel for thousands of souls; souls that had died of the plague, unwilling, and too young. He embodied their anguished pleas, their forgotten potential. The tears of a thousand mothers and fathers filled his psyche. Born from the plague but not of it, he had watched London for more than four hundred years, though time, for him, was inconsequential.

He had watched London endure bouts of epidemic and disease. He had seen fire rage through her streets, leveling homes and cathedrals. He had witnessed the destructive reign of brutal kings. But he did not choose this semi-existence, this purgatory, this limbus between the living and the dead.

He had gotten there by accident.

Every alchemist sought to understand the world around him. It was that curiosity that drove the inquisitive to experiment. While most alchemists sought the philosopher's stone, there were others who understood that small discoveries could be just as useful. He had been such an alchemist—once.

He had also been more successful than most. Basic understandings regarding the noble art came naturally to him, and he had laid the foundation for discoveries that would come later. Until Ferris Stannum, no one had delved deeper into the dark science than he.

Rarely does nature allow her secrets to be broached without a cost.

The Rat Man lifted his nose, catching the essence of alchemy, and tasted it on his tongue. Someone had discovered something of import. Someone had come as close as he had once done. Perhaps even closer. He moved his skiff without concern, for the river was void of wherriers for the moment. No one saw his boat glide out from beneath the span and disappear again under the drawbridge. The boat moved with such efficiency that it would have disappeared in the blink of an eye.

Such a passerby would have missed seeing a hooded figure whose eyes glowed green like a cat's. The creature's skeletal body had not seen the light of day in so long that his skin was gray and nearly transparent beneath a black woolen cape. Known as the "wraith of the Thames" to some, the Rat Man to others, he had existed in the imaginations of those who swore they had seen him and who believed in such entities.

What drew the wraith under the drawbridge to watch a skittish man hurry across it? Resolution. The Rat Man sought a solution to the one law he never mastered. A law that had punished him for even trying. He could not live and he could not die. He was the abomination of an experiment gone badly wrong.

And as he watched the steps of an alchemist tread across the drawbridge above, he smelled on that alchemist the solution to that depravity.

Thomas Plumbum cradled the ale to his lips, pondering what to do.

A steady stream of muckrakers and swindlers flowed in and out of the Dim Dragon Inn—mostly in, though it was growing rapidly late and more should have been flowing out. He studied their wizened faces coated in mud from the flats. Their entire persons from head to toe were encased in gray muck. Only the whites of their eyes, and if they were young, the whites of their teeth, offered any contrast in their dismal costume.

He should not have liked being a muckraker. He straightened

his doublet, realizing his attire set him apart from the denizens of the Dim Dragon. Even though he had gotten the smell of Jack Blade's piss out of the worn garment and mended its tear, it was still a sad thing that he did not have a second one to wear instead. Such was the lot of a failed alchemist.

Spiced ale should have dulled his overactive imagination. His intent was to sooth his rattled wits and come to a solid decision. But as he quaffed one tankard after another, his mind grew more fearful.

He felt the appraising stare of three sets of eyes. Setting his drink on the board, he concentrated on reducing the number of sinister pairs to one and had almost succeeded when he felt the overwhelming urge to relieve himself of the abundance of brew sloshing in his bladder. Plumbum staggered to his feet and pitched himself in the direction of the door.

Fumbling with his codpiece, he momentarily forgot the strange sensation as he wended through the tables on his way to the back alley. He held his breath so his fingers could loosen the leather strings snug against his gut. Perhaps it was his imagination, but he thought he noticed someone cupping his hand to a fellow's ear while keeping his eyes on him. Plumbum freed himself of the leather pouch that constricted but accentuated his most precious possession and gave over to the torrent of relief that followed. Emptying one's bladder after waiting overlong to do so was a kind of ecstasy. He could think of only one other act that was akin to such bliss.

But his felicity was short-lived, for as the alchemist's last few spurts fell into the dirt beyond his shoe, the point of a dagger found the attention of his cheek. He froze for just a split second as his survival instinct primed his already scatty nerves. Unwilling to give over to any request or demand, Thomas Plumbum summoned his inner badger. With a sudden burst of grit he drove his shoulder into his assailant.

The man stumbled, putting out a hand to catch himself against the stone of the tavern. His eyes locked on Plumbum's and the alchemist got a look at his face. In the instant it took for the man to draw back his arm, Plumbum connected the rogue to the man receiving the whisper inside the tavern. No doubt an angler looking for an opportunity to rob a man of his money. Perhaps the alchemist would have been relieved that the man had no further ulterior motive, but this did not occur to him. The man sprang with the force of a catapult and plunged the dagger into Thomas Plumbum's chest.

Fortunately, the ale dulled Plumbum's perception of pain. The alchemist looked down at the knife protruding from his doublet. He gazed up at his aggressor, bewildered. This man had meant to maim him. With a growl, Plumbum viciously butted his forehead into his attacker's vulnerable crown. The cozen staggered backward and Plumbum hooked his foot behind the rascal's knee, forcing him down. Plumbum nearly fell on top of him but managed to spring away and remain standing. The alchemist wheeled about, growling and scanning the shadows for more flicks. Satisfied the rogue acted alone, Plumbum did no further damage.

Grasping the hilt, Plumbum pulled out the dagger and felt the tip for blood. It was dry and he patted his chest where it had protruded. All was safe inside. Now his only doublet had a new hole in it. He sighed and pocketed the shiv inside his bootleg. One could never have too many knives.

Before heading for the waterfront, Plumbum paused to get his bearings. He considered what the night had brought him. His survival had to be a propitious sign. If before he had been fraught with doubt, his decision now was certain. His spirit rose and his step quickened as he congratulated himself on a brilliantly conceived plan.

CHAPTER 16

The black tiger cat sniffed Bianca as she slept at her table, her head buried in her arm. She had fallen asleep while working on her sublimation. The cat pawed at her tangled hair, trying to find her face beneath it. Bianca stirred to the sound of rough purring and a wet nose touching her own.

"Hello, tiger," she said, lifting her head and letting the cat nuzzle her cheek. "I suppose you think it is time I paid some attention to you." Bianca scratched the cat under the chin and it closed its eyes, tipping back its head and pointing its chin toward the ceiling. Finally, it flopped on its side and exposed a striped belly for more petting.

"You aren't a dog," she said. "But I suppose you don't even know you are a cat." She stroked its stomach and it stretched, rubbing its head on the board and looking at the world upside down.

The day shone brightly through the window and Bianca realized she must have slept past early morning. She wiped the sleep from her eyes and looked over at John. If he had stirred in the night, she had not heard him. Concerned, she went to him and sat on the edge of the bed.

Her sitting did not rouse him. She laid her hand on his forehead. He felt damp and cool to her touch. "John," she said. Getting no response, she leaned closer and shook him. "John, wake up."

An eye popped open, focused on her suspiciously, then snapped shut.

Bianca shook him more vigorously.

John groaned, rolling away from her.

"Well, at least you are with the living," she said, standing.

She found a pot and was about to go outside to the cistern when John rolled back to face her.

"Where are you going?"

"Ah," she said. "You do live. It is not my wishful thinking."

"I do live, but just barely."

Bianca returned and peered down at him. "How do you feel?"

"Tired."

"Perhaps another day of rest is what you need."

"I am fine." Glancing around, John saw the room brightly lit with a midday sun. "Why didn't you wake me sooner?" he said. "Boisvert will be in a French snit."

"I didn't stir you earlier because I was sleeping, too." Bianca turned back to the door. "I'll cook some porridge."

"No need," said John, kicking off his sheet. "I haven't the time." He swung his legs over the edge of the bed and sat up.

Bianca saw his face grow ashen, and he paused as if the room was telling him a secret. "John, you don't look well."

John focused on a fixed point across the room. In a moment he stood, but not with his usual vigor. Bianca watched him steady himself and, when he had stopped his slight weaving, checked her sublimation experiment. It had failed. She had been unable to stay awake and keep the heat constant.

John picked his way gingerly to the back alley door. When he returned he sat down at the board instead of getting dressed. "I'm already more than late," he said. "I think I will rest a little more before I go to Boisvert's."

"You should stay home," said Bianca. "It is hard labor at Boisvert's and he can manage another day without you."

"Are you going out?" asked John.

Bianca had planned to return to Ferris Stannum's to collect the retorts she had bought from Amice. She had been so distracted finding Tait there that she'd forgotten to take the alchemy equipment. But she couldn't let John know where she was going. "I need to go to market," she replied.

"To Newgate?" asked John.

"I can."

"Will you stop in and tell Boisvert I will be along?"

Bianca saw John back to bed and propped open the door so he would get a cross breeze. Taking the bowl she would have used to make porridge, she dipped it into the cistern and washed the sweat and grime from her face. A looking glass hung on the wall, exposing her rebellious head of hair to her scrutiny. She found a comb and started working on the snarls but lost interest and tossed the comb on the table. Appearance was of little concern to Bianca, but she had the benefit of youth on her side. Tousled hair could be covered with a muffin cap, and as long as she put on a fresh smock, she was presentable.

With a kiss planted on John's forehead and a gentle head butt bestowed on the cat, Bianca set bread and ale next to the bed. She headed out the door. Seeing John out of bed lessened her concerns. She told herself it was a combination of heat and fatigue that had momentarily slowed him. John had given her a task and an excuse to leave for a while, and she was not about to squander it.

A number of questions still bothered her regarding Ferris Stannum. She would collect the retorts and ask Goodwife Tenbrook if she knew where Thomas Plumbum lived. The alchemist had been conspicuously absent since Ferris Stannum's death. Perhaps he did not know his friend had died, but she would ask Tenbrook if she had seen him since Stannum's death.

Again it was low tide as Bianca rode the ferry across the river. The sun, as relentless as the day before, made for an uncomfortable ride. Stirred by the warm, damp air, the sand flies at Paul's Wharf attempted to make a meal of her as she stepped out of the

boat. She hurried up the steps and quickly put some distance between herself and the river.

The air lacked its usual tang of iron when she turned down
Foster Lane, home to other smiths besides Boisvert. She supposed the sweltering summer had slowed the ambitions of most
journeymen. Firing up a forge and working in its suffocating heat
would make for more misery than any coin or bauble was worth.

The door to Boisvert's shop hung open, which surprised her,
as Boisvert was a finicky man. An open door was an invitation for
stray animals, both four-legged and two-, to wander into his shop.
The amount of time and aggravation he spent chasing them out
generally defeated any pleasure he gleaned from an occasional
breeze. Bianca poked her head inside and saw the silversmith or-
ganizing his tools, a tumbler of wine in one hand, iron tongs in
the other.

"Boisvert," said Bianca, stepping into the shop.

The silversmith wheeled about. "Ah," he said. "I was expecting your husband, not you."

"He is overly tired. The heat seems to have exhausted him."

"It is never this unpleasant in France. *C'est vrai*, we may have
the heat, but it comes without the unpleasant stink of the river."
He looked at her accusingly, as if she had created the disagreeable conditions.

"John will be along later."

"*Il est malade?* Because if you think it true, then home he
should keep to. I do not want any *anglais* disease, *merci beaucoup*."
He swirled the tumbler under his nose while watching her.

"He thinks it matters more that you not think him lazy."

Boisvert huffed. "Lazy. I think nothing of the kind. John does
much of the heavy work. I am not so insensitive."

"Can I tell him you wish he would stay home until he is well?"

"As long as he is ill, as you say, and not looking to set up his
own shop."

John's apprenticeship was nearing an end, but it was premature for him to consider leaving Boisvert now, anyway. "Of course
he is ill. John still plans to work with you until he earns his li-

cense." She didn't know what else to say to reassure the peevish Frenchman, who eyed her skeptically. "Well," she said, backing toward the door. "Shall I tell him you wish him a quick recovery?" She dipped in a brief curtsy but did not wait for his answer.

With St. Paul's in sight, Bianca cut through a chain of alleys to the street off Ivy Lane where Goodwife Tenbrook lived. The shadowed way offered relief from the sun, but as Bianca neared the rent, she saw the disconcerting sight of a collector's cart next door.

The cart held one shrouded body, but there was room for more. Bianca approached, glanced around, and, seeing no one watching, pulled the linen back from the corpse's face. The face was still preserved, and belonged to no one she knew. As she tucked the cloth back in, she noticed the door to Goodwife Tenbrook's building open to the street. Voices carried from the second-floor window.

Down the lane, a child wailed and a door slammed. A cat watched a spot in a foundation, but other than a young boy across the way drawing pictures in the dirt, there were no signs of life, no activity in the lane. Alarm settled in the pit of Bianca's stomach as she stepped inside Tenbrook's building.

Again, Ferris Stannum's rent was closed, but this time she ignored the door and listened to the sound of conversation coming from Goodwife Tenbrook's quarters. All she heard was the muffled drone of men talking.

Bianca crept softly up the stairs, pausing to hear Barnabas Hughes speak. Amice responded. Another man, whose voice she did not recognize, asked a question. Unfortunately, Constable Patch enthusiastically chimed in. Bianca groaned at the thought of dealing with him yet again. Before ascending the final risers, she prepared herself for the inevitable scorn he would probably lob at her.

"Well nows," said Constable Patch, looking past the physician when she stepped inside. A third man stood apart from the others, trimming his fingernails with a knife. He had the grubby attire and insolent air of a man used to performing unpleasant work. Bianca took him to be the bearer. "What an incidence to see you here," crooned Patch.

"I came to collect some equipment from Ferris Stannum's. I paid Amice for them."

"That so?" He looked to Ferris Stannum's daughter.

"Aye, it is true," confirmed Amice.

Patch continued, "We seem to have another peculiar death on our hands. Two deaths in as many days at the same address. Do you not find that special?" The constable's eyes widened. "Or, if not special then at least—interesting?"

Surprised and doubting it possible, Bianca shouldered past the physician and Constable Patch for a better look at Goodwife Tenbrook. The landlady had drawn her hands near her chin as if pulling up her sheet. Her body lay in rigid repose; her eyes stared fixedly on a jagged crack running along the beam overhead. Flies inched along her frame, exploring her ears and nose, landing in her mouth. The lips had thinned, exposing Tenbrook's front teeth, her mouth forming an *O*. Could her final expression have been one of astonishment? Or perhaps she had taken a last gulp of breath. "Who found her?"

"I did," said Amice. "She has the key to my father's rent and if I wanted to get in, I had to see her first." Amice rested her fists on her hips. "It's my duty to tend to my father's belongings. The old bit wanted the last say on every move I made. Serves her right." She spoke directly to Tenbrook's corpse. "Ye reap what ye sow."

Bianca hoped Constable Patch recognized Amice's frustration and would realize the words were spoken in anger. She still cringed when she thought about her own interrogation at his hands. And though Amice was feisty, she did not think the girl would be adept in proving her own innocence. "How did you get in to find her?"

"The door was open. I imagine she kept it cracked last night like everyone else did. 'Twas another mucky one. I doubt she worried that anyone might do her in while she slept." Amice pinched her face in distaste. "Who would want to touch such an ugly old shrew?"

"So you found her this morning?"

"Aye, that. I have a rare day to myself. Shame to spend it chasing after a key and having to fetch a constable and all."

Bianca turned to Hughes, the physician. "Did Constable Patch send for you?"

"I arrived as the coroner was finishing. I had told Mrs. Tenbrook I would return and see how she was faring. I didn't expect to find her dead. My daughter is ill. I chose to care for her rather than indulge an old woman whose malady, I believed, stemmed from loneliness."

"Has a cause of death been determined?"

"The sweat," pronounced Constable Patch.

Bianca had thought Hughes had considered this when he attended her. He had not been concerned the disease was to blame for Tenbrook's complaints. She looked over at the physician. "Do you agree with the coroner?"

Hughes straightened and pressed his palms together, bringing the tips of his fingers to rest on his lips. "Patch and I were just discussing my visit with Goodwife Tenbrook yesterday. I suppose it is possible. The disease can act swiftly."

Bianca's distress was momentarily forgotten by her need to clarify the physician's findings. "But you did not suspect the sweat when you visited her, I thought."

"I took it under consideration. However, I believed she was exaggerating her symptoms in a play for sympathy. Nothing gave me pause to think her complaints life threatening. She had been drinking heavily and I believed her malaise was a result." The physician interjected a smile of assurance. "I often see this in older women, especially widows. A little attention and some kind words are a great consolation. When they get to be that age, they are often overcome with loneliness. Minor concerns can overwhelm them."

"You gave her a draught," said Bianca.

"I gave her a sleeping philter. You saw how agitated she was. A restful night's sleep is a great balm for an unquiet mind."

Bianca glanced at Constable Patch, who listened without comment. Just a few months before, he had accused her of poisoning her friend Jolyn, when all she had done was give her a tea to settle her nausea. Was this not similar? Yet Patch accepted Hughes's explanation without question. Perhaps being a physician had its advantages. More likely, thought Bianca, a man's explanation carried merit, while a woman's did not.

"I recall Goodwife Tenbrook had said she could not breathe. You were not concerned that she had the sweating sickness yesterday?"

"What I took as a wheezy chest when I put my ear to her back could have been a symptom. However, the elderly often have an accumulation of phlegmic humour. After examining her, I saw no other evidence for the diagnosis."

The streets murmured with rumors of the dread disease, yet the physician did not consider Tenbrook's symptoms indicative of the sweat. Bianca remembered John's fatigue and worried she would not recognize symptoms of the illness. "Can you tell me, sir, what symptoms do you look for?"

"Do you question my expertise?" said Hughes, turning haughty.

"Nay, sir," said Bianca. "I wish to understand the disease so that I may cure it."

"How pretentious to claim such a feat. What else have you—cured?"

"I am flattered you should like to know. Perhaps we might discuss my remedies someday. However, now I wish to learn more about the sweat."

Constable Patch's eyebrows lifted and his eyes shifted to Barnabas Hughes. Patch reveled in their brambly exchange. Apparently, he was not the sole recipient of the girl's impudence.

The collector snorted, breaking the strained silence.

Called upon, Hughes launched into an explanation, offering more information than anyone, except Bianca, cared to know. "The afflicted suffer from a stinking sweat," he said. "It is as if the disease opens the pores and drives every foul humour, every evil thought, every pollution, out of the body onto the surface of the skin.

Faces flush. Victims complain their heads feel gripped with a squeezing pressure. They often rant and claim fantastic visions."

Amice wandered off, searching Tenbrook's cluttered living quarters for the key to her father's room. She picked through the woman's endless collections of scrap rope, torn pamphlets, and cracked pottery, certain that even a woman so disorganized must have a special place for keeping keys or other necessities.

"I have heard hearts beat with rapid, shallow pulse," droned Barnabas Hughes. "I have seen the sick ask to have their thirst quenched, but it is never enough. They could drink a barrel of water and they would ask for more. But I have also witnessed the miraculous recovery of people so delirious that I suggested the family prepare themselves for their burial. Most often, by the time I am summoned, the short, panicked breaths and pressure in the chest have begun and there is nothing I can do to prevent the disease from running its course."

Bianca was the only one listening. She thought of John, and besides his sweating, which she could attribute to the mercilessly humid weather, she did not believe he showed signs of the disease. Still, it was a concern and she wondered if John might have concealed a symptom to prevent her worrying.

Barnabas Hughes finished his discourse.

Bianca walked around to the other side of the bed. She got within inches of Tenbrook and studied her face. "Have you ever noticed anything peculiar about a victim's skin when they die of the sweat?" She kept her eyes pinned to Goodwife Tenbrook's complexion.

"Peculiar?" asked the physician.

"Have you ever examined their skin, or the eyes of one who has died of the disease?"

Barnabas Hughes exchanged looks with Constable Patch. They both looked at Bianca, puzzled.

"I do not see a flushed complexion, a hallmark of the disease, as you say."

"If she died several hours ago," said Hughes, "the febrile skin would have subsided."

"How many hours does it take for the face to lose its color?"

"The process begins almost immediately."

Hughes bent down to examine Tenbrook's face. "Do you see something I may have missed?"

Bianca did. She shrugged, watching Amice and Hughes for their reactions.

Amice didn't appear in the least interested. She was on a hunt, lifting jars and peering into them, biting her lower lip in distraction. Barnabas Hughes simply looked irritated.

Bianca expected Constable Patch to intervene. Aware she was overstepping the bounds of her station, she sensed both men's growing disaffection. She moved away from the body and feigned interest in the table, which was strewn with the possessions of a woman who apparently kept everything.

Constable Patch was baffled by Bianca's insinuation and utterly irritated with her. He waved the collector over. "Well nows," he said. "I suppose we is done. It is too warm to further delay your duty." He grimaced at the smell of excrement wafting from Tenbrook's bedding. "Ye may take the body." He stepped aside so the collector could strip Goodwife Tenbrook of her night shift and the crucifix she wore around her neck. "Take that as payment," he said to the collector.

The man brought it up to one eye and squinted at the center garnet. He lifted his brow in thanks and positioned Mrs. Tenbrook on the bedsheet.

"If you do not need my further services, I shall take my leave." Hughes bowed from the neck to Patch and glanced at Bianca. As he strode to the door with his leather satchel in hand, Bianca suddenly remembered a final question.

"Sir," she said, hailing him back.

Barnabas Hughes reluctantly turned.

"Do you know where Thomas Plumbum lives?"

His voice weary, the physician gave her directions. "If that is all, God keep you."

The sound of his footfall echoed through the building as Constable Patch and Bianca watched him disappear down the stairs.

They turned back to the bearer, who finished tucking in the ends of the winding sheet.

"Ha!" said Amice, holding up a key with a length of hemp tied to it. She went over to the bed, where Mrs. Tenbrook's wrapped body lay looking like a link of gray sausage. "Thought you could keep me from claiming my rightful due, did you? All your mean and miserly ways got you nowhere. Well"—Amice jutted her chin forward to suggest some cordial advice to the deceased—"it got you dead is what it got you."

While Constable Patch watched Amice, Bianca scanned the table looking for the cup Barnabas Hughes had used to administer the sleeping tincture to Goodwife Tenbrook. It had a blue glaze near the lip, and she found it amid the jumble of objects on Tenbrook's table. She dropped it in her pocket. Also thrown onto the mess was the near empty bottle of wine Tenbrook had taken from Ferris Stannum's room. "Amice," said Bianca, stepping away from the table. "Can you open your father's door so I may get the retorts?"

Amice finished chiding the sausage and looked over. "Aye," she said. "Come on." She trooped from the room with Bianca in tow, leaving Constable Patch to follow the collector as he started down the stairs carrying the body.

CHAPTER 17

Bianca took a retort that looked like the head of an ibis with its long beak protruding from the side. She also chose two smaller retorts before leaving Amice to organize the leavings of her father's alchemy room. She told Amice she would ask Thomas Plumbum if he cared for any of Stannum's equipment, but that was not the only reason she wanted to meet with the man.

Tucking the smaller devices under her armpits and stashing the bottle of wine in her pocket along with Tenbrook's cup, she was able to carry the larger retort. She jangled as she walked, clattering with breakable goods. As soon as she took a precarious step into the lane, the boy across the way, who had spent the morning drawing pictures in the dirt outside his family's rent, skipped over to see what she was about.

"What's that?" he asked, pointing to the copper contraption she carried.

"It is a retort," said Bianca and the boy fell into step beside her.

"What's it do?"

"It helps separate liquids when I heat them."

"Why would you do that?"

"Because it is what I do." Bianca glanced at the child walking barefoot beside her. "I make medicinals."

"Medicinals?" he echoed, quickening his step to keep up.

Bianca's mind was on Thomas Plumbum, and she walked briskly in spite of her burden, in an attempt to lose the grubby gamin. But he kept pace with her.

"Is you a conjurer like that old man who just dieds?"

"I am far from being a conjurer. I cook balms to help people overcome illness and disease."

"Ah," said the boy, skipping backward in front of her. "For a penny I'll carry those for you." He pointed to the retorts under her arms. "You look as if your hands is full."

"I can manage well enough."

The boy ignored her rebuff. "I seen the collector carry out a body. Was it the old lady?"

"It was."

The boy picked up a rock and hurled it as far as he could in front of them. "First the old man, then the old woman. What they die ofs?"

"It is not certain," said Bianca, wishing the boy would lose interest. But she harbored a kindness to children, especially those with an inquisitive nature, having been so inclined herself. "Mayhap it was just old age."

The boy became thoughtful. "Well," he said at last. "I will miss the old lady."

Bianca glanced at him. "Were you on familiar terms?"

"I was. She used to give me a penny to run errands for her."

The two turned the corner and were thrust into the brilliant sunlight of a wider lane. With the sun came the cruel heat and their pace slowed. "What sorts of errands?"

"Delivering letters. Like I did when she found the old man dead. I guess I won't be making any more money from her."

Bianca stopped walking. She turned to face the boy. "You say you delivered a letter for Mrs. Tenbrook the day Ferris Stannum died?"

"Aye. It was to that puffer on Soper Lane. I seen him visit the old man the day before the collector came for his body. You was there, too. And that man with the leather satchel."

"Do you know what the letter was about?"

The boy shook his head. "But I was to wait for an answer after he read it."

"What answer did he give?" Bianca watched him intently, hanging on his every word.

The boy shrugged. "He said, 'Yes.'"

"Yes?"

The boy readily answered with a nod, hoping to win favor with her. But suddenly, those astonishing blue eyes bored into him, making him squirm under her scrutiny. He realized, too late, that he had shared too much of what he knew. He kicked himself for being smitten with her and for losing the chance to make some coin.

"Did the alchemist give you anything to return to Mrs. Tenbrook?"

The boy forced himself to look away. He might still have a chance to make a penny. He clamped his mouth shut and made no indication one way or the other.

Bianca repeated her question.

Still he remained silent.

She moved up against the side of a residence, set down the beaky-nosed retort and alembics. Feeling around in her pocket, she dug out a coin and held it up. "Does this help you remember?"

The boy snatched the coin from her hand before she could reconsider. "Nay," he said. "He gave me nothing for her." Gleeful he had made enough for a loaf of Carter's bread, he couldn't control his sudden appetite and skipped away, leaving Bianca to ponder what she had just learned.

Bianca tucked the retorts under her arms and stepped into the flow of pedestrians. What could have been in the note to Thomas Plumbum? Maybe Tenbrook sent word that Ferris Stannum had died. Bianca sniffed. Tenbrook was not the sort to inform people of Stannum's death out of consideration for those who loved him.

Nay, she would contact others only if in some way she could have benefited.

Tenbrook had taken exception to Amice selling her father's equipment because she believed she had the right to collect Stannum's back rent. The landlady purposely kept the key from Amice. If Amice wanted into her father's room of alchemy, she had to go to Goodwife Tenbrook first. It made sense that the landlady would contact Plumbum to see if he was interested in buying any of Stannum's paraphernalia.

Bianca regretted not having paid more attention to the boy. He was observant and keen to use his wits to make coin. She wondered what more she could have learned from him. At least she knew where to find him.

Overhead, laundry stretched between facing buildings, hanging limp in the languid summer air. Bianca would pay a visit to Thomas Plumbum once she deposited her retorts at home. She hoped John had recovered and gone to Boisvert's. If he had, then she could concentrate on finding answers to Ferris Stannum's death without inciting his comment.

She took a ferry back across the river, enjoying a rest from toting the awkward fittings. The tide had changed and the ferrier poled his skiff diagonally, landing near the bridge. A crowd of onlookers had gathered at its entrance to see the fresh display of miscreants enhancing the upper rim of the gate. The heads were bloody and exposed, probably because no one cared to heat tar on a hot day to dip them. A throng of ravens and gulls fought over torn bits of flesh, their screeches drowning out the shouts and jeers of onlookers below.

If the crowd was any indication, Meddybemps probably enjoyed the spectacle as much as they. He probably did a brisk business and she hoped he managed to sell some of her remedies in addition to his amulets. Avoiding the boisterous revelers, Bianca took a back alley to her room of Medicinals and Physickes.

When she arrived, her hopes sank when she saw the door wide open. John would have closed it if he had gone to Boisvert's. But the air was leaden and John's consideration for her collection of laboratory equipment was often contingent upon his mood. Perhaps he had thought it more important to circulate the air than to protect a few of her crocks from crooks.

Alas, when she stepped inside her eyes were drawn to the neighbor's chickens scratching through the rush that covered the floor. It looked to be the entire flock. Oblivious to their clucking and messing, John lay asleep on their bed with the black tiger cat sprawled beside him.

The sight was enough to make Bianca forget that John may have been too ill to shoo the fowl from their rent. She would have wished for a more responsible cat, but perhaps it had learned a long time ago that chickens were too large to bother with.

"John!" Bianca dropped the retorts where she stood and set upon the chickens, running after them. With arms windmilling, she chased them about, herding them out the door. Two particularly stubborn chickens managed to elude her. One scurried behind a stack of crockery and the other scooted under the table. Both refused to come out. Bianca grabbed a broom, a good scaring being a language the one hiding behind the pottery understood. Finally, Bianca got on her hands and knees and crawled under the table to catch the final holdout. She tossed the last hen into the air outside their door and slammed it shut. Removing her muffin cap, she hung it on a nail and picked up the retorts and the empty bottle of wine to carry them to the table.

John had propped himself on his elbows to watch the excitement.

"Didn't you hear them clucking and knocking things over?"

"I did, but I thought I was dreaming."

"You never made it to Boisvert's?"

John lay back on the pillow and stared at the ceiling. "I did not."

"Have you even gotten up?"

"Not much."

Bianca sat on the bed beside him. The black tiger, never one to refuse an opportunity to be petted, stretched and stepped on her lap.

"My head is pounding," said John. "It feels as if horses are galloping back and forth inside my skull."

Bianca blinked in alarm. She ran through the symptoms Barnabas Hughes had mentioned about the sweat. Pounding head, fever, shortness of breath . . . "Are you feverish?" She placed her hand on his temples and felt his cheeks. He did feel warm to her touch. "You will become parched if you do not drink. My mother believes one must drink to keep the river flowing inside."

She found a cup and poured John some ale from the cask they had gotten from the Dim Dragon Inn. "If you have a fever and you are losing your water to perspiration, you must drink." She reached for her pillow and wedged it behind John as he sat up.

"Where have you been?" he asked. His eyes closed as if he hadn't the strength to keep them open.

"I collected the retorts I bought from Amice." She watched John take a sip of ale. She could not expect him to gulp it down—only the most brave could guzzle that tavern's brew. "I thought I would have to ask Goodwife Tenbrook to let me into his rent. But when I got there, she was dead."

"Small favors," said John. "At least you were spared the inconvenience of having to convince her to unlock the room." John finished the ale and handed the cup to Bianca. "I know you wanted to collect those retorts. However, now that you have them, I see no reason for you to return to Ferris Stannum's alchemy room. The place seems to have a dangerous effect on anyone spending time there. I am rather fond of you and would prefer that you not drop dead. Now, if you have no objection, I shall rest." He removed the pillow propping him up and dropped onto his back.

"Are you having difficulty breathing?" asked Bianca, but John's breath had already lengthened into slumber. Bianca sat on the edge of the bed and watched him rest. His current fatigue was disturbing. True, the heat sapped everyone's strength. All of London operated at a more sluggish pace.

Bianca began to think about a tincture to cure the illness. Or, if not cure, then at least ease its ugly symptoms.

In the meantime, John's complaint took precedence. Bianca took down a bunch of dried feverfew from her collection tacked on an overhead beam and decided to make a poultice for his forehead. If he could sleep restfully he might be able to ward off the disease should it be trying to wear him down.

Finding her mortar and pestle, she ground the aerial parts until they were a fine powder. To this she added a measure of water and honey to make a paste. She slathered the mixture on a piece of thin muslin and laid it on John's forehead. Much to Bianca's disappointment, he did not stir when she put it on his skin.

If this was the precursor to the sweating sickness, she must be prepared. The shortness of breath that Barnabas Hughes spoke of could mean the victim's lungs were filling with phlegm. If the secretions were thick and yellow, a "hot" phlegm, she could use silverweed and elder. She had never combined the two, but the silverweed could help dry perspiration. Elder was an expectorant, so mixing them together should help with the copious secretions that the disease was known for.

But as Bianca checked her shelves for elder, she remembered that elder could induce sweating. It would counteract the drying effect of silverweed. The two would not mix. Disappointed, Bianca ran through other combinations of ingredients.

The black cat roused from its nap beside John and jumped to the shelf in front of Bianca. "If I had Ferris Stannum's elixir of life, I wouldn't have to figure this out." She stroked its back while thinking. Looking the feline in the eyes, she said, "I hope you don't mind living forever—though you have no choice in the matter." The cat butted her head affectionately as if in agreement.

"*Morus alba,*" said Bianca, snapping her fingers. She reached past the black tiger and felt around on the shelf behind it. "Ha!" she said, pulling out a chunk of mulberry root and sniffing it to be sure. She had seen the tree growing near a field in Horsleydown and had insisted John help her dig for some roots. He had not taken kindly to her using his knife to saw off bits of the stubborn plant, grousing that he had just sharpened it and now he would have to do it again.

"I can dissolve this and add the silverweed tincture to make a tea," she told the cat.

Confident she had the basis for a remedy, Bianca found the tincture of silverweed and made a decoction of root bark. Soon, a pleasant smell filled the room and Bianca hoped John might notice and sit up to comment. Instead, his sleep grew increasingly restless. He tossed about, briefly lying still before flipping over again, dangling his leg off the edge.

Bianca retrieved the feverfew poultice and asked if it had helped the pounding in his head. When he didn't respond, she shook his shoulder and spoke in his ear. His eyes blinked open and he moaned what she took to be an "aye," then turned away from her.

The tea finished steeping and Bianca wondered if it would benefit him if he took it now. However, doing so before symptoms appeared might be premature. The tea was not made as a preventative, and giving it too soon might have an undesired harsh effect on his system. So Bianca strained the infusion and set it aside, ready in the event that John's health declined.

Ferris Stannum's empty bottle of wine lay on the table, and Bianca picked it up and ran it under her nose. Bianca tipped back her head and closed her eyes. Spirits were always difficult for her to evaluate. The alcohol often dissolved and masked any questionable additions—such as ground apple seed or rat poison. She turned the bottle upside down and a single drop landed in her palm. She sniffed it. No notable smell hinted that it was off. She touched it with the tip of her tongue. Nothing. If someone had laced the bottle with poison and given it to Ferris Stannum as a gift, she could not detect the offending substance. It did not mean that it was not there, but she could not tell what it was.

But who would do such a deed? Bianca tsked. Smile and give a gift that kills. Several had reason to wish ill on Stannum—Tenbrook, Tait the lender, Amice, or rather her husband, Gilley. And there was Thomas Plumbum. But why would Plumbum want his old friend dead? To steal his journal of alchemy and claim glory as the discoverer of the elixir of life? Given his unscrupulous manner, it was entirely possible. Which led Bianca back to the question—where or from whom did Ferris Stannum get the bottle of wine? And when?

John rustled in bed and settled. Bianca poured herself some ale and settled on a stool next to the board. She watched John while she sipped, resting her chin on her fist.

Ferris Stannum and Goodwife Tenbrook could have died from ingesting something in common. They had both partaken of the wine. But so had Thomas Plumbum, she remembered. He had taken a hearty swig from the bottle. Unless, perhaps, it only appeared that he had taken a drink.

If the wine was laced, Stannum's death could have been planned, but Goodwife Tenbrook's death appeared accidental. Bianca pondered the similarities, but there were a couple of differences in their deaths that troubled her.

Bianca had found dried blood that had run down each temple from the corners of Goodwife Tenbrook's eyes. Weeping eyes was not a symptom mentioned by Barnabas Hughes when asked about the sweat. However, Ferris Stannum did not have dried blood on his face. It was on his pillow, indicating to Bianca that Ferris Stannum had been smothered.

If Goodwife Tenbrook had died from tainted drink, say, perhaps the wine, and if Ferris Stannum had not been smothered, would he have eventually died from poisoning, too? But neither of them showed overt signs of poisoning. There was no vomiting, no inflammation of Tenbrook's mouth. Bianca took another sip of ale. Perhaps it was a subtle poison. One she was unfamiliar with. But if the wine was not tainted, what did Tenbrook die of? Was the coroner correct in his diagnosis of sweating sickness?

Finding the tumbler with the blue glaze, Bianca tipped it toward the light to examine the remnants of tincture stuck to the bottom like dried sap. She recalled the physician's quip when Tenbrook asked if he was poisoning her. "I would not be so obvious," he had said.

Bianca pursed her lips. "Indeed," she said cynically.

A pan of water sat on the table and she stuck her fingers in and dribbled a few drops in the cup, swirling the tincture until it dissolved. She found a small dropper and rinsed it clean. Drawing up the residue, she held the dropper to the side of a cage, allowing a rat to lap it dry. She set the cage on the table and waited for the rat to react.

The lousy ale made her sleepy and she fought the urge to lay her head in her arm. She forced herself to think of another remedy for the sweating sickness. The only way to know if the tea would work was if John came down with the disease.

Of course, if Meddybemps came by, she could make more tea and send him off to sell it at market. Bianca propped her fist against her cheek and watched the rat push its nose against the cage. She stood and stretched her arms over her head, noting John's snores filling the room. The black tiger cat leapt to the windowsill.

Bianca wandered beneath the sprigs of herbs hanging from the beams. The sprays took up a large portion of the room and were unlabeled, but she knew what each of them was and where she had gotten it. She gazed up at the hyssop and goldenseal. Both were possible ingredients for a remedy. She snapped off a sprig of meadowsweet and ran it under her nose. The fragrant herb was another possibility. They all had varying effects on lung secretions. Bianca gazed up at the dangling display. She strolled along the herbs, running her hands under them. She was pondering what combinations might work when her toe stubbed on a lump in the rush.

A bound package wrapped in linen lay directly in front of the window. Bianca went to the opening and looked out. The lane was empty of anyone who might have just tossed it through without her noticing.

"Sudden do you sneak up on me," said Bianca, bending over

to pick up the parcel. "What are you?" She turned it over, running her hand over a slash in its linen covering.

Thinking she was addressing it, the black tiger leapt down from the windowsill and strode over. It followed her back to the table and jumped up to investigate the curiosity along with its mistress.

Bianca unwound the linen from the parcel. She sat down and blew out a long breath. "You never made it to Cairo."

Chapter 18

Bianca ran her hand along the binding, sniffing the leather imbued with fifty years of experiments. She slid her fingers under the cover, noted a thin slit, and opened to the first page, knowing even before she'd read his signature that this was Ferris Stannum's alchemy journal. He had not hidden the book from her when he had mentored her, nor had he chided her for studying a page as it lay open on his dais. In fact, he had shown her his *Decknamen* for gold. The reverence she felt to have his entire life's work at her disposal, in her hands, left her momentarily awed.

She carefully turned over the pages. Pages filled with his *Decknamens*, his drawings and methods. Some she recognized, and followed his process through putrefaction and calcination—stages she had grown familiar with as a child watching her father. Occasionally, Stannum had taken the time to create drawings using inks and paint to color the figures. She marveled at the fanciful renderings of mythical green lions devouring blood red hearts, the animated moons with sleepy expressions. The suns with wise faces sprouting dagger-sharp rays.

With no consideration, the black tiger walked across the treasured pages. It ran its back under Bianca's nose, waiting for her attention. Petting or scolding, either would be fine.

Bianca pushed the shameless egoist off and kept the little nuisance at bay as she hefted the pages over to the end, where she believed Stannum's latest and greatest work must be. She was not disappointed.

The final page showed a glass vesicle shaped like an onion bulb. Within the vesicle stood a woman with her arms outstretched. A gesture of disclosure. The woman could be Eve, the giver of life. From her waist down she was submerged in water—symbolic of amniotic fluid. A drawing of a peacock rich in hues of green and blue stood to the side, its head turned toward the woman in the flask. Bianca knew from her father that peacocks represented immortality. She stared across the room. This was Stannum's visual interpretation of the philter of life. The more she thought about it, the more she was certain. This drawing represented the elixir of immortality.

She turned back a page and studied the drawings, interpreting them to be about congelation. She turned back another few, trying to find the beginning of his final experiment—the beginning of the process to create the elusive elixir.

As she scanned the carefully written text, her fascination with the noble art displaced her long-seated contempt for it. For years she had denied its validity. She blamed her father and his obsession for her family's financial strife. For all the rancor and resentment, she could not deny alchemy's occasional usefulness.

And now she was presented with the recipe for concocting the elixir of life. She sat back and contemplated what that meant. Death was the end of a person's physical existence. But was it the end of that person's spirit? At the moment of death, some people claimed to have seen the spirit leave a body, though Bianca had never seen it happen.

Faith in God was no different from believing in the spirit. There was no physical proof of either. You could not touch God like you could a flower. You could not touch the spirit. Some argued that God was everywhere, that God was the flower. Then was it true for the spirit?

What was spirit? Was it simply—life? Or the memory of it? After a person died, his spirit remained with the living in memories. But as time reached into the future, the memories diminished. With each succeeding generation moments were forgotten, stories were lost, until finally, the memory was extinguished. And, if someone was remembered, that memory was reduced to a name. But was there eternal life elsewhere for that soul?

If the soul was immortal, why can't our physical bodies last forever?

Bianca wanted to believe that the soul was immortal. There was no proof for believing it so. It was not based on any rational proof. But if life, if existence, consisted only of the time we had on earth, what was the use in following a moral path? If there was no reward at the end of it, was life itself irrelevant?

Bianca shook her head. "Life has relevance *because* we die."

John turned over in bed. He kicked off the sheet, complaining again of the heat. Bianca left the journal along with her thoughts about alchemy and immortality and went to him. Halfway there she smelled the putrid stink of sweat.

Her first thought was a plea that this could not be the sweat. But she knew it served no purpose to hope that it wasn't.

"John," she said, shaking his shoulder. "You must sit up. If you become short of breath, you must stay upright." But he did not seem to hear or care. His hair stuck to his scalp and his skin was drenched with an unnatural, offensive smell. She stood over him, holding the brewed tea.

Would he become suddenly short of breath? She had never seen the characteristic symptom of the disease. A symptom rarely overcome. The sweat chose its victims randomly, and who could say why some were spared while others were not?

She thought how she might give him the brew when suddenly John's eyes shot open. He opened his mouth for a sudden gasp of air. Bianca set down the tea and jammed a pillow behind his back to help him sit. He gripped her arm, his eyes wide with panic.

"John," she said, bending over him. "Take small breaths." But she had no idea what he should do. She could only encourage him to keep trying for breath.

John gulped. His eyes rolled. Surrounded by air that could save him, he struggled, unable to take what he needed. Bianca regretted his not drinking the tea infusion earlier. It might not have prevented the dyspnea, but she worried that if his lungs filled with mucus, he would suffocate. He held his sides and tipped his chin up and down as if nodding, but it was only an effort to fill his lungs with life-giving air.

Forcing him to take the tea now could result in his drowning from it. Helpless, she stood by his side, unable to think what to do or how to comfort him.

His struggle to breathe went on for hours. She thought he would have fainted, but finally his panic and short breaths slowed. Bianca lit a wall sconce and tallow and paced the length of the room. His breaths grew longer, but with them came a disconcerting rattle. His lungs were filling with mucus.

The moment she felt he might be able, Bianca encouraged him to down the tea infusion. "John, drink this." She held the cup to his lips. His eyes found hers and she gently tipped the drink into his mouth. He settled back against his pillows.

Bianca returned to pacing, thinking what to do. She gazed up at the herbs, racking her memory for possible healing combinations. But with the sound of each labored breath, the rattle of congestion further unnerved her.

Bianca could think of nothing else to do. No poultice, no syrup, eased his pain or struggling. If his humours were unbalanced, she knew not how to balance them. The only possible way to restore his health would be to bleed him. With no alternative, she caved to protocol. She sought her neighbor across the way to summon Barnabas Hughes, the physician.

As she waited for Hughes's arrival, Bianca returned to the alchemy journal. Mostly she wanted to occupy her mind and distract herself. Perhaps the book might contain enough information to make a healing tincture without going through the entire process of creating the elixir of life.

Eventually she found the beginning of Stannum's last experiment. He did not make a notation of when he began the process. Dates were conspicuously missing in his journal, making it difficult to gauge the length of any one stage in the process. She was familiar enough with alchemical methods to deduce the time required for some of the stages; however, the journal kept its secrets. Stannum had never worried that anyone else might confiscate his work, probably because only a handful of experienced alchemists could correctly interpret it.

Bianca had no idea how long she had been studying the journal when Barnabas Hughes arrived. She heard a gentle rapping and inquiry and looked up from her reading. "Sir," she said, standing and crossing the room to greet him. "I fear my husband may have the sweat." She led him to their bed. John was oblivious to their presence.

"I have given him mulberry root bark tea and silverweed to help him breathe."

Barnabas Hughes set his satchel on the edge of the bed. "I will need a bowl." Withdrawing a bottle from his satchel, Hughes removed the rag stuffed in its opening.

Bianca went to the table and rummaged about for a bowl with dried ingredients that she could dump. In her concern for John she had forgotten about the rat she had given Hughes's tincture to. She lifted its cage and peered in. The rat lay unresponsive. True, he had said it was a sleeping philter, but even after a vigorous shake, the rat slid about, lifeless. Bianca set the cage under the table. She looked over at Barnabas Hughes, her stomach churning. Her hand shook as she poured the contents of the bowl into a jar, spilling most of it on the table.

Hughes didn't notice her difficulty holding the bowl still as he tipped the bottle's contents into it. Out slithered several leeches. Their flat bodies undulated gracefully as they swam in clear liquid. Unfolding a worn leather wallet, Hughes removed a polished lancet. He touched a thumb to the blade, producing a small drop of blood. Approving of its sharpness, Barnabas Hughes ran a finger along John's neck.

"Must you bleed him there?" asked Bianca, alarmed.

"Your husband is delirious from an accumulation of blood in his skull. This is the quickest and most effective way to release that pressure. I must ask that you turn his head and hold it still."

Bianca set the bowl next to Hughes and moved to the front of the bed. In spite of John's protest, she placed her hands on either side of his face and turned his head toward the wall. He had been unaware of the doctor's presence until that moment. "What?" he exclaimed, catching a glimpse of the lancet near his face. His eyes wild, he began to struggle.

"You must hold him still," said Hughes. He located the vein he would puncture and pressed his finger firmly against John's throat.

Bianca bent close and murmured in John's ear. Her reassurance worked, for the tension in John's body drained and he lay still, though likely he may have exhausted himself.

Her eyes welled as Barnabas Hughes pressed the lancet into John's flesh, causing John to flinch. A crimson ribbon of blood trickled down his neck. Hughes reached into the bowl and picked out a leech. He held it between his thumb and first finger. Carefully, the physician touched its mouth to John's wound.

"Couldn't you collect the fluid in a bowl? Why must you attach those?"

Hughes answered in a reassuring tone. "They prevent the blood from clotting."

Bianca could barely watch as it gloried to the taste of her husband's blood. Once it had secured its mouth against John's skin, its body began to constrict and pulse as it fed. Hughes attached a second leech to John's neck.

John kept his eyes tightly closed, placing his full faith in Bianca. She touched her lips to his ear, whispering words of comfort. Struggling to calm her growing unease, she laid her cheek against his and shut her eyes until the leeches were removed.

"I've done all I can," said Barnabas Hughes as he dressed John's wound with a plaster of herbs. "He is in God's hands now." He wiped the lancet on the bedsheet.

Bianca stared at the leeches floating in the bowl, lethargic from their meal.

"You may throw them in the stream," said Hughes, noticing her reticence. "There is no short supply. I have no more use for them." He packed his leather satchel, closed his bag. "If that is all, I shall bid you well." He rose, laying his hand across John's forehead for a moment. He took up his limp wrist to feel John's pulse. Hughes looked over at Bianca. He read the fear on her face, so like his own. So like that of anyone about to lose a loved one. Hughes felt the urge to assure her, to comfort her. Youth was so blissfully ignorant of life's painful misfortunes.

"Time moves slowly for those waiting to see what it has in mind," he said. He wasn't sure what he saw in her reaction. Was it gratitude? Or the naïve refusal to accept her husband's inevitable death? Bianca Goddard was especially difficult to comprehend. He started for the door. Halfway there, he paused at the table where the alchemy journal lay open. "You now dabble in the noble art?"

Still spent from what had just taken place, Bianca shook her head, distracted. She was holding the bowl of leeches and staring at them. "Should I not kill them first?" she asked, glancing up.

Barnabas Hughes studied her before answering. "If it should please you. Then certainly."

CHAPTER 19

Dusk settled over London, painting the sky vermilion. Though night had not yet fallen, Bianca couldn't shake an unsettled feeling as she hurried down the bridge's center. The lane was always dimly lit from the stately merchants' homes and shops lining the span. Every merchant or haberdasher worth a groat wanted his address to be Tower Bridge. And while some natural light seeped through the gaps between buildings, it was not enough to put her mind at ease. Bianca wished she had either left earlier or perhaps waited until the shopkeepers and residents had lit their lanterns.

After hours of trying to make sense of Stannum's final process, Bianca determined she needed the wisdom of the one person she knew who might be able to decipher some of Stannum's elusive *Decknamens*.

Her father.

She did not relish having to convince him to help her, but she knew it was futile to try to re-create Stannum's process without his advice.

So while John rested from his bloodletting, Bianca wrapped the alchemy journal in its linen cloth and dropped it in a satchel she slung over her shoulder. She considered asking her neighbor to check in on him, then worried he would be exposed to the contagion. Deciding she would not be gone long, she kissed John's forehead before leaving him in the care of the black tiger, which had groomed itself and was turning circles next to John's legs, finding a suitable spot to nap.

It had been months since Bianca had last seen her parents.

Albern Goddard worked in an abandoned warehouse near the Thames. She expected her father to have heard of the accomplished Ferris Stannum. Stannum had to have been one of the oldest practitioners in London. Alchemists, while feigning disinterest, were quite aware (sometimes painfully so), of other alchemists' achievements and purported wealth. But whether rumors of Stannum's elixir of life and his sudden death had reached her father, she did not know.

Bianca kept a hand on the shoulder strap of the satchel and met the eye of every pedestrian and loiterer she passed. Only a few gave her pause, but the feeling she was being followed never waned. As she neared the drawbridge, she found it difficult to shake an eerie sensation. It was not usual for her to feel apprehensive walking across the exposed span. She tentatively stepped onto its iron grate. Shaking off her fears, she dashed across.

On the other side, Bianca kept a lively pace until she emerged onto Thames Street and into the bustle of London. Even in the fading twilight she could see better than she had on the bridge. Relieved to be out in the open, she followed the road paralleling the river until it intersected with Lambeth Hill.

Her parents' rent was one of several lining the slightly inclined neighborhood, known for its tawdry cluster of residences. She turned onto the lane and noticed the small changes only those once intimately familiar with the neighborhood would see. Mrs. Templeton's front door had rotted through near the bottom, and a shutter that once hung squarely over the family Dodd's window now drooped, held by a single hinge. Bianca had forgotten how the fusty smell of moldering thatch roofs permeated the air. A twinge of apprehension settled in her stomach as she wondered what kind of reception she would receive. Hopefully her mother would be home, as she balanced her father's cynical disposition. Besides, Bianca missed spending time with her.

The timbers between the sorrel daub had darkened from mildew, almost black in some areas. A spreading mat of moss grew at the bottom of her parents' door from the perpetual shade and damp. The window shutter was open and Bianca stood back a distance to peer inside.

All was as she remembered, unadorned walls and an interior simply furnished. Her mother worked at a table tying bunches of herbs, tossing them into a pile to be hung overhead later. Bianca scanned the room for her father but did not see him. Perhaps he was in his room of alchemy. She decided to visit anyway.

She knocked, calling for her mother as she cracked the door open.

"Bianca, my child," said her mother, looking up from her collection of herbs. "Help me gather this mint." She pushed a mound of cuttings toward Bianca.

It would have been unusual for her mother to have acted surprised or even pleased to see Bianca. It simply was not her way. Instead, she treated Bianca as if she had merely stepped out for a moment. Their relationship continued where it had left off. The passage of time had not changed her mother, nor did her mother seem to think the passage of time had changed her daughter.

"How do you fare?" Bianca asked, ducking under a structural beam. She set her satchel on the table. Inquiring out of consideration was not a lesson she had learned from her mother. She snipped off a length of string.

"What do you mean, how do I fare?" Her mother looked up from tying off a thick bunch of rue. She pushed her wavy hair off her face with her upper arm. "I fare as I always do. I manage. I make my salves. I take care of my people."

By "people" she meant a group of neighbors who regularly sought her remedies and medical advice. Her mother's old-world mentality served her well. She could spout all kinds of nonsense and her patients believed every word. As a child, Bianca had been fascinated by her mother's outlandish cures, but more so with her clients' reactions. She recalled her mother had treated a plantar wart by cutting a dead mouse in half and binding its torso to the bottom of the man's foot. Once the mouse was in place the man's entire demeanor changed. He happily paid her mother and hobbled out the door. Bianca had never forgotten how pleased he had been to have a dead mouse tied to his foot.

It was that sort of appreciation that inspired Bianca to make her own remedies. But to her credit Bianca was able to discern between the strange and what could be thought of as reasonable.

Bianca ignored her mother's defensive response. She collected some peppermint and wound it with twine. "Some time has passed since I have seen you. How are you managing in the heat?"

"As long as I have the rain barrel to stand in when I get wilted, I can cope. The heat cannot last forever." Her mother tossed the bound bunch on a pile. "I only see you when you've got some news of importance or need help." She tipped her head back and looked down her nose at Bianca. "You with child?"

"Nay, do I look to be?"

Her mother tilted her head to one side. "I don't suppose you do. You're too thin." She gathered another handful of herbs and arranged them with their stems in one direction. "Last time you visited, you told us you married that John."

"Mother, 'that John' is now my husband. You may call him simply John."

"Well then. How is simply John? It doesn't look as though he feeds you."

"John is ill. I believe he has the sweat."

Her mother laid down the sprigs and put her fists on her hips. "Then what are you doing here? You should be with him."

"He is sleeping. There is nothing I can do for him at the moment." Bianca glanced around, avoiding her mother's disapproving stare. "I am looking for Father. Is he here?"

"You're looking for your father?" her mother repeated, surprised. She searched Bianca's eyes, puzzling over her daughter's unspoken intentions. Still watching Bianca, she gathered another bunch of herbs and motioned to the alley. "He is standing out back in the rain barrel."

Bianca had not spoken to her father since she announced her marriage to John. She had thought he would show at least a little joy having one less body to provide for, but she had been wrong. Her father met the news with typical disinterest.

His apathy no longer fomented her resentment. It was simply what she expected. Dismay served no purpose. However, she did believe she was entitled, on occasion, to seek his help, since she had once given him hers.

Bianca knew she would be received coldly, but she also knew her father would be unable to resist looking at another alchemist's journal. Especially Ferris Stannum's.

She walked through the rent, past where her pallet had once been—the space was now taken up by a cupboard. The door to the back alley was open. Her father did not immediately see her, which gave Bianca a moment to brace herself for his cool indifference.

He looked like a stork wading in a pool. His long, thin legs were bare and he stood in the barrel, which came up to his thighs. He wore a linen shirt that reached his knees and a straw basket on his head to protect his thinning pate from the sun. Even half-dressed and wearing unconventional headgear he looked forbiddingly unapproachable. He must have sensed his being watched, for he turned his head regally to look on her.

"Father." Bianca tucked her chin in respect.

His gray eyes ran down her person and up again. He returned his gaze back to his previous view, which seemed to be a fissure in the building opposite.

"Father, I've come to ask your assistance." She detected a subtle lift of an eyebrow as the basket slightly wobbled. Appealing to his sense of humanity, his sympathy, would be useless, so Bianca did not mention John's illness or her desire to cure him. Instead, she solicited her father's help by interesting him in the journal.

And interested he was. He removed the straw basket and

placed it on the ground beside the barrel. Lifting one leg to his chest and then the other, he stepped out of the cistern, reinforcing Bianca's comparison to a stork. She followed him inside.

"Where is this book?" he asked, glowering at the table piled in herbs.

Bianca's mother returned his glare and maneuvered a stool under a beam to hang the sprigs of herbs. She snapped up an armful of sprays and endeavored to teeter upon the stool.

Bianca removed the swaddled tome from her satchel and laid it before her father. He stared at the journal for an extended moment before speaking. "Do you plan to remove the cloth, or do you expect me to first comment on the wrapping?"

Bianca bit her tongue and pulled the covering off the book. Her patience nearly drained, she opened the journal to Ferris Stannum's final experiment—his recipe for the elixir of life. "I was able to decipher most of his symbols and *Decknamens*, but I am confounded by this final process."

Albern Goddard scoured the elaborate illustrations, the brilliant colors, the inspired and fanciful drawings depicting his beloved science. Not only was the text filled with ingenious combinations of base metals with minerals, but the presentation of Stannum's methods, his detailed yet subtle drawings, was a work of art. Albern dropped onto the bench and moved the book closer to better study it.

"Find my spectacles and bring me that light." Albern waved his hand in the direction of an unlit candle.

Bianca's mother cheerfully ignored her husband's requests, allowing Bianca to answer them. She continued to hang her bunches of herbs, stepping down from the stool and collecting more armfuls from the table while being sure to dispense a withering look at her husband before returning to her task.

Luckily Bianca found her father's magnifiers without too much trouble but spent more time searching for a working flint to light the candle. She set it beside him.

Albern ran his finger along the page, muttering to himself. He chuckled intermittently, enjoying some private jape only alchemists would find humorous. He nodded; he scowled; his eyebrows lifted; his eyebrows furrowed. His wife could have fallen off the rickety stool and broken a leg, Bianca could have jumped on the table and danced in front of him, and he would never have noticed.

He ignored Bianca's request that he look at Ferris Stannum's final experiment and turned back the pages to some other process that seemed to be interesting him more. Unable to wait for her father to meander through the journal, Bianca boldly reminded him that her question concerned the final experiment.

Albern Goddard froze. His eyes widened with annoyance, sliding sideways before he turned his head.

Bianca expected a snide retort. However, none was forthcoming. Without comment, he returned his gaze to the book. He heaved the pages back to the final process and began to study it.

The longer Albern read, the more intense his interest in Ferris Stannum's final accomplishment. As the candle was about to burn out, he looked up. "He has created the elixir of life."

Bianca had remembered seeing him this excited only once when she was a young girl assisting him in his alchemy room. Such zeal was reserved for that extraordinary moment of grasping some truth, some kernel of sublime understanding that made every sacrifice, every tortured moment of self-doubt, suddenly worthwhile.

"Aye." She nodded. "He was about to send the journal to Cairo for verification. Unfortunately, he was murdered before he could send it off."

"And the journal mysteriously appeared in your rent?"

"It did."

Albern could have questioned her on its inexplicable arrival, which sounded suspicious at best, but chose to leave his daughter to her own dangers. After all, she was his child and as such was predestined to travel an unconventional if not difficult path in life. Instead, he concentrated on the elixir.

"So you are trying to re-create the elixir of life?"

Bianca refrained from telling him why she was interested and distorted her explanation by avoiding the topic of John's potentially fatal illness. "I merely wish to glean useful information from his recipe. Perhaps I can find a remedy that might help those suffering from painful disease."

"Do you wish to grant these sufferers immortal life?"

"I only wish to ease their suffering."

"But if you were to impart immortality—how would you answer to God?"

Bianca refrained from arguing. She had never understood why a higher entity did not intervene on behalf of His creation. God stopped Abraham from murdering his only son, but where was He when her parents' neighbor Mallon was accused of witchcraft simply for being old and keeping a cat? The parish constable set her in a dunking stool, and if she had not drowned she would have been burned alive. Where was He to prevent such a grievous miscarriage of justice? It seemed to Bianca creating a little bit of immortality might not matter to such an unreliable God.

And yet, Albern stubbornly ascribed to matters of morality with God in mind. He adhered to the old religion, though his belief nearly got him killed for resisting King Henry's changes. These days Albern caused no stir. He lived a life of demure experimentation. His wife made a meager pittance that kept them fed. But then, he had always relied on her to sustain them.

"Surely I do not have to create the entire elixir for it to do some good."

"And which part of the elixir do you suppose would serve your purpose?"

"I was hoping you might advise me."

Albern gave a dismissive snort and fixed Bianca with his pale gray eyes. "One cannot stop a process at some arbitrary point and hope that it does what you want. It takes months or years to learn the advantages, if there are any, of any one particular stage. This is a recipe for the elixir of life. If you create it, you create all the moral and spiritual consequences that go along with administering it to a person. You cannot give someone a little bit of immortality. You either create the elixir of life. Or you do not."

Albern waited for her to speak, and when she did not, his response sounded condescending. "You have not fully considered the consequences."

Bianca did not tell her father about John's illness, though she reeled from a feeling of desperation welling inside. She had to argue that creating the elixir was important to her without divulging the true reason behind wanting to create it.

But Albern had exposed a fault in reasoning that Bianca simply could not accept. She did not agree that creating the elixir was an all-or-nothing proposition.

"How can you assume there is no useful purpose in creating even a portion of the elixir? Where does it say that I must create the entire potion or I will have nothing of value? I am willing to take that chance. If I can create even one dose of syrup that might ease another's suffering, is it not worth trying?"

At this, Bianca's mother stopped hanging herbs and leveled a keen stare at her husband. "Listen to the girl's argument. It speaks of her ambition. Why deny her your expertise if others might gain from it? What do you fear?"

"Fear?" said Albern Goddard. "I fear nothing about this child. But I worry for her eternal soul. She must consider the consequences if she is to challenge God's will. This desire to alter God's intent is not natural. It is not for her to change the fate of any man."

Bianca's mother stepped down off her stool. Her grave face and dark eyes pinned her husband from across the room. "Natural? What is natural about spending your life obsessing to project gold from lead? Is that God's will? I believe it serves God more to want to ease the suffering of the sick."

Albern started to speak but thought better of it. If there was one thing he had learned in all his years, it was to avoid arguing with ignorant women. Instead he changed his tone. If his daughter did not care whether she lost her soul to eternal damnation, then why should he bother trying to save her?

Albern settled back on the bench. He looked at his wife and

daughter. After taking a breath and blowing it out, he managed to keep his voice even. "Tell me what you wish to know."

Bianca's face shed some of its worry and she flashed a brief smile at her mother. She leaned over her father's shoulder, peering at the text, and pointed. "Be labored so with heat both moist and temperate," she read, "that is all white and purely made spiritual. Heaven upon earth must be reiterated, until the soul with the body be incorporated, that earth become all that before was heaven."

Her father thought a moment and turned back a page and then another. He studied for a moment and returned to the text in question. "You must subject the dross that you have gotten up to now to sublimation. But you will fail unless you use a special instrument." Albern shook his head. "You need a kerotakis."

"Kerotakis," echoed Bianca, thinking where she had heard the word. "Ferris Stannum showed me one." She frowned. "Is it necessary to the process?"

"Only Stannum can answer that. But I would assume it is likely, if he has so written it."

Bianca straightened. "Do you have one?"

"I do."

"May I use it?"

"You may not." This was one argument he had no intention of losing. He refused to lend his most fragile instruments to anyone. And that included his heathen daughter.

"I shall return it by tomorrow."

"You will not. This is a process that will take you longer than an evening. If you want to dabble in the noble art, you must have the proper equipage. But more important, you must have the right destiny. And you do not possess it."

"And you are the judge of that?"

"Have you spent years in single-minded pursuit? You create a salve here; you mix a concoction there. You have not shown the vital reverence my science requires. You will not succeed."

Bianca gritted her teeth, avoiding an argument. She snapped the alchemy journal closed.

"I believe you have helped me more than you thought," she said. She snatched away the book and returned it to her satchel, wadding up the linen cloth and stuffing it in on top. "It is always an education when I am with you, Father." She hoped he felt the sharp prick of her intimation.

CHAPTER 20

The unease Bianca felt earlier when crossing the bridge into London doubled on her return home to Southwark.

Earlier, the Rat Man had smelled her coming. He sensed her approach as he lingered under the drawbridge waiting for nightfall. His nose caught the whiff of alchemy carried on her person. His curiosity had been piqued when he saw the bearer of the book was different from before.

It was not true that the wraith showed himself only to those who knew how to look for him. That was a story perpetuated by those whose imaginations were overactive from too much drink. But the wraith did have a sense of when he might be seen. And he had a sense of who might see him. And drunks, more often than not, were the only ones around at such perverse hours.

The wraith was familiar with Bianca, the daughter of a disreputable alchemist. He knew her smell. He knew the feel of the air when she passed through it. He had watched her as a young girl collecting plants along the riverbank. And had seen her watch a man die in the early morning hours when she should have been at prayer.

Her curiosity intrigued him. There had been a time when his character was not unlike hers.

She was a lonely child. But perhaps she chose to be alone. Either way, she stood apart from others her age. A keen observer, he'd seen her sneak into the Tower on the morning of Catherine Howard's execution. It had been a private dispatch, but the girl managed to slip past guards unnoticed. And later, she managed to leave without their notice. He imagined the spectacle had made an impression on her. How could it not? He saw the result of that experience—her shunning of the affections of a wheaten-haired rascal who followed her like a smitten puppy.

What woman isn't changed by watching another executed? Especially a woman condemned to dying who had once been so dearly loved? The king had his reasons for seeing Catherine dead, reasons tremulously written in a letter and deposited anonymously where Henry would find it. The Rat Man snickered. Love—man's impetuous lunacy.

But now he sensed Bianca's desperation. He smelled that she was driven by love. She was older now and, unfortunately, had entered into love's most unpredictable folly. He wished he could advise her, tell her that love, like life, is ephemeral. She should not invest her heart in such transient pursuits. But communication was a privilege he had forfeited long ago. The Rat Man could only watch and observe. Just as Bianca had done.

The second source of Bianca's unease came not from under the bridge, but from the streets on which she walked.

She left her parents' rent on Lambeth Hill and felt her spine tingle once she started down Thames Street toward Paul's Wharf. Ahead stood St. Benet, its bells silent for the night. A few graves were marked in its yard, the stones leaning and the inscriptions worn from time. A lone oak stood guard, its leaves quivering in the slight breeze. Shadows darkened the ground where she stepped, spreading up the sides of buildings, swallowing her as she passed. She turned the corner abutting the churchyard and had taken no more than a couple of hurried steps toward Burley House when her suspicions that she was being followed were confirmed.

She felt a brazen tug on her satchel, and as she yanked back in resistance, the force of her weight was used against her. Whoever had wanted the satchel suddenly let go and she stumbled forward, falling on her side, clutching the bag against her body. She had not suffered from the fall and instinct told her she should not lie there long. She reached out to brace herself to stand and was instantly punished for that effort. Pain exploded in her hand as it was crushed by a well-heeled boot. She yelled, and with her good arm clung to the attacker's leg to prevent his driving his heel into her hand again.

Her shoulder lurched upward as her arm was pulled up by the strap. Bianca yowled at seeing the satchel disappear over her head.

To prevent further protest, her assailant swung the satchel. Bianca felt the impact to her head and toppled from its force. She lay in the dirt, stunned. The black night spun about, making her dizzy. It was easier to close her eyes.

Thoughts of retrieving the satchel retreated into a gathering muddle of memories jostling about inside her head. For now, whosoever wanted the journal could have it as far as she was concerned. Her head pounded. A piteous cry escaped her lips, sounding distant even to her. She rolled onto her back and tried to open her eyes.

If she had any sense left, she would not have been able to use it. Like a scene from a play she had seen in Pike Garden, a scoundrel launched himself through the air, using a low stone wall from which to catapult. Bianca heard the thud of feet against a chest. She heard a gasp of breath being knocked out of someone.

Bianca tried to focus on the brutish scrabbling beside her. Two men wrestled, their legs entwined almost like lovers. But there was no mistaking their intent. Arms flailed and legs bent, trying to find purchase against the compacted dirt of the road. Their bodies rolled into the building's shadow. The dull smack of punches and grunting was all she could hear. They snarled and growled, the language of animals—not men.

With effort, Bianca dragged herself in the opposite direction, distancing herself from the tangled fight, and sat against a building. She pulled her legs up to her chest, keeping completely hidden in shadow while the men continued their brawl.

Still dazed from the blow to her head, she laid her cheek against the stone building. The ground looked more comfortable. Bianca relented to its allure. She closed her eyes and the world faded away.

CHAPTER 21

Barnabas Hughes did know something of alchemists. His medical practice familiarized him with apothecaries (whom he had come to rely on), herbalists (whom he regarded with some suspicion), and alchemists (whom he regarded with even greater suspicion). But Ferris Stannum had been different.

Ferris Stannum was so old that his devotion to and knowledge of the noble art were practically mythical. Stannum had perfected enough chemical methods to impress Hughes, whether he understood them or not. At least the physician was astute enough to realize that this chemistry, this dabbling in minerals, temperatures, and metals, might be beneficial. How? He could not say. Nor did he have any idea where all of this experimentation could lead.

While his opinion of alchemy was essentially one of dubious interest, a small portion of his mind remained open to its possibilities.

As his daughter's condition wavered, his desperation led him to ponder the dark science and its strange achievements. He wondered if Ferris Stannum had any remaining elixir of life. To his recollection, he thought it had been completely used. Even if Stannum had remaining elixir stashed in his room, how would he know how much to dispense? What was the correct balance? Was it like mercury, in that a little might help but more might kill? No, it was senseless to even consider the possibility.

Verity called out to him, her voice feeble yet so endearing that the sound of it made his throat catch. He savored its sweet lilt. He committed the sound to memory, forever imprinting it on his heart. How many more times might he hear her speak? Please, God, let this not be the last.

"My child," he said, finding her hand and cradling it in his. He sat on the bed next to her.

She stirred slightly from his touch. Her lips curved into a smile that flickered and disappeared like the sun peeking through a bank of swiftly moving clouds. Her eyes opened slightly. "Papa," she said. She settled back on her pillow.

"Rest, dear one. Do not exhaust yourself." He held her hand until her breathing evened and the tiny creases of worry and pain relaxed from her brow. He laid her hand by her side.

He had considered it before. Possession of the journal was not a cure. He had no means by which to interpret its mysterious language. He knew of no apothecary who could even begin to deduce any of its meaning. But who could create the coveted elixir? Certainly not Thomas Plumbum. Hughes had agreed with Stannum's decision not to entrust his journal to that desperate mountebank. Plumbum could not be trusted.

Barnabas rose from the bed and winced. His limbs ached. He was not so young anymore. Holding his side, he went to the door and leaned against its jamb to gaze up at the night sky. Another gypsy night. He hoped for rain to match his mood and to quench his growing frustration.

How had the journal come into Bianca Goddard's possession? More important, what was she planning to do with it? Did she possess the ability, the knowledge, to create the elixir of life? It had been within his grasp. So close . . .

He knew about her father's reputation and ability. Years ago,

Hughes had served at court when Albern Goddard had been in favor with the king. He had seen the alchemist impress His Majesty with his discoveries and explanations. Albern Goddard was a strange character. Since his fall from grace he avoided public scrutiny, rarely showing himself except when walking between his home and his decrepit room of alchemy. Without Bianca to fetch his ingredients, he relied on young boys to run his errands. Of all the alchemists Barnabas Hughes knew, Goddard was probably the one most able to interpret Ferris Stannum's journal.

Perhaps it was for the best that Albern's daughter was in possession of the coveted work.

Barnabas Hughes turned his head and observed Verity. Fortunately, she seemed at peace, for now. He closed his eyes, wishing to be spared life's senseless sorrows. Indeed, as he collapsed into a chair, he wished the world could be spared all senseless sorrows.

Thomas Plumbum stopped at the Royal Poke and ordered a pottle pot. He hoped he'd made a lasting impression on the loathsome coward. Plumbum straightened, assuring himself he had definitely trounced the gutless dastard and had chased him off.

A pretty maid of fair complexion and copper hair set the ale in front of him and collected her coin. He was weary enough to allow his gaze to fall upon the dewy shade of cleavage hovering at eye level. There his interest lingered happily while she collected empty tankards, exchanged tart words with a patron, then caught him nearly cross-eyed for a better look at her cleavage.

"I would say you need more than an ale tonight," she said, straightening, ignoring his leer. She was used to such wanton ogling. "You're bleeding from a gash on the temple."

Plumbum did not respond, but neither did he drag his eyes from her display. He took another sip, continuing to stare.

The maid scowled, gathering a fistful of empty tankards on one hip. "I know from where I have seen you. You're Plumbum, my father's friend. An alchemist."

This got Thomas Plumbum's attention, and he jolted upright as if prodded by a hot poker. He scrutinized the girl's face. Ferris Stannum's daughter—Amice. The last he had seen her she seemed but a child.

He felt the unwanted attention of a table of men giving him black looks. Having it announced one is an alchemist does not particularly ensure a safe passage home.

Plumbum shook his head. "Nay, you have me mistaken for another," he said. "I do not know your father." Like Peter denying Jesus, he shirked and listened for a cock to crow.

Amice insisted, trying to shog his memory. "You hid at my father's when you had a band of men after you. Didn't the father of a young lad take exception with you? I remember you were perhaps overly partial to his son."

"Nay, I am not that man. It is possible another may resemble me. But I am not he!" Plumbum glanced nervously at the table of inquisitive stares. "I do most thoroughly assure you." Seeing no sympathy from his tablemates, he took on an indignant tone. "I am appalled at what you are implying. I do not have to sit here and be accused of heinous behavior."

"Then what is it ye do?" asked one of the patrons. The man had the kind of intelligence, a perceptiveness, that set him apart.

One glance was enough to worry Plumbum at ever having his true nature painfully exposed. His lie had better be a good one. And he had better tell it as smoothly as he could. "I am a tailor," he said, hiding his face behind a long drink of ale. Inwardly, he cringed at his lack of imagination.

The man's eyes worked their way down his person and up again. "A tailor, ye say?" The corner of his mouth lifted in a condescending smile. "By my measure, not a very good one."

"I was recently set upon. Tangled in a scuff. My garb is a bit frayed."

"Frayed? Sirrah, tattered is a better choice of word. A more shapeless and unsavory doublet I have not had the misfortune of seeing. Indeed, I have witnessed beggars more handsomely clad. It does not speak well of your vocation."

"I would thank you not to judge. I have fallen on difficult times as late."

"As late as the day ye were born?"

Amice snorted, expecting to be vindicated. She ignored the whistling and waving imbibers ready for refills.

Thomas Plumbum took another lengthy drink of ale, hoping by the time he set his tankard on the table, the man would be gone. Or at least would have lost interest in him.

"What might a tailor be in a scuffle about?" the man persisted to Plumbum's chagrin. "And why might a tailor be havin' his ale in this puny boozing ken?"

"Did you not hear? I have fallen on difficult times."

"Aye, by the looks of ye, I say ye have certainly fallen. Ye got an eye swelling bigger than a bull's bollocks from the looks of it." The men at the table roused with gusty accord, further encouraging the provocateur to grow more brazen. He held out a flap of Plumbum's torn sleeve. "Gentlemen, I ask what construct of fashion might this be?"

"I would offer he wears the garment of a Spaniard."

"Nay," said another, "methinks it is the new French fashion." He batted his eyes and kissed the air, elbowing his neighbor. The table of men launched into jeering their horse-eating foe across the sea. For the moment, Plumbum was spared further harassment. The king's preparations to invade France were greatly despised by the commoners. Their taxes had increased and they were being enlisted to risk their lives for the glory of their peevish king.

The alchemist took advantage of this shift in attention and, as unobtrusively as he could, rose from the bench and sneaked toward the door.

But his exiting had not gone unnoticed. Amice watched with baleful eyes. She resented being made a liar and disappeared into the kitchen.

Still dazed and bleary, Bianca opened her eyes. At first she was completely baffled. With her cheek against the ground, she saw nothing but dirt and the legs of an abandoned shop stall across the way. She pushed herself to sitting, wincing from the pain in her hand, and leaned back against the stone building. After a few minutes of waiting for her head to clear, she was able to remember where she was and why.

Night had not yet given way to dawn. She figured that at least she had been lying in the street for only a few minutes. No night watchman called the time, but by the deep black sky overhead, she thought perhaps it was the small hours. She held up her hand and worked her fingers. Fortunately, they all moved as they should, but she expected her skin to be purple by the next day. She rubbed her cheekbone and opened her mouth, feeling her jaw. Her body ached a bit, but she was relieved she'd escaped with a minimum of hurt.

If she had not heard the faint cry of a baby and the distant clop of hooves, she would have wondered if the town was even inhabited. A visitor arriving at this neglected hour would think London abandoned. Bianca got to her feet and straightened her bodice, brushed the powdery dirt from her kirtle. Looking down toward the water, she wondered if she might still find a ferrier to take her across to Southwark. No doubt the bridge would be closed for curfew.

Her thoughts flew to John, and she worried how he was faring. Was he still sleeping or had he woken and discovered her gone? Would he even be aware of his surroundings? Just the thought of him alone and needing her help spurred her to action. She glanced around before heading to the river and caught sight of her satchel. It was pushed against the stone wall next to the building where she had lain.

She looked around and, seeing no other living soul, went to the bag. Was it not the reason for her being followed and attacked? Someone had tried to steal the satchel and had made sure she could not object to its being taken. Yet, there it was, in plain view.

Bianca had little recollection of what she had seen. Who had attacked her? And who had intervened? Cautiously she opened the satchel. She removed the linen cloth stuffed on top and found the journal underneath. Whoever wanted the satchel, or the journal, had not taken it. Bianca crammed the cloth back into the bag and tied the flap closed.

She glanced around. Was someone watching her? Watching to see that she took the satchel? Bianca slung it across her chest, trying to remember the person who had come to her aid. Why had he come to her defense and not stayed? Why leave the satchel? Perhaps he had no interest in it.

Her muffin cap lay nearby and she shook off the dirt and stuffed it in her pocket, keeping a watchful eye out. She headed for the water. This time, she gripped the bag with both hands and kept it in front of her. A night watchman called, "Two in the night and to all a good night."

But perhaps she was wrong to think her rescuer had no interest in the satchel. Could he have intervened to make sure she kept it? A chill ran up her spine, and it wasn't from the night air.

The moon shimmered on the river, luminous silver, like flowing mercury. A lone ferrier answered her whistle. Soon she would be home.

Thomas Plumbum slipped into the night air, distancing himself from the Royal Poke and its atrocious clientele. He made a mental note to avoid the unsavory ken in the future. Perhaps if he had not been recognized by Ferris Stannum's daughter he might have gone unnoticed. He could have enjoyed his pottle pot in peace. The alchemist unbuttoned his doublet. It was too hot and too late to bother with appearance.

The gash on his temple oozed. Plumbum removed his cap and wiped the sweat trickling into the wound. He would soon be home and could tend to it then.

He turned a corner, and a mongrel drinking from a puddle of city filth decided the alchemist was more interesting and fell in pace beside him. Plumbum was in no mood for company. He reared back and kicked the dog in the side, launching it into the air. It landed, whimpering pathetically, and scrambled to be gone.

It was damnably dark this time of night. Lanterns had been extinguished; candles had burned out. The only means of illumination was the light of the stars and the Queen Moon sneering at him from behind St. Paul's Cathedral, refusing to rise above its roof and light his way.

London suffered from a disconcerting lack of respectable alehouses—essentially a contradiction in terms; there probably was no such establishment. Well, thought Plumbum bitterly, at least not an alehouse that he could afford.

He trudged on, avoiding the Crooked Cork and Jack Blade's territory. Ever wary, Thomas Plumbum hesitated, thinking he'd heard the squeak of leather behind him. He wheeled about, squinting into the inky night. It took a moment for his eyes to thoroughly focus on the street behind him.

"I know you are there," he said, warning whoever followed him. He withdrew his dirk from its sheath and held it at the ready. "What do you want?" He slashed at the empty air. "If it is coin, I haven't got any." The pottle pot from the Royal Poke had been no watered-down swill. It affected his vision and compromised his better judgment. Sober, he would never have conversed with a ruffian whom he could not even see.

Blood dripped in his eyes and he dashed the cut with his sleeve, resuming a menacing pose. "Come, now," he squawked, losing his nerve. "Show yourself."

No one did.

He waited another minute, ears straining for any telltale hint. He was rattled to the point where he thought he might puke; his attention wavered. His singular notion was to make it home.

He started walking backward, still watching for a stalker to show himself. Seeing no one, Plumbum turned back to face the road ahead of him and quickened his step.

If he weren't so anxious to be home, he would have circled back to St. Benet's to see if the satchel was still against the wall. His head throbbed. He was so weary he didn't even think he could make it there and back.

Blood continued to trickle from the gash, and it ran down his face, dripping onto his front, further aggravating him. "Ach, and now the doublet is staining with blood." He muttered how he would have to soak it in his rain barrel but remembered this was not possible since the barrel was now empty. He had dumped the water—fouled with Jack Blade's piss—into the alley. "And no rain in a fortnight," he said, feeling demoralized.

He stopped to look at something orange in the road that caught his eye and bent down. "Aw, poor bird," he said, picking up the dismembered foot of a duck. He envisioned the creature trying to walk on one leg and burst out laughing imagining it. The sound of his guffaw startled him. He was drunker than he thought. He glanced around to see if anyone had heard him. Seeing no one, he reasoned aloud, "Well, he just stays in the water." He wondered how a duck would look swimming with one foot. Would it wobble in the water? Or would it swim in circles? He tossed the foot over his shoulder and continued on.

As he neared St. Paul's Cathedral, he paused to watch the young gamins sleeping in the shadows of its massive stone exterior. A pang of desire stirred his membership, and he adjusted his codpiece but thought better of it. He was nearly home and mustn't risk his chance of getting there.

His jittery nerves and drink caused him to suddenly appeal to the heavens. "Have I not proven myself?" He did not wait for an answer, but forced himself to keep walking. "My past may have been filled with poor decisions, but have I not redeemed myself?" Somewhere a dog began to bark. "Do I not deserve some reward? Some mercy, some compensation for my atonement?" He stopped and stared up at the stars, looking for a sign. Was that a shooting star? The red planet? "At least acknowledge that I have proven myself worthy."

But Thomas Plumbum would get no commendation on this dark night. He dropped his head to his chest.

With an exasperated sigh, Thomas staggered on. It would soon be morning, and with it came the promise of a new day. From now on, he would live a virtuous life. If God didn't feel like bargaining today, maybe He would tomorrow.

Within sight of his neighborhood, Plumbum smiled with relief. As he turned onto his lane, he mistakenly clung to the corner instead of keeping to the center. It would have given him a few extra seconds.

Had he not partaken of the Royal Poke's noxious swill, he would have had enough sense to avoid a grim situation. But God turned an indifferent shoulder to Plumbum's redemptive plea. He had something else in mind for the alchemist.

Thomas Plumbum's eyes opened wide in surprise at the sudden recognition of a rogue lunging forward, seemingly out of nowhere. He did not hear the knife being plunged into his liver, only the bestial utterance of the man doing it. A searing pain caught up to his surprise as he looked down at the hilt of a dirk protruding from his side, and the man's hand still upon it. Seconds inexplicably lengthened as the alchemist realized that these precious moments would be his last.

Hunching over, he reached for the knife just as his assailant withdrew it. Plumbum dropped to his knees, withering from agony.

It was not by accident that Thomas Plumbum breathed his last. It was with cause that the alchemist saw his end. He had been warned. But being distracted by a ludicrous belief was as much to blame as it was his nature. In the end, Thomas Plumbum was a victim of his fatuous pursuit of an unobtainable dream. And, as he lay crumpled in the lane and took his final breath, he thought that if this was his reward, then God had a sadistic sense of humor.

CHAPTER 22

The last few steps took longer than all that had come before. Bianca slowed as she neared her room of Medicinals and Physickes. Not only did she ache from her brutal attack, but her trepidation over John and what she might find weighed her down. She scolded her fears into submission and dragged herself up the stoop.

She had left the door ajar, hoping for a cross breeze to keep John cool. Doing so had left the rent and John vulnerable. Aware that perhaps it had been poor judgment on her part, she cautiously pushed on the door. It creaked open and the black tiger approached to greet her.

Bianca peered into the dark, her eyes finding John in their bed. She set the satchel on the board and went to him.

At first she thought he was sleeping peaceably, and for that she was grateful. She quietly sat on the edge next to him, not wishing to disturb his rest, but hoping he would respond to her weight. But he did not. Bianca brought her face close to his.

"John," she said, hoping he would stir.

When he did not, she gently shook him.

Her query went unheeded.

Alarmed, she rocked him enough so that his head lolled from side to side.

"John!" she said louder and more firmly. When he did not answer or open his eyes, she laid her head on his chest to listen for the beat of his heart. The black tiger walked across John's legs and sat observing the two of them.

Though the cat's boisterous purring made it difficult, Bianca finally caught John's heartbeat, faint and slow. She pulled his eyelids back. The whites glinted in the dim light. John stared, unseeingly, at the ceiling overhead.

If she had stayed and not gone to her father's, could she have prevented his slipping into the heavy sleep? She chided herself for leaving, but how could she have prevented him cascading into the world between the living and the dead?

She observed his chest expand shallowly, worrying that the rattle in his lungs would worsen. He could not continue to lie flat or the phlegm would drown him and he would never stir. Taking her pillow, she maneuvered it under his head, raising his shoulders to a slight incline. She sat beside him and thought.

Despite her tears, Bianca knew she must not despair. She must not sit in regret of what she had or had not done. Her reason for leaving him was to find out what she needed to know in order to cure him. She reminded herself that her intentions were born from love.

The cat, sensing her distress, gave a short chirp, as if asking if she was all right. She ran her hand down its back, feeling the need for reassurance. In return, the cat gave her an appreciative rub against her chin.

Night would soon give way to day's boisterous arrival. Sleep would elude her, but neither did she have any desire to rest. Her mind galloped on, thinking what she could do to save John. She wandered over to the shelves of ingredients, medicants, and syrups as she had done earlier in the day. Was there some combination, some mixture or technique that she had missed?

She ran through the possibilities. But her mind could still think of nothing.

Her father claimed she could not make any one part of the elixir of life and expect it to help. Bianca disagreed. Surely at some point, the elixir would start to wield its healing powers.

The cat jumped on the table and knocked a wedge of cheese to the floor. She reached down and shaved off a few slivers for its meal.

And what if she did succeed in creating the elixir of life and gave it to John?

Indefinitely extending *one* person's life would not disrupt the course of humanity, she reasoned. Extending everyone's life certainly could.

"Well," Bianca said to the cat, "I only seek to save John."

Besides, did it matter if one person lived forever, walking the earth for eternity? Belief in God ensured an everlasting life after death. Did it not? If one believed, did one get to sit at God's table and pass Him the plate of potatoes?

But was it right, was it just, to keep John from joining this ethereal divinity? She refused to entertain the thought that her pursuit to save John was a selfish one. She could no more think of continuing life without him than she could face that his fate, whether he lived or died, was not hers to determine. She refused to consider the notion. She must do everything she could to save him.

Bianca untied the satchel's flap and removed Ferris Stannum's book of alchemy. She cleared a space on the table and opened the journal to his final experiment.

The first page of the process was an elaborate drawing of what Stannum hoped to achieve. Bianca interpreted the symbols, determining what the first step entailed and what equipment she needed. She read aloud from the second page, committing the verse to memory and repeating it until she thoroughly understood the direction of the projection.

> "Our bodies be likened to the sea,
> And shall lose their first form,
> Awash in a liquid that must be bound.
> Contained in flask bottom round."

Eager to begin, Bianca collected the ingredients and set up her table with clean mortars and bowls. She filled a jug with rainwater from the cistern and washed several flasks. Though the night was still uncomfortably warm, she would need a fire for the first stage. She gathered kindling and dung patties to stoke her furnace.

Once she had ground the gentian root and zedoary, she searched her shelves for stibium, which she had nabbed from her father years before. He had once performed a process similar to the one she was about to try. The result had seemed like magic, and she had stolen some ore as a reminder of what she had seen and to someday create her own "magic."

The first step required calcinating the ore until she obtained "the wolf of amber glass"—the transformation she had witnessed as a girl. She lit a fire in her furnace and pulled a stool next to it. The process required constant stirring and attention to heat until the ore melted. Once the ore melted it would go through a transformation and solidify.

Day began to break and Bianca's arms tired from stirring. John had not moved the entire night, and the black tiger slept curled against him. Fatigue tempted her to abandon the experiment and take a quick nap, but she fought the seductive lure of sleep. She kept herself awake by reading aloud snippets from Stannum's alchemy journal . . .

> "The wheel is now near turned about
> Through air flies earth,
> And fire slain by water.
> Of element's nature there is no doubt
> Begin thy process

This circulation begin you in the west
Then into the south 'til they come to rest."

A rooster crowed from across the way and London began to wake. Bleary-eyed from reading in the dim light, Bianca recited whatever came to mind—her father's discourse about alchemy, Meddybemps's street patter. She kept dogged attention to the process, to her stirring, and suppressed her weariness and dread of failure.

Hours of work seemed to have produced nothing, and she wondered if the calcination had failed. As she pondered what she had done wrong, her enthusiasm waned. Should she start over? She glanced at John, worried.

How long would John stay in that deep sleep? The sweat usually killed its victims quickly. But the deep sleep was a different matter. She had heard people could linger insensible for days. Even weeks. Finally, the afflicted withered from lack of drink and starved. But if she stopped the process and accepted failure, John would surely die.

The thought of losing him spurred her on. Bianca stubbornly kept on stirring.

Again she turned her thoughts to Ferris Stannum.

It seemed entirely possible that the alchemist had been murdered by someone wanting his alchemy journal. Bianca envisioned the murderer creeping into his room while he slept and smothering him with his pillow. She wondered if Stannum had heard his murderer approach. But there was no indication that he had put up a struggle. In her mind, the hidden bloodstained pillow she had found was proof of treachery. Though John thought Stannum could have slept on his stomach and caused the stains, there were three facts that ran counter to his theory. One, the pillow was far from Stannum's bed, and two, the pillow had two perfectly spaced stains. Three, the journal was missing the next day.

But why had *she* been given the journal? Was it given to her for safekeeping or because someone believed she might be able to interpret it?

Bianca gazed over at John. It occurred to her that she had not followed up on her experiment with the rat, testing Hughes's tincture to see if it had been poison. Originally, when she had checked the cage, she had found the rat unresponsive. It had appeared dead. Bianca stopped stirring the solution and found the cage under the table. She slid it out and lifted the cage onto the table. The rat was alive.

So Barnabas Hughes had not poisoned Mrs. Tenbrook.

Bianca set the cage back on the shelf with the others. Perhaps the coroner had been right in his diagnosis. After all, she had no direct knowledge of the sweat or its process. Like other diseases she had seen, the sickness could probably manifest differently in its victims. The coroner had been quick in his decision, declaring the landlady succumbed to the disease without giving it a second thought. But a swift diagnosis did not always guarantee a correct diagnosis.

What if Goodwife Tenbrook had not died of the sweat? Both she and Stannum had unusually red eyes. It was a symptom not associated with the disease. Bianca returned to her furnace and took up the stir rod.

If the landlady had smothered Stannum, the mischief would have ended with her. But the arrival of the book of alchemy in Bianca's room of Medicinals and Physickes and the attack on her near Burley House contradicted that.

So who gave her the book and how did that person first get it?

Bianca dipped the rod back into the flask. As she began to stir, Amice and her husband, Gilley, came to mind. She wondered if he had married Amice for love. Or did he marry expecting a dowry that he believed was his right? Bianca sniffed. Anyone marrying an alchemist's daughter should know that the reward for doing so is paltry at best. Unless he expected to benefit in some other way. Bianca gave some thought to this. Perhaps he wanted the journal but had been prevented from acquiring it. Bianca's face darkened. Perhaps he had been the man who had attacked her.

Bianca dropped her arms to give them a rest. She rubbed the back of her neck and threw another dung patty in the stove. The fire snapped, throwing sparks in the firebox.

She had just gone over to check on John when the transformation she had been hoping for began.

The ore passed through a stage of hardened grayness and began to dissolve. Transfixed, Bianca gaped at the inexplicable magic happening before her. In a moment, a brown fluid covered the bottom of the flask. Bianca resumed stirring. The liquid thickened around the iron rod, solidifying into a deep yellow, brittle-looking glass. It was the "glass" that Stannum had written of.

Thrilled by her success, Bianca cackled in delight. The black tiger lifted its head and eyed her suspiciously.

"At last! The moon of perfection!" Bianca clapped her hands together and brought them to her lips.

She removed the flask from the heat and hurried to the front door to examine the glass in the early morning light. "I have never seen a more beautiful wolf," she cried.

Her neighbor, throwing handfuls of grain to his chickens, looked over his shoulder in alarm. "Wolf?" he exclaimed. "Where? Where is wolf?"

Bianca waved the flask over her head and smiled. She disappeared into her rent and shut the door, leaving her neighbor gawping after her as if she had lost her mind.

In a way, she *had* lost her sense. Her mind was in a haze from lack of sleep, and her concern for John had left her nerves frayed. She consulted Stannum's journal of alchemy to see what stage was next.

> Grind thy livered wolf into a fine, flower dust,
> That blown by puff of air, into it would float,
> But look thee to element three,

Must in dissolution of red most soured.
And then in sublimation lives.
The fellowship knows the stone which we seek,
Is of red man and white of wife,
Fools follow but Philosophers find.

Bianca closed her eyes, concentrating. "Grind thy livered wolf" was simple enough. She fished the yellow solid out of the flask and pulverized it in a mortar.

"But look thee to element three, must in dissolution of red most soured." She read the line over and sat back in thought. "Element three," she mused. The four elements were air, water, earth, and fire, but which one was the third? Bianca considered the riddle. She read over the second half of the sentence, "must in dissolution of red most soured."

Dissolution was a liquid process. The third element must be water. "Dissolve the livered wolf in a liquid that is red and sour." The only liquid that came to mind was a bottle of wine that had turned to vinegar. Bianca retrieved the bottle and poured the soured spirits in a flask. Next, she shook the ground "wolf" into it.

The particles of powder disappeared into the liquid. Bianca swirled the solution and the liquid became cloudy. She ran her finger under the next line of text, understanding what she must do, but a lump settled in her stomach at the thought of it—

"And then in sublimation lives."

Sublimation—the method she had yet to perfect. Her failure being the reason for seeking Ferris Stannum in the first place. She looked over her new retorts and wondered if she should chance using them. She had no more stibium to repeat the process if she failed. She also had no kerotakis. The hard-earned amber wolf sat at the bottom of the flask. She had one opportunity to make it work.

She froze, demoralized. Perhaps her father, with his years of alchemical expertise, was right in saying she could not produce the elixir of life. According to him she had not been given that destiny. Nor did she have the correct apparatus—the kerotakis—to even attempt the next step.

Should she take the risk of sublimating using her inferior alembics? Bianca set down the flask and went to John. She stood quietly by, following his breath, wondering how many he had left. How long could he stay in the deep sleep? Another day? Another hour? She didn't know. But she felt the press of time against her.

CHAPTER 23

For what felt like the twentieth time in three hours, Joseph Tait unlaced his codpiece and strained to pass his water. He thought if he stood in his patch of lavender, the scent might relax him enough to help. Only a trickle dribbled from his pizzle, and most of that was blood. His entire body felt puny, and this included his knees. He braced an arm against the stone wall that separated his yard from his neighbor's.

If he did not pass the gravel in his bladder, he would surely die. Or his bladder would burst and then he would die. Neither outcome provided much solace. He'd never seen a physician manage the condition with any success. It was a circumstance left for God to decide.

Tired of fumbling about with his codpiece and hose, he removed the former's ties and threw the elaborate contrivance against the wall in frustration. It was better to let his member dangle than constantly lace and unlace the thing.

He'd suffered from stones before and had always passed them. But this one seemed damnably different. It felt the size of a bean and was probably spiked like a mace. Another wave of nausea cowed him and he vomited in the bergamot. Luckily he had abandoned his damask in favor of his shirt, which was soaked now from perspiration.

He attempted to straighten but thought better of it when another stabbing pain coursed through his back. Consumed with agony, he doubled over, holding his sides and taking tiny steps in an attempt to go back inside.

If he weren't so miserable he would curse. Instead, the condition made him cry. He barely got inside before he dropped to his knees and blubbered like a baby.

He wanted to shake his fist at his God, but he could barely lift it. "Take me now, damn you. I want to die."

But, as it had been earlier in the night with Thomas Plumbum, God wasn't answering calls.

Joseph Tait would be forced to suffer.

And why shouldn't he?

Had he not caused untold misery to another? So it was that Joseph Tait wallowed in self-pity, and no one, including God, heard his anguished plea.

Another wave of pain and the usurer curled like a fetus fresh out of the womb. He whimpered and shook, tasted the salt of sweat coursing into his mouth.

Shouldn't the force of so much piss against the pebble push the confounded thing out? He knew nothing of his anatomy, but he'd seen how dams could be breached. The pressure of a river was too much for a single boulder. Was this not the same? Joseph Tait rolled onto his back as the latest wave of torture started to subside. He stared up at the ceiling, panting.

What made the whole affair more wretched was the sweltering heat. It had not cooled much from the height of day. He longed to drink but dared not add to his already inflated bladder. Instead, he clawed his way up the leg of his elegant table and staggered to his feet. A ewer filled with ale sat on the edge. With a weak arm he seized the flagon and poured it over his head. So what if it stank and was sticky? He lapped at the brew running down his face, hoping to quench his parched tongue and cool his feverish skin.

Tait had a brief respite before yet another contraction started. Woozy and exhausted, he wondered if childbirth was easier than passing pebbles. Perhaps this was man's punishment for causing women such trials.

But this cramp felt different from the others. He felt a great urge to aim his pipe at his pot. He spread his legs as much as he was able and pointed his bloody member at the jordan. With a great rush of excruciating pain and relief, his water gushed forth, spraying the pot and splattering the floor. Joseph Tait sighed in ecstasy. He felt as if he had just experienced the most sublime fuck of his entire life.

And indeed he *was* completely spent.

The pain he felt as he collapsed and hit the chair was nothing compared to what had come before.

CHAPTER 24

The next morning, Bianca kissed John, hoping that when their lips touched, he would return the gesture. She would have sooner kissed a wall. His lips did not answer. He gave no clue that he even knew she was near.

Her hand went to her heart as if steadying it. John lay in bed, his chin tipped to the ceiling, his skin flushed. His breath was shallow, but at least it was even. Bianca pulled the sheet to his chin and left a mug of ale next to the bed.

"Watch over him," she told the black tiger and gave its jaw a scratch.

Bianca found the rucksack and stuffed Stannum's journal into it. She would keep the book on her person rather than risk having it stolen while she was gone. Whoever wanted it seemed to know more about her than she knew of him—if even the book was what was wanted. At least with day's light she would have a better chance of keeping it.

She hoped she could secure the kerotakis from Amice for modest coin. Bianca regretted not buying the part when she had the opportunity, but at the time it had seemed more of a curiosity than a crucial piece of equipment.

The air was thick with humidity. The sky had lost its blue and was the color of mollusk shells. Rain would settle the dust that kicked up on the hem of her kirtle. Bianca longed for a change of season. A change in weather. The summer heat had been unremitting. Plants withered; people were short of temper.

From the dock at St. Mary Overie, a low-lying haze bathed the London skyline, masking the steeple of St. Paul's. The whole town seemed to bear the stultifying air with sullen resentment. Heat had a way of stretching time, of making it slow. Perhaps it was only one's doleful reaction that made it appear that way. Fortunately, Bianca did not have long to wait before a ferrier poled his skiff alongside the pier.

Bianca stepped aboard and had just settled when a man came running down the dock calling for them to wait. Dressed in a rough canvas jerkin of the country, he turned to yell at two children lagging behind, a small boy of around eight and his younger sister.

The father waved his arm, trying to hurry them along, but the two children ignored his impatient gestures, advancing at their own tentative pace. When the girl was within a few feet, he pulled her roughly toward him and lifted her into the boat. The boy shirked from his father's reach. Uncertain, the boy stepped back, gaping at the river as if he had never seen it before. The man swore. He lunged for the boy, but the child was quick. He escaped up the dock.

"Ach," cried the ferrier, as the man gave chase. " 'Od rabbit it! Does he expect me to sit all day while he runs after his bootless, ill-bred spawn?"

The little girl's eyes grew round with alarm and she started to scramble out of the boat, reaching for the dock and trying to pull herself up onto it. The ferrier had already lifted his pole and the skiff had begun to separate from the dock.

Bianca caught the girl by her middle and pulled her back in. "Now, child. That is not so wise." Bianca sat her in her lap, speaking both to the girl and to the ferrier. "Wait, give him leave. He must be back. He cannot leave his daughter to strangers."

"Paa!" said the boatman, looking up the length of the dock and not seeing either man or boy. "I've seen it before," he said. "The man is overwhelmed and canno' take care of them. Heed my words. He will leave them on the streets to fend for themselves like abandoned dogs."

"It is not for sure," said Bianca. "Do you know the man's mind?"

The ferrier spat into the Thames. "It is double the fare if we leave without 'im, and you will have to pay it."

"I should put her out now so she can wait for her father to return."

"Nay, he will not. That is what I am telling ye," said the ferrier. "It is a trick that a man of his sort plays. Find an unsuspecting, able woman and leave a child with her while running off for the other. It works artfully well most of the time."

The girl began to cry, which only proved to further aggravate the boatman. Bianca expected he would put them both out. "Now, lass," she said, rocking her. "Shh, do not waste your time crying. Here, here." She wiped the girl's face with the sleeve of her blouse, turning the dust from the girl's travels into a dirty smear. "You must have been walking a long way."

The girl responded with only a shuddering breath.

Bianca looked at the ferrier, who shook his head. "I am telling ye," he said. He reached for a flask at his feet and took a long drink. He jammed the cork back into it. "Make up your mind. I am losing fares sitting here."

Closing the monasteries had inflicted untold hardship on the poor and destitute of London. The sick and the disabled, the orphans, had nowhere to go. They wandered the streets, begging. And even this humiliating and barely sustainable labor required a license, for it was a punishable offense to beg without one. Orphans roamed the streets, some starving and some forming packs of mischief-makers. Because there was no organized system to collect alms or dispense charity, only the rich benefited from

Henry's decision. They bought church property, dismantled chantries, and sold their stones.

It was poor luck that Bianca found herself in this predicament, and poor timing. She couldn't abandon the child on the other side, but she could not afford to linger in Southwark, waiting for the father to return. Time was precious.

"Well," said the ferrier, "it looks to me like you have made yeself ward to the brat." He stuck his pole in the water, turning the bow into the current. Bianca's choice had been made for her.

Bianca began to run through possible solutions. She might be able to leave the girl with her mother until she had a chance to tend to the matter. Her mother would not be pleased, but she wouldn't turn the girl out.

"Wait!"

Bianca turned to see the man running down the dock, hailing the ferrier. He carried the boy over his shoulder like a sack of grain and waved his arm.

"Turn back," shouted Bianca. "He's returned."

The ferrier lifted his pole out of the water and glanced over his shoulder. "Ye is daft if ever I seen it. He'll dump the child, then ye'll have two."

"Either way, you'll get more fare."

Encouraged by this idea, the ferrier looked at Bianca. "Alrights," he said. "I shall hold ye to it." He jammed his pole into the still shallow river bottom and swung the bow about, returning to the pier.

The skiff bumped gently along the wharf and the man dropped the boy into the hull. For a breathless second, Bianca thought he would turn and leave. But, holding on to a bollard, he eased himself in beside the boy. "I was afraids I would find ye gone." He settled on a seat and pulled his son next to him. "Sits still or I shall throw ye in," he said into the boy's face. The boy sat beside him, sullen, avoiding Bianca's gaze by fixing his to the bottom of the boat.

Bianca felt the girl squirm and push out of her arms to scramble into the man's lap. From that vantage point, she stared solemnly across at Bianca, her eyes dark and accusatory.

"We thought you were abandoning her," said Bianca to the father after they were on their way.

The man held her stare and said nothing. He turned his focus on the bridge as the ferrier pointed the skiff into the current. As for Bianca, she continued to study his inscrutable expression. She waited for a reply, hoping her disapproval might shame the man into better behavior. Eventually she looked over her shoulder at the ferrier, who grinned back at her cynically.

Bianca shifted the satchel, resting it on the seat. The bag caught the children's interest, but when Bianca met their eyes, their father shot them a disapproving glance, and they dropped their stares to their laps.

Other ferries trekked across the river from the opposite side, filled with men. There were far more skiffs heading to Southwark than to London. A bear-baiting was on the docket for later that day, and Bianca assumed they were getting an early start on the festivities.

When they reached the stairs near Three Cranes Lane, the tide was high enough to prevent an attack by the relentless sand flies. Bianca waited for the father and his two children to disembark before stepping out. She could have hurried past, dismissing their fate to the beleaguered father, but his general manner troubled her.

Carrying the girl upon his hip and taking hold of the young boy's hand, he struck a course up Thames Street. Bianca trailed behind, feigning interest in a stand of fruit and slowing to allow them to gain some distance ahead of her. The three moved at a creeping pace. Bianca was torn between abandoning this probably futile endeavor and striking out for Stannum's room of alchemy. Finally, she reasoned this was a waste of time and the father was probably stalling until she passed. She quickened her stride, and as she approached the slowly plodding family, the confusion on the father's face was impossible for her to ignore.

"You appear lost, sir," she said, walking up and touching him on the arm. "I know this town's twisting lanes. Where are you going?" She realized she was exposing herself to another curt dismissal, but his expression softened.

"I seek St. Thomas Lane."

"I can take you; it is on my way." It was not. Bianca calculated the distance from Ivy Lane and Ferris Stannum's room of alchemy, where she hoped to find Amice. Though not overly far, St. Thomas was a detour and a delay nonetheless.

Bianca fell in step beside them. She hoped to learn his intentions, but the man carefully guarded every word. Apparently his wife had died and he was bringing the children to live with his sister. He fell into silence, and after they cut through alleys and plastered themselves against buildings to let carts pass, Bianca felt a tentative hand touch hers. She looked down into the little boy's soulful eyes peering up at her. She took his hand.

"Your sister lives on St. Thomas Lane?" asked Bianca.

"Aye," said the man.

"What is her name?" Bianca asked. "Mayhap I know of her."

"Likely you do not. She is just moved here," he answered.

"There is no hiding if one lives in London," said Bianca. "Someone always knows someone who knows another."

But the man did not offer his sister's name. A silent rift grew between them. Bianca named a nearby ordinary where they could buy a reasonable meal if they needed. She was hoping to put him at ease, talking about food and offering a traveler such as he a native's advice. But the man only grunted in reply. Finally, he let go of the boy's hand and doffed his cap to Bianca. "Good day. This is where we part."

"But I have not seen you to your sister's," said Bianca. "Do you know where she lives on St. Thomas?"

"I can manage," said the man. "Am I far?"

Bianca saw no use in arguing. She would make a point to visit St. Thomas Lane another time. She gave him directions.

"God give you a good day," he said, taking hold of his son's hand and pulling him on.

Bianca watched them walk up the road. The little girl peeked at her from her father's shoulder. The boy kept glancing at her as his father hurried him along. She couldn't decide what the father's intentions were. Perhaps he mentioned a sister in order to put her off. She hoped the children would take to their aunt and that all would end well. Bianca sighed, knowing it was rare that anything ended well, especially the care of children.

Bianca turned in the direction of Ferris Stannum's alchemy room, cutting through back alleys to avoid the main thoroughfares as they grew congested. She hurried, making up for lost time, dipping under lines of laundry strung between buildings and maneuvering around dumped kitchen scraps slimy with rot and teeming with flies.

Emerging at one end of Ivy Lane, Bianca was surprised to see the neighborhood more alive with activity than she had ever seen it. The heat must have driven people out of their rents. The street clamored with voices heard from windows and doors that had been flung open. Passions roused and Bianca passed one tenement, listening to an accusation of adultery, and another, hearing evidence that it housed those possibly committing it.

Across from Goodwife Tenbrook's, the boy who had weaseled a penny from her sat on his mother's stoop. With his chin resting in his hands, he looked the portrait of boredom. At the sight of Bianca he trotted over.

"Ye be back?" He ran in front of her, skipping backward.

"So I am," said Bianca. She stopped in front of Goodwife Tenbrook's rent. A heavy padlock hung from the latch.

"They put that on to keep folks out."

Bianca stood back and peered up at the second story. "I don't suppose anyone is here." The shutter had been nailed closed.

"Ye suppose right," said the boy.

"Has anyone cleared out the old alchemist's room?"

"They did that yesterday. A man and a woman came and loaded a cart with all kinds of strange-shaped copper and crockery."

"The old man's daughter?"

The boy shrugged and nodded. "I suppose."

Bianca looked up the street and down it. Rather than go to the Royal Poke to find Amice, she figured she was closer to Thomas Plumbum's room of alchemy. She wondered if she should trust the man. She had wanted to ask him about Ferris Stannum's death and watch his face for signs of deceit. But visiting him served a more important need. She could scope his room of alchemy and steal his kerotakis.

The boy pulled on a board nailed across Ferris Stannum's small window. His thin fingers were of little use prizing it off.

"It's not worth trying," said Bianca. "It's a new plank and they didn't spare any nails securing it." She considered the little rascal, who seemed curious and exceptionally observant for his age. "You spend a lot of time sitting on your mother's stoop."

"I like it better outside."

Bianca began walking up the road, expecting the boy would follow. "You never told me your name," she said.

"Fisk," said the boy, bending down for a stone, then hurrying to catch up to her. "You never told me yours."

Bianca obliged. "Mostly you sit outside and watch the street?"

"Mostly."

"Do you sleep well these hot nights?"

Fisk shrugged, wiping his hair out of his eyes. "Sometimes I get up and bring a blanket out on the stoop. I sleep by the door." He had no sooner said this when a woman's shrill voice called after him. Fisk stopped walking and answered. "I've got to go, miss. Me mother wants me."

Bianca watched him run down the lane and disappear inside his family's home. She wondered how much he had noticed of the various goings-on at Goodwife Tenbrook's. A minute passed as she considered this before returning her thoughts to Thomas Plumbum.

Besides nabbing a kerotakis, she hoped to learn the alchemist's intentions and in the process find out where he thought the book might be.

Bianca slowed on the street where Barnabas Hughes had said the alchemist lived, studying each shop front, every door she passed. She followed her nose, but no errant odors of liver of sulfur or putrefaction gave a clue to the alchemist's whereabouts. Finally, she was forced to rely on a neighbor leaving his rent partway down the lane.

"Might you know of Thomas Plumbum?" she asked. "I am looking for him."

The neighbor's thin shirt snugged around his thick middle. In the crook of one arm was a blood-spattered apron. He had the thick shoulders of a man accustomed to hefting sides of beef. He screwed up his nose as if reacting to the peculiar smells of the alchemist's work, or perhaps something more offensive crossed his mind. "Aye, the man lives there." He pointed to the decrepit exterior of the building opposite his. "The third door, the one with the crooked stoop."

All three entrances were far from level, but one slanted markedly worse than the others. Bianca crossed the lane, and in order to stand on the block of stone, she bent one knee and kept the other straight. Balancing on the stoop required some attention, so that she failed to notice the door was unlatched. When she pounded on it, the door swung inward from the force of her knock, pitching her forward into the room.

"Master Tait," she said, catching herself up.

The usurer was on his toes reaching behind a stack of crockery when he heard his name combined with the sound of her stumbling. He whirled about, narrowing his eyes at the sight of her. "It is a matter of courtesy to knock," he said.

Bianca recovered and straightened her bodice. "And what courtesy are you exhibiting?" She swept her eyes around the room. "Where is Thomas Plumbum?"

The usurer's lips curved in an indulgent smile. "He is not here."

"Sir, I question the liberty with which you riffle through alchemists' belongings when they are not at home."

"I am afraid Thomas Plumbum won't be home anytime soon." Tait shook his head with regret. "His body was found at the corner. Dead from an abdominal wound, imposed by a dagger, it seems."

Bianca's mouth fell open. "When?"

"Last night. The time I cannot say." Tait picked up a flask and sniffed its contents. One eye closed as he registered the smell. Apparently he found it objectionable, as he quickly returned the flask to the table. "I cannot say when it happened, because I was not there."

"Then how did you learn of his death?"

Tait's dark eyes considered her a moment before answering. "It is a matter of business. The delicacies of which are complicated for a woman to understand."

"Sir, you misjudge me." Bianca stepped forward. "But perhaps you will not say because you have a guilty conscience."

"My dear, I assure you it is not *my* conscience that is tainted with guilt." His gaze ran over the strap crossing her chest.

Bianca shifted the satchel behind her back and their eyes met.

Tait continued. "I would advise you to stay to matters of medicants or whatever it is that you trifle with. These matters are not your concern."

"I find it interesting that within hours of Ferris Stannum's and Thomas Plumbum's deaths you are busily rummaging through their belongings. It seems too much of a coincidence."

"The only coincidence is that they were both alchemists. And as you know, I have made my living lending alchemists money. I am simply collecting my due before word travels of Thomas's death."

"I should think the constable would secure the property pending proper investigation into his creditors, of which you may not be the only one."

"One might as well open the door to looters as have a constable secure it. My dear, you are so innocent. I lent money in good faith to support Plumbum in his work. And I seek to recover what he owes. I have no time for incompetent men of law." Tait turned to a shelf and lifted out a jar. He peered into it. "I can see you are ignorant in matters of business. I shall not waste my time explaining finances to you." He reached into the vessel, withdrew some powder, and let it trickle through his fingers onto the floor.

Bianca regarded all moneylenders with skepticism. They spoke of their profession in terms of "service"—supporting individuals in their pursuit of self-sufficiency. But beneath their self-aggrandizing twaddle were men who profited off the hopes and dreams of others.

"Why would you lend money to an alchemist? Would not a more reliable venture prove more profitable? A wool merchant or a chain-mail maker is a more dependable and needed trade. I would think a man as prudent as yourself would avoid such a risky endeavor."

As Bianca was saying this, she noticed the usurer limp as he moved down the shelves, examining Plumbum's possessions. He had not shown a hitch in his walk the last time she had seen him. She might ask how he came by it. Had he been involved in last night's skirmish?

"Such condemnation coming from an alchemist's daughter. You ridicule the means by which you were fed?" He tutted with disapproval. "It is a well-known adage that risk garners the greatest reward," he said. "I had a considerable amount of faith and money invested in Ferris Stannum. His death was an enormous disappointment to me."

Tait grew thoughtful, appearing genuinely contrite.

"However," he continued, "Thomas Plumbum was a dabbler by comparison. He was a conniver. Good alchemists often are. I found Plumbum to be a man of his word—at least when it concerned our agreements. He paid me on time and I made a modest sum of money from lending to him. But lately he had been negligent. I had hoped he would curb his less admirable inclinations and get back to the matter of alchemy."

"And those less than admirable inclinations were?"

Tait pinched his lips, appearing coy. "You are venturing into dangerous waters, my dear." He continued to sort through a collection of bottles, holding them to the light, uncorking them, and cautiously sniffing. After a moment, he continued, "Ferris Stannum believed in Thomas Plumbum's abilities. The old alchemist must have seen some potential in Plumbum. He would not bestow his attention on just anyone." He shook a bottle of pickled cow eyes and watched them rearrange themselves in the fluid. "A man had to show merit. They had to prove themselves worthy of his attention. He had to believe in them." He set the bottle back on the shelf. "And unfortunately, to my detriment, I believed in Stannum."

Tait gazed across the room at Bianca. "And how was it that you earned Stannum's faith?" he asked, his eyebrows lifting. "You only knew him a day." Tait picked up an alembic, turning it right side up and then flipping it over. "You must have made quite an impression."

"I shall not speculate about his interest in me. Perhaps, as you say, he saw some potential."

The usurer looked her up and down. "Indeed," he said.

Bianca riled at his implication. Unable to keep silent, she said, "You favor your left side. I don't recall your limping the last time I saw you." She watched his face.

Tait continued to feign interest in the copper still head.

"You walk as if you have been hurt," she added.

"I suffer from gout," he answered. The usurer set the alembic back on a shelf and calmly reached for a leather purse. "My footwear must be specially made."

Bianca noted Tait's fine boots and decided he must have spent good coin on them. Such a pair would have cost her several months of earnings.

"My mother prescribed eating porridge of barley and vinegar followed by the application of a poultice of ground worm and pig's marrow." She mentioned this as a way to gauge his interest. No one suffered the disease with resigned acceptance. Gout was painful and debilitating. Anyone afflicted with the condition was willing to try almost anything in the hopes of curing it.

Tait looked up. He did not ask how warm the poultice should

be, or what type of vinegar worked best. He loosened the draw-string on the purse and stuck a finger into it.

Bianca found his lack of interest surprising. His indifference, while certainly unexpected, did not prevent her from trying to engage him. "Who found Plumbum's body?"

"I suppose some poor fool who happened upon it." He plucked out a lump of cinnabar. "Never an enjoyable experience, I can as-sure you." Having held the ore to the light and examined it, he dropped it back in the pouch and cinched it closed. "Have you ever come upon a shivved body in your travels?"

"I have not."

Tait tossed the pouch back onto a shelf, frowning in disgust. "I am not fond of crimson."

Bianca took advantage of Tait's disinterest and scanned the room for a kerotakis. If Plumbum had one, it was not sitting out for her to see. Feeling their conversation had reached an impasse, she backed toward the door. She might find out more about Plumbum's murder from just about anyone other than Tait.

"I shall leave you to your . . . business," she said, taking a final searching glance around the room. The needed piece of equip-ment had eluded her once again.

CHAPTER 25

Bianca did not believe in curses. Verbal profanity, however, *was* acceptable and at times necessary. She did not shirk from using it on occasion. In fact, she embraced the art of a well-placed expletive with gusto. It was the other definition of "curse" of which Bianca was skeptical.

She *did* believe in ghosts. Who didn't? Pinning down suicides with a knife through the heart seemed the only way to prevent them from wandering around and making life miserable for their loved ones. Nor did Bianca think Meddybemps's talismans and amulets were frivolous. Wearing a badger's tooth to prevent getting robbed served a useful purpose. The wearer conducted his affairs with more confidence under its protection.

But Bianca did not believe it was possible for a person to conjure evil and misfortune upon others. Truthfully, she had often thought a generous dose of bad luck humbled those needing a lesson in compassion. And while hexes, potions, and curses worried the average citizen, to Bianca the only one capable of heaping untold misery on a person was oneself.

Bianca believed that she was responsible for creating her present circumstance. Certainly, waggery was everywhere. One need only look around to see skullduggery and murder. But standing over a burning candle and summoning evil spirits to spite another person just because someone asked them to seemed a dubious proposition.

But as Bianca made her way to the Royal Poke, the subject of curses did cross her mind. Could the alchemy journal be her ruination? Had Ferris Stannum or even the force of nature—or dare she admit it—God, in His infinite wisdom, imbued the journal with a way to prevent the elixir of life from ever being projected again?

Was the journal, or perhaps the path to creating the elixir, a cursed undertaking? Bianca could think of no other word to describe the accumulating difficulty and deaths associated with the book. Ferris Stannum's death, or, as Bianca believed, murder, came soon after his discovery of the elixir of life. Now *she* held the recipe for the secret of immortality and someone had made an attempt on her life. Whoever had the journal before her must have known or experienced its inherent danger and chose not to jeopardize his life by keeping it.

But why toss the journal through *her* window? Did the person expect her to succeed in creating the elixir, or had the person wanted her to die trying?

If John's bloodletting had helped relieve the pressure in his skull like Hughes believed, she might be able to save him. She saw how he was sleeping more soundly, but there was no sign that he was any closer to recovering. John seemed to be trapped in a state of quiet suspension. How long would he have? How long did she have to find the kerotakis and concoct part of the elixir?

Bianca snaked through the stalls of Cheapside Market and, without slowing, filched a plum while the tender was busy with a customer. She bit into the fruit and paid no attention to the juice trickling down her chin. Should she heed these warnings and rid herself of the journal? Was she being dissuaded from creating the elixir by unknown forces or, dare she think it—a curse? Then again, it could be mere coincidence that someone tried to steal her satchel while the journal just happened to be in it.

Her other thought was that someone might be killing alchemists. The killer might have a profound distaste for those practicing the noble art. First Ferris Stannum was murdered; then Thomas Plumbum met his end. "I'm not an alchemist," she said aloud, eliciting a curious glance from a passerby. But perhaps someone mistook her for one. Bianca glanced over her shoulder. "Nay," she said aloud, admonishing herself for letting her imagination get the better of her. She finished the plum and tossed aside the pit.

Bianca wiped her sticky chin on her sleeve and thought about Tait, the usurer. It was the second time she had caught the man going through an alchemist's belongings within hours of his death. True, he may have only been trying to recoup some of his loss. But his avowed strategy of knowingly investing in more risky ventures seemed ill-advised. Being the daughter of an alchemist, she knew what it was like to wrap strips of wool around her feet for shoes or to go without eating because her father had melted the last coin for some alchemy experiment.

Could Tait have suffocated Ferris Stannum with a pillow and murdered Thomas Plumbum? Was he after the alchemy journal? Bianca relieved the weight on her shoulder and crossed the satchel to her other side.

He had run his eyes over the strap as if it were of interest to him. Could he have been the one to attack her? Had he known she had the book and carried it in the satchel?

But if Tait had wanted the book, why didn't he try to take it from her in Thomas Plumbum's alchemy room? Bianca kicked a stone and sent it careening off the wheel of a passing cart.

Gout could flare, creating intolerable pain. Mentioning her mother's remedy barely elicited an acknowledgment. Sufferers were desperate to learn what could relieve them of the excruciating pain. No matter what the topic, all pretense was forgotten when a new remedy was mentioned. But Tait had remained aloof.

Perhaps he had lied about his gout. Perhaps his limp was caused from something else. Had he been involved in the brawl over the satchel the night before? She tried remembering the details of the attack. The feeling of being followed was similar to the one she had now. Again Bianca stopped and whirled about to face the crowd behind her. No one caught her eye; no one suddenly pretended to be interested in the plaster of a building. Bianca resumed walking.

She had felt a tug on her shoulder strap and had instinctively hung on to it, pulling against whoever was trying to steal the satchel. She had stumbled and fallen forward, rolling to her side, still clasping the satchel in both hands. When she had tried to stand, her outstretched hand had been crushed under the heel of a boot. A heel that had delivered a painful blow. A heel of hard wood, she thought.

With her other arm, she had wrapped herself around the assailant's leg, trying to prevent a repeat stomping. The satchel was wrenched over her head and savagely used against her.

Bianca leaned against an oak tree and concentrated. She closed her eyes as a finch squeaked from a branch overhead. It had been dark at the time of the attack, making it difficult to see any distinguishing features of the attacker or the fight that had followed. She ran through the order of events.

The bark of the tree was rough against her cheek. The leather of the boot had been soft against her face. The leather had the smooth feel of a supple hide.

As she remembered the feel of the leather in her hand as she clung to her assailant's leg, she placed herself in the scene again, experiencing the smells of that street in London on a warm summer's night.

She could smell the river, the brackish mix of silt and decomposition. Across from where she lay, the smell of refuse merged with the contents of a dumped chamber pot. Moldering timbers and thatch permeated the air. She tasted the gritty dirt of the road in her mouth.

But as she stood with her eyes closed, a smell filtered through her memory that was more distinct than the others. The scent of roses.

Bianca opened her eyes. She had smelled roses when she was attacked.

CHAPTER 26

Constable Patch leaned back in his chair and closed his eyes, intoxicated by the smell of its leather upholstery. How had he managed so many years without? Only a few months into his new position and its novelty (the leather, not the job) still had not worn off.

In his mind, the promotion had been long overdue. Patch had spent years patrolling the unsavory ward of Southwark for little pay and even less notice. He had often gazed across the river at the seductive skyline of London and dreamed what it might be like working on the other side. He imagined the crimes and misconduct to be more sophisticated, less unseemly, less unruly in nature, since that was Southwark's domain.

He grimaced with distaste remembering London's wanton sister. The bear-baiting and dogfight venues had grown in popularity and number. So had the number of brothels and the foolishness that went along with them. He had done his best to recruit men willing to help enforce the king's law, but without enticement such as pay, he had had to appeal to their more charitable inclinations.

And in Southwark it was nearly impossible to find a man of altruistic disposition.

No one of any scruples lived in Southwark by choice. Only divs and lowlifes called it home. How he came to be a constable there was another story. But a better one was how he came to be a constable in a peaceful ward within sight of Christ Church with mainly candlemakers to protect.

Less than half a year had passed since he had discovered the cause behind a disturbing influx of rats. To be truthful, he had not made the discovery, only reported it. But by doing so, he had saved London from a scourge of vermin and pestilence the likes of which the citizenry had never seen. And, thanks to him, they never did.

It began with a muckraker. A young woman who benefited from a spate of fortunate circumstances—fortunate, of course, until she was murdered. The corner of Constable Patch's mouth turned up in a snide smile.

She was friends with Bianca Goddard, an alchemist's daughter who fancied herself industrious creating remedies by dubious methods she had learned from her atypical parents. Goddard lived and worked in the area called Gull Hole, claiming she could afford the rent there. But like most residents of Southwark, her type would not have been welcome across the river in London.

A woman alchemist in London? Patch snorted. She would have ended in the dunking chair.

Bianca Goddard had said her friend had suddenly dropped dead while visiting her. He'd found her explanation fraught with emotion and he had left unconvinced. But the entire story unfolded in a rather astonishing way, and he had been the recipient of an unexpected windfall of useful information that he was able to leverage for his benefit.

Thus the rich popingay blue doublet and shiny brass buttons.

Patch turned one button to examine its insignia and ran a finger over its embossment. To think he had scrounged for years to put food on the table in that vile ward. He had never seen his wife move faster than when he announced they were leaving. The bribes he enjoyed these days kept her well fed—which was necessary since she was immoderate in appetite.

He propped his legs upon the table before him, clasping his hands across his stomach. He wished the woman could rid herself of her lice, but as long as she allowed him to dock her once a week, he could squeeze his eyes shut and imagine she was that saucy Catherine Howard. (When she was alive, of course.)

Patch thought he might take a nap before strolling the streets. Nothing of any great importance ever seemed to happen. Robberies and occasional assaults kept him from growing bored, but most often he arrived too late and merely had to assure a distraught shopkeeper or citizen that he would do his best to find the culprit. Luckily, Patch had not been there so long that the citizens could accuse him of indolence.

He positioned himself so that a breeze might find him and closed his eyes, content with the world. Street sounds lulled him into a mild, languorous respite. A horse clopped by; a boy shouted after another; a mongrel barked just to hear its voice. It was a sure measure better than hearing sots shouting at whores and the women's lurid banter in reply. Aye, he had come up in the world.

Constable Patch was in that dreamless state of sleep, jerking and twitching as he tumbled into its soft embrace, when he heard his name buzzing around his ear. Aware of sounds but not cognizant of them, he swiped it away as if it were a bee. But the mind has a way of calling one back when needed. And it was needing him now.

The calling persisted, and with a groan, he opened his eyes. Before him stood the source of his annoyance.

"Constable Patch," she said. "If I may speak with you."

Patch stared a moment to get his bearings. Aye, he was still in his quarters—that part was good. He looked out the window and saw it was still daylight. He had not slept very long. He removed his feet from the table and sat up in his chair. Yes, it still smelled of leather. He was still in London.

But before him stood a reminder of Southwark.

"What brings ye to these parts?" he asked. "Out of your elements,

I would say." He eyed Bianca Goddard suspiciously. It did not matter that she was the source of his promotion to this ward on the opposite side of the river. The girl still had a way about her that made him wary.

"Is it true that Thomas Plumbum has been murdered?" Bianca wasted no time in niceties. She had just come from the alchemist's rent and needed to confirm what Tait had told her.

Constable Patch leaned forward, propping his elbows on the table, and rested his chin atop his steepled hands. He paused before answering, appraising her and the motive behind her asking. The coroner had pronounced the alchemist dead of a stab wound to his stomach. He saw no reason to withhold this information. "It appears he has been murdered, aye."

"Have you any suspicion by whom?"

Patch leaned back in his chair, considering. "Suspicions?" He grimaced as if the notion pained him. Which it did. No family member or paramour had shown up distraught and demanding justice. It was not unusual to be on the wrong end of a blade. Wrong time, wrong place; it was so common as to be ordinary. Patch was disinclined to delve further into the matter. But he took exception admitting his negligence and anticipated her wanting to know why he had not investigated further. "Nay, I have not pursued the matter. Apparently it was a robbery. "

"A robbery resulting in murder?"

"It happens," said Patch defensively. He had no idea why Thomas Plumbum was stabbed.

Bianca said nothing in response, but Constable Patch read her expression of disbelief. He reached for a quill and dipped it into an inkpot. There was a proclamation lying on the table and he whisked it in front of him and signed his name at the bottom of it. "Now, if you have no further business with me, I must get back to my work." Patch kept his head down, scribbling his name a second time on the document, the only words he knew how to write. He found a second document and wrote his name, clueless as to what he was agreeing. Why would she not leave?

Patch glanced at her from under his brow. She waited patiently for him to finish.

He laid down the pen, releasing a long, audible sigh.

"What is it you want?" he said, exasperated.

"I want to know more about Thomas Plumbum."

"Ye should have befriended him when he was alive. He isn't much of a conservationist now."

"Conversationalist?" corrected Bianca, annoyed by the smirk on his face.

Patch's face fell. "Perhaps ye would do well to question the patrons at his boozing ken of choice. I am still just learning the ward. I am not privy to blether and gossip. I can be of no more help to ye." Patch decided there was no better time for his stroll than now. There seemed to be no getting rid of her, other than leaving. The legs of his handsomely appointed chair scraped the floor as he pushed it back and stood. He straightened his doublet and rearranged his bollock dirk on his belt.

Bianca did not move. He started to come around the table, then stopped.

She had pinned him with that piercing blue stare.

"There is something you must do for me," she said with an earnestness that he could not ignore.

CHAPTER 27

Bianca stood outside Constable Patch's, deciding which direction to take. The sun was dropping in the sky, prodding her with urgency beyond what she already felt. She looked toward Southwark on the other side of the river and thought of John. She had already been gone too long.

Strange how volumes of feelings could be crammed into a single moment. Overwhelmed by the intimidating stab of realization that she could do nothing to prevent time's passage or the changes that inevitably accompanied it, Bianca wavered in indecision, paralyzed with doubt.

She regretted not being with her husband. Her mother was right. She should be with him. What had she accomplished by leaving John to look for a piece of equipment? He could be asking for water this very minute. And she was not there to give it to him.

All for a piece of equipment her father claimed she needed. Her lack of faith in her own methods had prevented her from trying to create the elixir without it. Perhaps her inability to secure the necessary kerotakis was a sign. Should she just abandon the idea of trying to create the elixir? Or was her inability to secure the equipment an indication that she should believe in her own technique?

Again her mind wound through the convoluted logic of whether she possessed the destiny, or even deserved the chance, to manipulate nature's plan. Or was it God's plan? She sniffed. She was wasting precious time.

Besides, John might still be adrift in a deep sleep. He might not have broken its spell. She didn't know what it would take to rouse him, nor could she reasonably expect that he would ever return to her. Or return to her complete in body and mind. He might just wither away. She had heard of similar cases where the victim had lain in such a state for weeks, refusing to die and, yet, refusing to live.

Admittedly, she was scared to return home. Scared at what she might find. Bianca drew herself straight. For the moment at least, she would push away her morbid thoughts and focus on finding the kerotakis. She would find the required cylinder and she would create the elixir.

Bianca looked away from Southwark, up the lane toward the Royal Poke, where Amice and Gilley lived. If she hurried she might at last secure the needed piece and return to Southwark before dark.

Along the way, prentices were shuttering up shops and clearing the stalls. The bustle of activity declared an end to the day, and Bianca quickened her step. She again experienced the eerie feeling of being followed.

She glanced over her shoulder and, seeing no one suspicious, hurried on. At one point a cart lumbered toward her and she pressed herself into a doorway occupied by a woman bearing a basket of eggs. A whiff of chicken manure stirred her to full attention like a slap in the face.

Emerging from the alcove, she let the trundling cart shield her and took a long look at the street beyond. She wasn't sure whom she should be looking for, who could be trailing her, but Tait's name kept whispering in her ear.

The strum of a lute floated over the discordant clamor of street noise, taming the sound of shouting children and bleating goats, reminding Bianca of what peace there is in song. She longed to stand beneath the window and listen to the tune—but such leisure was not possible.

Consumed with what or who might be behind her, Bianca scarcely considered what danger could lie ahead. She rounded a corner onto a narrow lane where houses jutted over the road so close that neighbors across the road could pass a pottle pot between them. Immediately it was as if the light of day had been secreted away. She strode purposefully, but each step took her deeper into the lengthening shadows. The lane grew darker and became more congested. Its suffocating lack of air was another unwelcome reminder of her poor decision. A crush of bodies soon pressed against her, slowing her progress until she could barely move.

Ahead, word spread that an overturned cart blocked the lane. There was no turning back, as others who had made the same mistake pushed in behind her. An unsuspecting driver followed with a second cart, further preventing escape.

No gap between buildings or intersecting alleyways could relieve the congestion. Those who had sought the lane as a shortcut began to grouse. No one moved forward and there was not much movement back.

"God's tooth, if I had wanted to feel the press of bodies I would'a gone to the Addle Hill stew!"

"Methinks you might enjoy a similar experience here, without having to pay," another answered helpfully.

At least one man could see a possible advantage to the bottleneck.

Bianca could not tolerate standing in one spot, doing nothing. She thought of John, which was all the prompting she needed.

"By your leave," she said, squeezing through the crowd. When refused, she squashed toes and poked ribs with her bony elbows. Leaving a wake of bruises and outcry behind her, she worked her way to a cart tipped across the lane. It lay on its side, its back axle snapped and a wheel off the rod. A load of grain had tumbled out and was strewn about the road. Bianca hitched her kirtle, exposing her ankles, and scrambled up the sacks to reach the other side.

"Ho there!" said a man, peeling her off like a beetle whose claws had caught in fabric. "You shall wait like the rest of us."

"I need to get through. I cannot wait."

A woman tipped her chin to be heard. "Wait she must," she shouted, still sore from Bianca's aggressive campaign. "She punched me in the ribs."

"Aye! She punched me, too!" called another.

"I did not punch," declared Bianca emphatically. She looked at the burly man holding her arm. "I nudged."

"Oh, that was not a nudge," said the woman stepping forward. "If that were a nudge, a blow is a bump and a clouting is a clip."

"If everyone were to scrap their way out, what an utter muddle we would have." The man yanked Bianca's arm to underscore his point. "You will wait doubly long since you have not the sense to behave civilly."

Bianca started to object, but her voice was drowned by another.

"Nay, let me through," proclaimed a man, a red cap waving at the end of a thin arm.

A group of men cursing the driver as he unhitched his horse stopped their sport and listened to the new distraction.

"This matter does concern me. I am responsible for her rude temperament." The cap flounced as if it were indicating the start of a race, and a group of men trying to rock the bed of the cart upright paused to see who was creating the commotion.

"I agree her impertinence is shameful, but allow me to dispense her punishment," said Meddybemps, tripping the last few feet and arriving to stand next to them.

"And by what right? Who are you?"

Meddybemps removed the man's hand from Bianca's arm and drew her behind him. "I am her father."

There was a reason Meddybemps placed himself in front of her. Bianca began to protest and received a painful pinch for her effort. The streetseller's insistent if not theatrical objections successfully covered her yowl.

The man eyed them skeptically. "She favors you not."

"Sir," said Meddybemps, looking wounded. "What are you implying?" He glanced round at the interested faces leaning in. "Are you questioning her mother's honor? Because if you think my dear . . . Bess . . . strayed . . . well, sir, that is a slander I shall not allow you to indulge." The streetseller straightened and met the man's eye. "My dear . . . Bess . . . good sir, let me tell of her attributes so that you may know how very mistaken you are. Her breath whispers of fresh-picked mint and her kisses are cool and as stirring upon my brow as if she had laid such sprigs upon it. She would want for none other, for she hath told me, my dear . . . Bessie, my . . . Bess . . . that I love her like none other. That I pluck her as sweetly as a daisy's petals so her face shineth like the sun. Her flower doth smell as sweet as a violet in purple display, her petals so colored and primed for me to inhale. Bess, sweet Bess. There is no more faithful . . . whore . . ."

Meddybemps felt the skin twist painfully beneath his jerkin. "—ible, aye, horrible how this cart has caused such an inconvenience." He smiled, then glanced over his shoulder to glower at Bianca.

Their drama gained more interest now than the overturned cart. The man, who was not a constable or even a deputy, was not inclined to encourage Meddybemps in more purple prose, and sought to end the confrontation quickly since he had no authority to do anything about Bianca's behavior.

"My good fellow, I merely sought to bring some order to this unfortunate situation. Your . . . daughter . . . was likely to cause an uproar. I was trying to impose a sense of order."

"And well you should," agreed Meddybemps, clapping the man on his shoulder. "It is the proper, indeed, the commendable citizen to inflict order on his neighbors."

The man, nonplussed, responded with a weak smile.

"My dear . . . daughter," said Meddybemps, turning to Bianca. "Let us take our leave and wish this fine fellow a good morrow."

He nodded amiably to the parting crowd as he roughly pushed Bianca back through it.

An oft-frequented boozing ken was tucked into an inconspicuous building on the lane, not twenty feet from the overturned cart. Meddybemps pulled Bianca through the door. He had hoped for a chance to sit with her and tell her what he had learned; however, other pedestrians looking to escape the congestion were successfully creating a new one inside the tavern.

Afforded the gift of above-average height, Meddybemps spotted an open bench and motioned her to follow.

They jostled their way to a back corner and sat opposite each other next to a boisterous group of men, possibly fishermen or workers from the fish market. Their close proximity bothered Meddybemps more than it did Bianca, but he put on a brave face and angled away from them.

After several attempts to wave down a serving wench, he took off his cap in exasperation and set it on the board in front of him. "Zounds," he said. "I could do with an ale." He scratched his thinning scalp.

"I suppose I should thank you."

"Methinks you are not particularly pleased with me. I could not stand idly by while that jackdaw made an example of you. I suspect he wanted some sort of lewd favor before giving you leave."

"Not every man thinks like you."

"Ha! You defend him?" Meddybemps's left eye circled while the other held her with a contemptible stare. "I shall not take issue. But unless you sit inside a man's skull, you cannot know why he does what he does. And one thing every man does, that may not be what every woman does, is think of how to profit in any given situation. That man saw a chance to have sway over you. I will not mention what could have happened if I had not intervened."

Bianca looped the strap over her head and set her satchel on the table between them. She rested her hands palm down on top. "If it should please you," she said. "Thank you for saving me."

The streetseller duly noted the sardonic edge to her voice. He laid a hand on top of hers and nodded, accepting her appreciation and knowing full well she gave it grudgingly.

"Do tell me the source of your worriment," he said. "Your impertinence does not serve." He removed his hand and distractedly looked about for the serving wench again.

"John has fallen into a deep sleep."

Horrified, he looked at her straight on. "A deep sleep? Meaning the kind from which you may never wake?"

"He has not died. Not yet, anyway." She glanced toward the door, a rueful expression settling on her face. "He is unresponsive to my touch. He doesn't react to my voice." Bianca absently ran her fingers over the coarse material of the rucksack. "Perhaps it is the sweating sickness but I am not sure. I have not heard that victims linger so."

"It could happen. I have heard it," said Meddybemps. "He is a strong lad; he may well recover." He knew no words that could comfort her. He had always liked John and thought them a suitable pair. They both had a bit of rascality about them, and since marrying, they had tamed their reckless behavior and pursued more respectable, if somewhat dull, livelihoods. Ventures definitely not to his taste or desire. "You have left him alone?"

Bianca's throat became tight. "There is nothing I can do for him, so, aye, he is alone." She glanced over his shoulder and leaned in. "I am seeking the final piece I need to create the elixir of life. And I fear someone is after me."

Meddybemps scowled. "Who should want to follow you?"

Bianca lowered her voice. "I believe someone wants Ferris Stannum's alchemy journal." She patted the satchel between them. "The journal contains the complete process for creating the elixir of life."

"Ah. Perhaps another alchemist would want it," whispered Meddybemps. "Or someone who could sell it to an alchemist."

"I had thought perhaps that Ferris Stannum's friend, Thomas Plumbum, could have wanted it. However, Tait, the usurer, told me Plumbum was stabbed last night near Soper Lane. And Constable Patch has confirmed it."

"Constable Patch," said Meddybemps with a shudder. "Not him again." He stuck out his tongue as if the man's name had left a bad taste in his mouth. "Must you bring that iron-witted doddypoll into it?" Reading the look of chagrin on Bianca's face, he saw that she must. Meddybemps sighed. "I was going to tell you what I knew, but it seems you already know. But, aye, Plumbum is dead."

"Tell me everything. Tait has been less than forthcoming and Patch doesn't know much."

Meddybemps lowered his face so no one could see his lips. "You had mentioned Plumbum and I became curious about the man. It seemed to me that perhaps he had the most cause for seeing Ferris Stannum dead. Being a less than accomplished alchemist, I figured he might be jealous of the old man's discovery. I had no difficulty finding the man, and with a little more inquiry, I learned he owed a sizable sum of money to Jack Blade—the rampallian who frequents the area around the Crooked Cork. Apparently Plumbum had a few obsessions he was known for." Meddybemps's eye began to skitter. "One is a traitorous offense. I shall suffice it to say, he was a man whose wanger was most wanton." Meddybemps tittered with contempt. "His other disgrace was playing primero. And this he played badly. He gambled more than he should have and had a debt that followed him from one table to the next. His reputation on both counts was less than sterling." Meddybemps snickered and glanced around. He finally caught the eye of the serving wench and she made her way over. "Have you a thirst?" he asked Bianca.

"I'll sip yours. I cannot linger. Surely the cart will be cleared away before long."

"It will, but the crowd will not have thinned."

The wench rested a fist on her hip with three empty tankards looped through her fingers. "What is your pleasure?"

Meddybemps ran his eyes up and down her person, which was of stout proportion. Unable to restrain himself, he reached for her buttocks and squeezed.

She slapped his hand away. "I hadn' the time for that kind of pleasure."

"Then a tankard of your bitter," he said, rubbing his smarting hand. "For it must be the house's drink."

The wench had no use for Meddybemps's tart remarks and replied with a scathing stare. She quipped to Bianca, "Your father needs a lesson in manners, lass. What will ye have?"

"Nothing, my lady."

The wench raised her eyebrows to hear such a formal address. She cuffed Meddybemps on the back of his head so that his cap fell over his eyes. "My lady," she repeated, ambling off.

"Well, *she* thought I could be your father."

Bianca scanned the room for familiar faces and, in particular, Tait's. Their chance meeting at Thomas Plumbum's had left her edgy.

"My sweetum," said Meddybemps, noticing her jump when addressed. "I need to tell you more of this Plumbum fellow." He held his hand beside his mouth, masking his lips. "The rumor is that he was run through by one of Blade's men. Plumbum never paid his gambling debt. After several warnings, Jack Blade's patience ran out."

"He owed the usurer, Tait, a sum of money, too. I wonder if Tait had anything to do with it."

"I can't imagine a usurer wanting a man murdered before collecting his due. Unless he wanted to make an example of him." Meddybemps shook his head. "That does not seem a prudent course for a man with such a business. However, a man who has crossed Jack Blade more than once should not expect the rascal to forget his indiscretions." Meddybemps snorted.

The patrons sitting next to them grew quiet and a couple of the men turned interested eyes on the pair. One man in particular took a lengthy accounting of Bianca. He addressed Bianca and hooked a thumb at Meddybemps. "Fair lady, what do ye see in this ragged coot?"

"He's my father," said Bianca.

The fellow lifted an eyebrow and the side of his mouth turned up in a half grin. "Aye, well, I suppose ye do take after him." He turned back to his friends, and after they had each taken a long gander and shrugged, they decided it was of no further interest to them and continued their boisterous camaraderie.

Meddybemps grinned. "So, my turtle, I wanted to tell you about Blade's crew. A young rogue has taken on some of his territory and works in partnership with the cozen. He does Blade's most atrocious deeds and in return he is well compensated for his trouble."

"And its import?"

"Thomas Plumbum had more than a few brushes with Blade. Plumbum was a man who was being watched."

"Did Blade stab him?"

"I have been frequenting the Royal Poke, where Amice works. It has been taxing, but I have managed to blend into the background and keep my ears open. I have refused games of dice and primero. And I want you to note I did not ogle the help."

"Commendable."

The serving wench returned with Meddybemps's tankard and set it before him. She held out her hand for his coin.

Meddybemps's eyes narrowed at her astringent treatment. He plunked his coin in her palm. "Keep the change, love."

Her hand remained open and waiting. "Ye owe me a ha'penny more."

The streetseller and she locked eyes and he stood up. Bianca dreaded another brazen confrontation like the one in the road. Meddybemps's stare never wavered as he dug into his purse, withdrew the coin, and plopped it in the serving maid's palm. The wench's face softened and she smiled in satisfaction, dropping it in her apron pocket.

"It must have taken some effort to stay unnoticed at the Royal Poke."

Meddybemps sat down. "Some alehouses are easier than others." He took a long quaff from his tankard. "Some women are easier than others." He glanced over his shoulder and, seeing the wench a safe distance away, lowered his voice. "And she has the face of a cow and the pendulous teats to match."

Bianca glanced at the door impatiently. "As you were saying?"

"I was sitting at the Poke last night having some fare, when in should walk three cozens. Two of them seemed to be shielding the third from view as they hurried through to the kitchen. The man they were hiding wore his hat pulled down in front of his face. I think they did not want to draw notice, but their behavior succeeded in doing the opposite. Rarely does a group of men come into a ken and not sit for a brew. It was dimly lit, as most taverns are, but I smelled the iron tang of blood when they passed. I glimpsed over and saw the man's dagger tucked in his waistband, dark with blood. I was not mistaken. A man I was sitting across from saw it, too.

"The three disappeared out back. A moment later there was a loud clatter from the kitchen and we heard a man and woman arguing. The commotion caused the entire establishment to quiet. Nothing stirs a man's sympathy more than the sound of another being scolded by his woman. There is not a man in God's creation who doesn't pale at the sound of a woman screeching. And then there was a slap. Everyone heard it."

Meddybemps took another drink and wiped his mouth with the back of his hand. "No one had time to blink before Amice came charging out of the kitchen. She was angry as a boar, red-faced and choking back tears as she bolted for the door. I couldn't say if her cheek was red from her being slapped or if she was just upset. Someone stood and made to comfort her, but she shirked away and whipped off her apron. Just before heaving open the door she threw the thing on the floor, glowered round at the clientele, and disappeared into the night."

"Sounds like good theater."

"It got the whole lot of us talking. And it comes out that Gilley had just murdered a man. Perhaps it was mere speculation. Tongues are loose after a few pottle pots, but with drink and conjecture comes a wee bit of truth."

"Do you believe Gilley murdered Thomas Plumbum?" Bianca helped herself to Meddybemps's ale.

Meddybemps arranged himself so his back blocked them from their tablemates. "Words flew that Gilley must have killed a man. Others surmised who he had murdered. One cuffin said he had been at the Crooked Cork a few days before and heard that Jack Blade had caught the alchemist, Thomas Plumbum, buggering a young boy. Blade had no use for Plumbum. He wanted his money back and if it was not forthcoming, he was the sort of man who would exact his own personal justice.

"It was presumed that Gilley and Blade had come to an arrangement between them. Blade no longer frequented the Royal Poke and moved his operation south of Knightrider. Likely, Gilley got the area around the Royal Poke in exchange for a few favors."

Meddybemps polished off his ale. He caught sight of the wench to order another but thought better of it when she glared back at him. "The reason I think Gilley is the culprit is because I stopped at the Poke earlier in the day and saw Amice accuse a man of being an alchemist. Apparently, Amice recognized him and mentioned his not-so-flattering conduct. The look she had when he tried making her look foolish was hard to miss. She is a woman who does not like to be crossed."

"So, Gilley's reason to finish Plumbum may be twofold."

Meddybemps smirked. "His sort doesn't ponder matters of conscience. As long as he sees some personal benefit, he doesn't question what is asked of him."

Bianca sighed. "I doubt Amice expected her husband to go as far as murdering Plumbum. If Gilley was found out, which sounds likely, it would be the ruination of them both." Bianca got a distant look in her eye. "Amice strikes me as a woman just trying to get by."

"The lot of an alchemist's daughter, wouldn't you say? Making do with nothing."

"Amice mistakenly saw Gilley as a way out of her misery. Instead, he is causing her plenty."

"Reminds me of someone else we knew."

Meddybemps was referring to her friend Jolyn Carmichael, the muckraker who had lived a hard life and had believed she was on the verge of a better one. She put her faith in the wrong person and it ended badly for her. Bianca was still pained at the mention or thought of Jolyn. She missed her friend terribly.

Meddybemps sensed Bianca growing morose and immediately regretted mentioning Jolyn. He quickly engaged her before she slipped into maudlin introspection. "Bianca, I doubt that Gilley would murder Ferris Stannum."

"But Gilley was his son-in-law. It seems an unhappy coincidence now."

"But why would Gilley murder Amice's poor father?"

"Maybe for the alchemy journal? Or the valuables in Stannum's room of alchemy?" Bianca massaged her temples. "My thoughts keep going to Tait. Both Plumbum and Stannum owed him money. I wonder if Tait could have some connection to Blade." Bianca gazed at a fixed point across the room, her eyes glazing over as she thought.

Meddybemps refrained from talking. Bianca often sank into silence and took issue if he interrupted her thinking. However, he wanted to remind her that her immediate consideration was John's welfare. He couldn't understand why she had taken it upon herself to find Ferris Stannum's murderer. Dismiss Stannum's death to natural cause and save yourself the bother, is what he wanted to tell her. Stannum was an old man, feeble and not long for this world anyway. But Bianca believed he had been murdered and was consumed with proving it. Meddybemps studied her determined face. If there was any way to connect the two alchemists' deaths, she would find it.

"I need you to take this satchel," she said, rousing from her rumination and pushing it across to him. She leaned over the table, then said in a low voice, "I warn you—you might be followed."

"I have been followed before," he whispered. "It is not the first time."

Bianca sat back and looked around. She tipped forward, meeting his eyes. "Meet me on the bridge in an hour," she said. "And bring the satchel. I have someone to visit first."

CHAPTER 28

Bianca found the crowd outside the boozing ken had thinned substantially. The overturned cart had been successfully angled, relieving the earlier congestion. She emerged on Cheapside Street—a wider thoroughfare that was considerably less dark and ominous feeling.

The sensation of being followed lessened, though she still cast searching glances over her shoulder with a mind for spotting anyone suspicious. If Tait or anyone else had followed her as far as the alehouse, he might notice she was no longer carrying the satchel. She hoped Meddybemps would be able to meet her at the bridge at their agreed-upon time.

When she had left Gull Hole that morning, she had not intended to be gone the entire day. Her main objective was to find a kerotakis. It seemed an unexpected string of events conspired to keep her from returning to John.

It would have been understandable to abandon the search and return home. A pang of guilt stabbed at her heart, but realistically, she did not know what she could have done for him. Sitting and waiting would have driven her mad.

But Bianca believed she would soon secure the elusive cylinder from Amice. And the sooner she had it, the sooner she could start working on the elixir.

She ignored her niggling conscience and followed the slightly curving route to the Royal Poke, where Amice and Gilley lived above the tavern. Night had fallen, and with it came fast-moving clouds and the sprinkle of stars in between. A northern breeze accompanied their appearance. A change in weather was in the air.

An errant goose took exception to Bianca and honked in loud protest as she neared the ignoble establishment. She ignored the bird's bluster and sidestepped around the creature. Unhappy at being brushed aside, the goose ran up and nipped her, eliciting a chuckle from a patron just leaving.

"God's wounds!" she exclaimed, waving it away. The aggressive beast retreated long enough for Bianca to scurry inside and slam the door in its face.

Bianca stood next to the entrance and scanned the rows of tables and raucous clientele. A new serving wench appeared from the kitchen clutching two fists of tankards. Bianca waited until she had finished serving. Before the girl got caught up with another order, Bianca tapped her shoulder.

"Amice is not working this evening?"

"She's ill." The maid motioned with her head in the direction of the kitchen. "She and her husband both. Haven't seen them since this morning." She put her mouth next to Bianca's ear. "We suspect the sweat." She reared back and gave Bianca a serious look. Her eyes flicked to one side and she leaned in again. "Best keep that one to yourself."

Bianca squeezed through the crowded tables with the pretense of finding a place to sit, watching until the serving wench was occupied, then ducked into the kitchen. No one noticed her slip past and head for the back stairs.

The candle on the stairwell had not been lit. Once she had felt her way up the uneven treads to the landing, she saw the door to Amice and Gilley's rent was closed. Bianca pressed her ear against the wood and, hearing nothing, knocked. After a moment she tried the handle. It was not locked.

She called into the dark but heard no reply, so she stepped inside. The shutters were closed. No candles or lanterns had been lit. She allowed a moment for her eyes to adjust, and the first thing she saw was the table where Gilley had played primero. It was piled with copper coils. Still heads and retorts cluttered the room. Their quarters had been transformed into a warehouse of alchemy equipment.

Bianca felt around for a candle on a high shelf next to the entry and, not finding one, sufficed by cautiously picking through the collection of alembics and crockery. A myriad of sizes and shapes, stacked in leaning heaps, created a tenuous maze for her to step through. She squinted in the dim light, navigating to the opposite wall to open a shutter, though doing so would only marginally illuminate the interior with moonlight.

The silence made her wonder if Amice and Gilley had feigned sickness and escaped together. They could have abandoned their rent and London in the hopes of avoiding Gilley's arrest. If Meddybemps had figured out Gilley's crime, someone else certainly would. Again Bianca called out. Hearing no response, she continued to the opposite wall.

She bent over, running her hand along a pile of copper, feeling the shapes, hoping by chance to find the cylinder with the curved glass top. Her fingertips had just touched the cool feel of metal when something hit the floor in the adjoining room. Bianca froze. She looked in its direction. A shutter banged, blown by a gust of wind. Dismissing the sound as something knocked over by the wind, she waited a moment. Hearing nothing more, she continued to the wall. Bianca pushed open a creaky shutter.

Moonlight was blocked by the roof across the way, affording little improvement. Bianca swept her hand along the wall to feel for a sconce. She crept forward, tiptoeing along the wall. Something ran over her foot. She yelped, disturbing several retorts and causing a clatter as they toppled over. In the dim blue light, a mouse disappeared under the jumble of equipment. If anyone was in the rent, they would know she was there now.

But no one called out.

Bianca resumed running her hand over the wall and found a sconce caked in dried tallow. She worked out the stub and patted her pockets for her flint. She often dropped one in her apron instead of leaving it next to a stove in her rent. Pleased that her forgetfulness had served her, she lit the candle and ran her eyes around the room.

She concentrated on the shape and size of the kerotakis. She had often found that visualizing her desire brought it to her. It was an amusement she often played, especially when she was creating salves and medicinals. She knew the location of every ingredient in her room, but, since John had moved in, he often put jars back in unexpected places. Sometimes it was a monumental task to locate her ingredients, requiring her to think like John, or remember where he had been and what he had been up to, before eventually finding what she wanted. But if she imagined the appearance or smell of an object, within a few minutes she would find it.

She turned, raising the candle in front of her. Her mind was a muddle. She paused, gazing at the display of equipment but not really seeing it. Worry and lack of sleep had worn her down. Her stomach protested, reminding her that she was not only tired, but hungry. She couldn't remember the last time she had eaten.

Bianca decided her weariness was a state of mind. The exhaustion and hunger were temporary discomforts that she needed to suppress. She tucked a loose strand of hair under her coif and rubbed her eyes.

When she opened them, she spied a vessel sticking out of a bowl. Excited, she hurried over and grabbed it. Unfortunately, it was just a simple copper cylinder, not a kerotakis. Disappointed, Bianca laid it on the table.

Hot tallow ran down the candle. She turned the stick sideways as the flame consumed the tallow near her fingers. Dropping the spent tallow, she heard a night watch call as she stamped the wick on the floor. Soon she must meet Meddybemps on the bridge. Time was running out and she hadn't found the kerotakis.

A loaf of bread sat on a table and Bianca tore off an end. The lump went down like wood, but she was so hungry she did not care. She glanced around for something to drink and found a keg of ale. She poured herself a mug, took a sip, found it potable, and polished it off, glad to slake her thirst. The humidity still sapped her strength in spite of a slight cooling breeze, but the ale revived her. She poured herself another cup and poured it over her face to cool her skin, not caring that she would smell like she'd taken a bath in it.

As she set the mug down, she noticed a copper vessel lying in a crate on the floor next to the table. She bent down and held it up in the dim light.

The kerotakis.

She pressed the cool metal cylinder to her chest. Finally. She closed her eyes and took a deep, invigorating breath. The elusive apparatus needed to sublimate the elixir of life. She had found it. Bianca bit her lower lip, hoping John was still strong enough to survive until she'd created the mythical brew.

Finding the kerotakis instilled Bianca with confidence. Confidence that this was indeed her fate. She would create the elixir of life. How could this not be an auspicious sign? If she had never found the crucial piece of equipment, she would have assumed before she had even started that her efforts were doomed. But now, with the kerotakis in her possession, her fate was awaiting her.

The thought of saving John made her giddy with joy. If someone had peeked through the window, they would have seen her toss her head back and laugh like a lunatic. She cared not a whit whether granting immortality might be immoral. All that mattered was John and their future together.

Bianca kissed the kerotakis, wagged a finger at it, and dropped it in her pocket. She lifted the hair off the back of her neck, fanning her damp skin with her hand. It was time to meet Meddybemps at the bridge.

Bianca turned to wend her way back to the door when she heard
a strange sound from the room off the main living quarters. Puzzled,
she hesitated. If Amice and Gilley were home and sleeping, surely
they would have heard her long before now. She looked over her
shoulder at the door of the adjoining room. Perhaps it was her
imagination.

Shrugging it off, she turned back to the door. She had taken
only a couple of steps when she heard the sound for a second time.
Eyes wide, she stopped and searched the dark, her senses primed.

A disconcerting shriek startled her. Her hand flew to her mouth,
squelching the cry that came out of it.

What was that unearthly sound? It was not in Bianca's nature to
flee. Her inquisitiveness was often a detriment to self-preservation.
Guardedly, she crept toward the room. In the few seconds it took
for her to reach it, her imagination had run the gamut of possibilities.

She paused just outside the door and slowly looked in.

It took a second for her to comprehend what she was seeing.
Moonlight shone through an open window. She followed its sil-
very beam across the room and saw where it illuminated Amice
and her husband. Gilley lay on a pallet and Amice was curled on
the floor beside him.

At first, Bianca thought them asleep. But Gilley's head was
turned toward the door, as if he had heard her coming. For a second she thought he might speak. His face was a sneer as he
stared right at her. The wind blew and the shutter smacked shut,
plunging the room into complete darkness.

Bianca froze.

Another gust of wind blew open the shutter and Bianca saw in
detail the horrible scene before her. Gilley's face was caked in
blood. A dried red trickle ran from his mouth down his chin.
Streaks of blood ran from his eyes. His nostrils were caked in it.
The whites of his eyes were dark, yet still reflected the dim light.
An arm dangled off the bed, his fingertips grazing Amice where
she lay on the floor.

Curled in a half-moon, Amice faced Gilley with her back to the door. Bianca went over and crouched beside her. She laid her hand on the girl's shoulder, feeling it cold to the touch. She rolled the girl over.

Amice's face was the mirror of her husband's. Lines of dried blood crisscrossed her skin. She had suffered the same fate as Gilley. She had bled from every orifice.

Bianca retreated. The bloom of death had not yet tainted the air. She had never seen a disease manifest in this way. She ran her eyes over the pair, seeking stab wounds, but their clothing showed only the stains of blood that had dripped from their faces.

As she stood and thought on their wretched end, she heard a scrabbling. The noise shot down her spine, jarring her to her core.

In a dark corner, Ferris Stannum's parrot thrashed. It writhed on the floor, attempted to get to its feet, and fell over. Bianca watched it push its unwieldy beak against the floor in a vain attempt to stand. A wing flapped helplessly; the other hung paralyzed and limp. What used to be a rainbow of red, green, yellow, and blue plumage was completely crimson now. Its pale golden eyes were blinded by streaming blood.

Helpless to ease its suffering, Bianca wished the bird passage from its misery. Its pitiful caw—a mournful, eerie cry—pulled at her heart. Finally, exhausted by its struggle, it lay quiet, its chest heaving. Its beak parted for a final breath and its body relaxed. Its agony was over.

"Peace be," she said. "You are free."

Bianca looked round at the scene before her. What kind of cruel malady would cause such a death? The symptoms were unlike any she had ever seen. Not even the sweat was as malevolent. The buzz of flies soon drew her notice. She looked about for sheets and found one folded at the foot of the bed. She covered Amice, leaving the flies to alight on Gilley.

Had the bird contracted the disease from the dead couple? Or had the parrot been the source of the contagion?

Strange creatures and birds from the new world had been

brought over by Spaniards, and these living novelties had a way of showing up on British shores. Bianca remembered seeing a turkey at Cheapside, its owner keeping it tethered to his stall to attract attention and buyers. At least the parrot had been beautiful, with its crest of red, its green- and blue-tipped feathers, and its magnificent beak. The turkey only drew notice for its homely appearance, with its red, wrinkled wattle and dull plumage.

Bianca crouched over the parrot and took a moment to look it over. The tongue protruded between its parted beak, black and lolling to one side. It lay in a pool of blood from its mouth and eyes.

At her visit with the elderly alchemist, Stannum had warned her not to get too close to the bird. He said he had been nipped. Bianca sat back on her heels. And Goodwife Tenbrook, she remembered, had been bitten.

Ferris Stannum's preoccupation with dabbing his eyes had seemed like a peculiar quirk until she noticed how bloodshot they were. His pillow had been stained with blood, separated by the width of his nose.

Bianca covered the bird and got to her feet.

If Ferris Stannum had *not* been smothered by a pillow, would he have died of the same infection that had claimed Amice and Gilley?

Bianca thought back to Goodwife Tenbrook lying in her darkened room with the shutters closed. She had complained of the light hurting her eyes when Barnabas Hughes opened the shutter. She, too, had bloodshot eyes. But perhaps the infection had not reached the point that it had with Amice and Gilley. Perhaps the landlady had only the beginning symptoms. Bianca shook her head. According to the coroner, Goodwife Tenbrook had died from the sweat. And apparently Barnabas Hughes had not poisoned her when he gave her the sleeping draught. There seemed to be no clear reason why the landlady had died. Unless, perhaps, the combination of several factors contributed to her demise.

Some deaths might always remain inexplicable.

A shutter clacked against the house as a gust of wind blew through the window, startling Bianca. She shook off her contemplation. She would have plenty of time to ponder while creating the elixir. But for now, Meddybemps was expecting her.

CHAPTER 29

Meddybemps stood beneath the drawbridge tower, peering up at the impressive display of heads impaled on pikes. He had done a good business at the Tyburn execution. The crowds had been raucous and irreverent. Minstrels entertained before the condemned were wheeled through to boisterous cheers. He had enjoyed himself thoroughly, until he realized one of the accused was his cousin. Seeing his sorry countenance trembling and terrified sobered the streetseller. He wished at least Winfred had shown some spine. Alas, he had not. Now Meddybemps spied his cousin staring down at him, his teeth glinting in a final grimace. "Poor Winfred," said Meddybemps. "Dear fellow, you have not much to grin about now."

The streetseller withdrew a pipe and turned his back to the wind, which had suddenly come up, blowing away the haze of humid, murky air that had plagued London of late. He huddled over the spark of a flint, igniting the bowl of dried tobacco, savoring the smell of its smoke. He had arrived with time to spare. Bianca was late but not so dramatically that he should be concerned. He whiled away the minutes in conversation with the rare passerby brave enough to cross the bridge at this late hour.

By the time he'd left the tavern the cart had been dragged from the lane and deposited at the edge of a wider one. A casualty of London's deterioration, it would cost the poor drayman plenty to repair the axle. He knew, for he had just repaired one on his pushcart not a month before. If King Harry weren't so intent on reclaiming his French land and proving he was more virile than King Francis, he might spend some money on patching the roads.

Bianca's satchel dug into his shoulder and he irritably shrugged it off, setting it beside him on the bridge. Why suffer needless discomfort? It would not be long before she arrived.

Meddybemps took another puff on his pipe and blew the smoke out over the water. A merchant vessel was mooring off Romeland, and he watched the crew haul up the sails. The great sheets of canvas billowed in the wind, tugging the ropes as the seamen lashed the sails fast. The hands furling the triangular sail off the foremast had particular issue with the gale. The line running through a block caught in the outermost pulley. The sail flapped about, and the sagging line flailed in the wind.

He listened to the crewmen curse and saw a young mate singled out to shimmy up the bowsprit. This made for great entertainment. Meddybemps puffed contentedly at his pipe as he watched the sailors and their antics.

Below, the water grew choppy and Meddybemps watched with increasing interest as the lad clung to the bowsprit, which dipped and rolled with the ship. The streetseller had little interest in sailing the seas. London was world enough for him. He had not a mote of desire to see the wonders of other lands. Even descriptions of women with their tawny skin and exposed bosoms did not entice him enough to take up such a life. If God had intended him to cross the seas, he would have been born a fish.

His interest drew the notice of another pedestrian walking the drawbridge as the moon lit the surface of the water and illuminated the poor sailor inching down the spar.

"They had better give him an extra ration if he makes it without falling in," said the man, a bawcock by the looks of him. He was dressed in merchant's clothing and did not seem to mind sharing the view with the likes of a streetseller—at least for the moment. Meddybemps gave him a sidelong glance, sizing him up and deciding if it was worth trying to wrangle a coin from him in a bet. If he hadn't been tasked with meeting Bianca, he might have prattled on about some such nonsense, then followed him into the darker recesses of the bridge to put a knife on his neck and scare it out of him. The fellow was probably good for decent coin, for Meddybemps noted a heavy-looking purse swinging from his waist.

Instead, Meddybemps forced himself to look away from the man's wealth and contented himself with conversation. "And if he does fall, and if by chance they manage to haul him out before he drowns, I say he deserves another three rations on top of the two."

The man nodded solemnly. "Have you ever stepped aboard one of those beasts?" he asked.

"Nay, no opportunity," replied Meddybemps. "Nor have I any desire."

"I have gone as far as Deptford," the man offered. He seemed happy to tell of his adventure, and Meddybemps did not mind listening, as long as he was not long-winded and humorless.

"Deptford is not so overly far," commented Meddybemps, wondering why the man would think that a worthy adventure.

"Far aplenty if you haven't the love for sailing." The man kept his eyes on the poor lad struggling with the line on the bowsprit. "I grant you, I most enjoyed watching the countryside roll by. But the life of a sailor is not for me."

"Why so brief a float?" Meddybemps held his pipe near his chest to keep the bowl burning. The wind blew, then died and blew again.

"I delivered a missive to the Royal Yard. The ship was to be refitted with a block of cannons."

"Ah, for our king's latest conquest?"

"To be at the ready. Aye, it is the desire of the Crown to call upon his merchant vessels when needed."

"And when might they be needed?"

"When the king is ready to take back his beloved Boulogne."

Meddybemps took a long draw on his pipe and tipped his chin skyward, blowing the smoke overhead. "Why does our king desire French land? Is their soil superior to ours?"

"I think one finds each a suitable surface to walk upon. The French till and piss on it the same as us."

"Then why desire it so?" Meddybemps cupped his hand around his pipe's bowl. The leaves were struggling to remain lit. "Be it so magical?"

"It is our liege's pleasure to think so." The man could not be lured into disparaging Harry or his policies. He was canny enough to know to keep his counsel. Meddybemps cared little for a man who so cautiously curbed his tongue. He decided to offer a wager.

"I've a pouch of leaves that says the boy does not return to deck," said Meddybemps. He had noticed the man's interest in his pipe and knew a covetous look when he saw it. He waited for the man to ante.

"I'll stake a crown," offered the man.

Meddybemps chuckled indulgently. Not only was this man niggardly with his words; he was stingy with his stakes. "Nay, my leaves are worth more than that. An angel and we shake."

The fellow considered this. He glanced at the boy wrapped desperately around the bowsprit. "Well matched," he said, putting out his hand to shake.

The two gamblers watched the lad fumble with the pulley. The gusting wind caused the ship to bob and yaw, and the lad frantically worked to be done with his task.

At one point the boy lost his footing and hung by his hands, dangling precariously over the surf. Meddybemps became excited and started shouting for him to let go. An angel in his pocket would be a nice addition. But Meddybemps underestimated the capacity of youths to engage their more limber abilities. The boy swung himself up like a monkey. Working his hands and then his legs, he inched down the spar to the waiting hands of his crew.

Meddybemps grumbled and removed his pouch of tobacco. It would be a while until he would secure more, if even there was any in London to find.

Delighted, the man pocketed his newly acquired cache. "A good eve," he said, touching a finger to his hat, spun from expensive silk. Whistling a discordant air, he disappeared through the dark interior of the bridge tower.

Meddybemps stifled the urge to follow. It would have been so easy to get back his pouch of smoking leaves.

A loud cheer went up from the deck of the merchant ship, and the monkey was made a hero. Meddybemps watched the crew heft him over the side and dangle him over the water in reward. Odd humor, these sailors. It confirmed his belief that days spent on the ocean with nothing but blue water before him made a man strange, if not mad.

Meddybemps tapped the ash out on the railing and tucked the pipe back into his jerkin. The Thames needed replenishing, and in a momentary lull in pedestrians, Meddybemps loosened the stays of his codpiece and aimed between the grates at his feet. He heard the tread of an advancing bypasser and turned his back on the approach.

It is a bodily function that cannot be hurried. Nor is the act of tying one's stays a quick exercise. Meddybemps floundered with the slippery cords, hoping the traveler was a man, because as such he would be sympathetic to the travails of securing these complicated fashions. Of course if it was Bianca, she would not much care, but the streetseller did not want to embarrass either of them.

Meddybemps did get his wish. A man stepped onto the grate of the drawbridge. However, instead of passing him by, the man strode up, grabbed the satchel, and made haste to be off with it.

"Ho there!" yelled Meddybemps, abandoning his project. He came about, snatching the strap of Bianca's satchel, and hauled back against the fleeing cutpurse. He was surprised to find his strength evenly matched. The thief would not let go. A tug-of-war ensued and the streetseller clung to the strap, hoping it would not fray from the strain.

In the dim moonlight, Meddybemps glimpsed the man's face but did not recognize him. His dress was not that of a typical scrounging vagrant. In fact, his attire implied a man of some professional station. His neatly clipped beard and ringed fingers certainly bespoke a man of refined taste. For the life of him, the streetseller could not figure what a man of such standing would want with an old satchel.

But whoever he was, Meddybemps was surprised with the man's determination. The thief clung to the rucksack like daub on a wall.

Still holding the strap, Meddybemps maneuvered them to the middle of the drawbridge so that the man had his back to the river. He then charged forward, yelling through gritted teeth, pushing the man into the railing.

"Leave off the satchel!" cried Meddybemps, yanking the strap. The motion tugged the man's arms so that Meddybemps drove his knee into the rascal's gut. But the move was not delivered well and the cozen fended off the bony appendage with his forearm.

Meddybemps stumbled. His grip lessened. The crook saw his advantage and quickly slid one hand up the strap and wrenched it away. As Meddybemps recovered his balance, the man turned to run. If he did not act, the satchel would be gone forever. Growling with a burst of strength, Meddybemps launched himself at the man's back.

Fortunately for the streetseller, the scoundrel caught his toe in the drawbridge grate. He fell forward, taking Meddybemps with him. Their bodies hit the grate with a thud. The satchel skidded inches out of reach.

Meddybemps scuttled after it and got his side punched. The thief scrabbled after it and got his arm bit. The two grabbed on to each other. They tussled, they grunted, they cursed. Finally,

Meddybemps managed to get the better of the man, seizing his wrists and pinning them down. But the rogue bucked the streetseller off and rolled free. Meddybemps swiped after his ankles as the man threw himself over the bag. Incensed, Meddybemps dove onto his back. This time the streetseller pushed the man's head into the grate and held it there.

" 'Tis a shame your nose isn't as thick as your head," said Meddybemps, feeling his hands grow wet with blood. "Maybe you might leave off that satchel, like I asked." For good measure, the streetseller grabbed the man by his ears and drove his face into the grate.

The crook said nothing in response. He offered no resistance when Meddybemps lifted his head for a third bashing. Remorseful, but not sorry enough to be gentle, Meddybemps let go. The thief's head fell heavily on the grate.

Heaving for breath, Meddybemps stood and picked up the satchel.

No pedestrians or travelers witnessed their scuffle. Only the wind, the stone façades of the bridge, and the river Thames attended the brawl. Meddybemps looked down at the filcher and felt a twinge of panic. The man lay motionless. Not even a moan escaped his lips. Had he killed him?

Meddybemps hadn't thought his strength was superior. He had dashed the thief's face into the grating only enough to stun him. His intention was merely to stop the scoundrel's frenzy. His heart thudded. Nay, that was not true and he knew it. He had enjoyed his moment of unbridled ire.

Meddybemps looked around. Had anyone seen him? He swiped his hat off the grating and pulled it down low over his brows. He pulled the collar of his jerkin up under his chin. If someone had come upon their struggle, surely they would have intervened. Surely someone would have stopped them. He stared down at the lifeless body in disbelief.

But a witness might have fled to find a constable. Meddybemps looked back in the direction of London, peering at the dark passage through the tower. In fact, they might be on their way now. Where was Bianca? He couldn't just stand here with a dead man at his feet and wait.

She had told him he might be followed. He had expected that. She had told him to protect the satchel. And he had. But she had not told him he had to kill a man in order to keep it.

"God's wounds!" he exclaimed. "From now on, I only sell your godless salves!" Since Bianca was not there to hear him, he voiced his rancor to the Queen Moon smirking at him from her lofty perch.

It would not do to stay a moment longer. His better sense told him to run. He glanced in the direction of London, willing Bianca to appear. In that still moment, the sound of sloshing water gave him an idea.

Meddybemps slung the satchel over his shoulder and went to the railing to peer over the side. It was far enough down and the tide was high enough that a body could be swept out to sea by morning. And if the man were not quite dead, a fall into the drink would surely finish him. No one would know the better, and he would bear the secret to his grave.

True, Bianca might never know the identity of Stannum's killer. Perhaps this thief was the old alchemist's murderer, but how was he to know for sure? Certainly, the man had wanted the satchel. But a man dressed as fine as this did not seem the dastardly type.

He would note the man's dress and his features so he could describe him to Bianca when she finally showed. He would tell her of the attack and that he had fended him off. He would tell her how the man ran away. Mayhap she would know who he might be from his description. Mayhap she would revel in the knowledge of Stannum's killer. Let her go to the foolish constable or justice of the peace and tell him of her thoughts. They would never find the man, and though Bianca might worry that he would be after her, in time, her fears would fade. And she would forget.

Meddybemps stepped beside the body, nudging him with his

boot to roll him over. He would get a long look at the man's face and remember it to Bianca.

Meddybemps was mistaken. The man was not dead.

His arm shot out, holding Meddybemps's ankle with a firm grip. Before the streetseller could regain his balance, the man had pulled him down. Meddybemps fell straight over, like a tree given the axe. His back slammed onto the bridge.

The man jumped on Meddybemps's stomach, pinning his arms to his sides. Unleashing a spate of pent-up fury, he pummeled Meddybemps in the jaw.

Meddybemps thrashed about, trying to avoid the man's determined fist. The taste of blood filled his mouth; his neck became damp from it. The man kept to his merciless assault for longer than Meddybemps had kept up his.

But Meddybemps sensed the man tiring. The punches slowed and they lost their brutal edge. It would take more than a nattily dressed professional to do him in. Stirred by indignation, Meddybemps rose in a surge of strength. He spewed blood and saliva in the man's face and threw him off.

"Now," said Meddybemps, scrambling to his feet. He spoke between heavy gasps of breath. "Suppose you tell me who you are and why you have issue with me?"

The man struggled to his hands and knees. He brought his legs under him and staggered to his feet. He wavered before Meddybemps, breathing heavily before speaking.

"Nay," he said. "That would serve no purpose." His eyes flicked to Meddybemps's waist, then met the streetseller's stare.

Meddybemps would have preferred the dirk in his hand, not sheathed at his waist. But he knew the rogue sensed it, too.

With a vicious whoop the man rushed at him. Meddybemps desperately tried to pull the dirk from its sheath, but his assailant got to him first and pushed him into the railing. Meddybemps felt the man's hands close around his windpipe.

The rogue bent him backward over the railing. Meddybemps gripped the man's wrists, trying to pry the man's thumbs off his windpipe. But with his blood flow constricted, an excruciating pressure began to build behind his eyes. He gasped repeatedly for a precious ounce of air. Unable to find the strength to throw off his aggressor, Meddybemps felt his consciousness begin to wane.

A burst of red was all he saw. His struggle was over. His arms dropped and his body went limp. The satchel slid down his shoulder.

CHAPTER 30

Bianca closed the door to Amice and Gilley's and dashed down the stairs. Bursting through the back door of the Royal Poke, she ran into the alley, leaving the discovery of the dead couple to someone else. She hoped Meddybemps had not lost his patience and that she would find him waiting for her on the bridge.

In an attempt to take the most direct route, she cut through back alleys, avoided derelicts, and jumped over heaps of refuse. Meddybemps would be watching the time. If the bridge was about to close to curfew, he would not wait.

At Thames Street, Bianca took the broad avenue to London Bridge. The moon lit her way as she barreled down the road, panting and holding the stitch in her side. Ahead, the clock by St. Magnus showed minutes before ten. She turned the corner onto New Fish Street within sight of the bridge.

The gate hung suspended over the entrance, not yet lowered for curfew. By the entrance, a gibbeted woman seemed to taunt and call after her as she scurried past.

Candles flickered behind windows on the bridge, affording her just enough light to see. Few people were out walking and soon the tallows and lanterns would be extinguished. Shopkeepers had closed, retreating to their residences in the upper stories. She kept a wary eye on dark recesses and hurried her step.

Bianca clamped her mouth closed and tried to keep her panting from announcing her arrival. It would have been best if she had paused long enough to catch her breath and calm her pounding heart. She did not know if Meddybemps would be followed, but she had sensed someone watching her up until they had gone into the alehouse. If her plan went as hoped, she would soon know the identity of her stalker.

Though she had seen no familiar faces, it was possible her pursuer could have avoided her notice. It was a bet she was willing to take that *she* was not what the murderer was after.

She entered the last section of bridge before the open span. Plunged into complete darkness, Bianca lifted her skirt to avoid tripping over its hem and charged ahead despite a rising sense of unease. Her eyes trained on the tower gate opposite, she kept to the center of the lane. The stones of the turret glowed blue in the moonlight.

Near the opening, Bianca heard a strange guttural sound coming from the drawbridge. Hesitating, she tried to identify the noise.

It was the unmistakable sound of a person choking.

Bianca rushed into the open. She saw the back of a hulking figure strangling Meddybemps against the railing.

The streetseller clung to his attacker's wrists, trying to pull his hands from his neck. His back arched perilously over the railing. Moonlight glinted off the whites of his eyes.

Bianca screamed. Her arrival had no effect on the man's determination to finish her friend. Horrified, she witnessed the final agony of Meddybemps's struggle. His tongue extended from his mouth and his eyes rolled upward.

Bianca ran forward, digging into her pocket, and pulled out the kerotakis. She wielded the weighty metal cylinder as if it were a cudgel. With a bloodlust even she found surprising, she bludgeoned the back of the attacker's head.

The man flinched, hunching his shoulders to protect himself. Bianca hit him a second time and he staggered backward, releasing Meddybemps. Bianca put every ounce of weight and strength into her third effort.

The assailant fell, his heavy body knocking the kerotakis out of her hand. It clattered on the grate, bouncing on the metal rods. Recovering from the surprise at seeing his face, Bianca spied the precious piece of equipment rolling toward the edge of the bridge. She lunged to save the kerotakis, threw her body toward it, but was too late. The kerotakis fell through a gap and tumbled into the river.

Bianca dropped to her knees. She stared through the trusses at the water beneath the span. It was not the loss of the crucial piece of equipment so much as the realization of what it meant. Her efforts were for naught. With the kerotakis gone, she could no longer save John. She could not make the elixir of life.

Bianca squeezed her eyes closed.

Dull with disillusion, she got to her feet. She wrapped her arms around her chest and held herself, remembering John's embrace. So much of her life was entwined with his. How would she survive?

Fear flashed through her mind. The pain of loss stabbed at her heart. A second of sorrow lengthened into what felt like a lifetime.

Overcome with grief, Bianca opened her eyes.

Before her, Meddybemps tottered over the railing. His assailant lay at her feet. She leapt over him and grabbed onto the streetseller as the satchel slipped down his shoulder. Bianca pulled Meddybemps off the railing and reached for the strap. She was a second too slow. The satchel freed itself from his arm and plummeted toward the water.

Meddybemps dropped onto the deck like a sack of flour.

Beneath the shadows of the bridge, the river swallowed the satchel like a hungry beast. Bianca turned away from the railing and knelt beside her friend.

"Meddy!" she cried, shaking his shoulders. The thought of

losing him was more than she could bear. She had lost her friend Jolyn not five months before, and she might have already lost John. Now Meddybemps's life was wavering and she had herself to blame. "Breathe! For God's sake and mine—breathe!" She reared back and searched his face for signs of life. Frustrated, she balled up her fist and hit him square in the chest.

To her astonishment, Meddybemps took a loud wheezing breath and began to cough. He rolled to his side, clutching his throat, coughing and gasping for air.

Bianca sat back on her haunches and wept.

The bridge was silent but for her sobbing and Meddybemps's wheezing. A gale drowned the sounds of their struggles, blowing their anguished cries over the river, where they faded into the night. Finally, Meddybemps's color returned to his face and he lay on his back, blinking up at the sky. He looked over at her. "I lost your satchel," he said in a barely audible, hoarse voice. "I know you had your mind set to save John. I've lost Stannum's journal. I am truly sorry."

"Nay," said Bianca, wiping away her tears. She shook her head. "I am truly thankful."

Meddybemps looked confused. "You have a peculiar way of showing it."

"You are alive—you foolish knave!"

"I am alive as you. Because of you."

"You were nearly dead because of me."

"I shall be content with my version." He turned back to stare up at the sky. Then mustering what little strength he had, he pushed himself to his elbows and propped himself against the railing. "I am a bit wobbly just yet."

"There is no need for you to try to stand. Sit and rest." Bianca found his cap and brushed it off. She waited until another bout of coughing stopped and he was sitting fairly comfortably before handing it to him. "I'd give you a drink if I had one to offer."

He attempted a faint smile of appreciation. "Never you mind. I don't think I could swallow it just now."

Bianca sat next to him until his dazed expression began to subside. His breaths lengthened and he began to look like himself again.

The still unconscious body lay in a heap before them. Bianca rolled him onto his back. "So, it was him."

"Who is 'him'?" said Meddybemps, his voice a soft croak.

"Barnabas Hughes, the physician."

"Well," said Meddybemps, rubbing his neck. "He certainly wanted the satchel. Do you think he murdered Stannum?"

"It is possible." Bianca felt for a pulse and jumped when Hughes moaned. "We shall learn the truth soon enough. He is not very dead."

"What did you do to the man? He had the better of me, last I knew."

"I hit him over the head."

"Pray tell me, with what?"

"Never mind," said Bianca, disconsolately. "It is water under the bridge." She looked up at Meddybemps. "Meaning, it is in the water under the bridge."

Meddybemps shrugged and made to stand. He thought better of it after his head started throbbing. "Well, I am grateful you finally decided to come along."

"I had to pay a visit to Amice and Gilley. Unfortunately, they never heard a word I said."

"A man might listen and ignore your good word, but it is rude when they refuse to hear you."

"Nay, it was not from being rude. It was from being dead."

Meddybemps shook his head. "It is a miracle I have survived this long in your acquaintance. You leave bodies in your wake."

Bianca ignored his comment as a connection suddenly became clear. "Hughes gave Ferris Stannum a parrot and a cat. He thought their company would ease Stannum's loneliness from his estranged daughter. But the bird and Amice and Gilley all suffered a horrible end."

"How could an end be anything but horrible?"

"This one was particularly so. I have never seen such hideous symptoms. And I hope I never shall again." Bianca met Meddybemps's inquiring stare. "They bled from every orifice."

"What do you mean? I don't understand."

"I found them in pools of their own blood. I could have thought their eyes had been gouged, but it was obvious they bled from their ears, nose, and mouths. Then, when I heard the parrot in its death throes and saw its eyes blinded with blood from no one's hand, I realized the sickness had started with the bird."

"The bird may have only been another victim."

"I do not believe so. The parrot bit Goodwife Tenbrook and Ferris Stannum. When I had spent the day with the alchemist, he kept dabbing his eyes. The cloth he had used and his pillow had two bloodstains, separated by the width of a nose." Bianca watched Hughes slowly stir. "I have a few questions for him concerning that pillow."

"Continue with this theory," said Meddybemps, interested in spite of feeling nauseated. He rubbed his eyes, then examined his fingers.

"Like I said, the parrot also bit Goodwife Tenbrook. She complained about being sensitive to light. She later died, but the disease didn't have time to ravage her before she died from another cause." She glanced down again at the physician. "Hughes gave her a draught to help her sleep the night she died. In combination with all that was ailing her, I believe he may have administered a high enough dose to have killed her."

Meddybemps glowered at the physician. He gave Hughes a peevish jab with his foot.

"Amice took the bird because I suggested she might sell it. I suspect the bird bit Amice and Gilley and the disease ran its course, unfettered."

"How can a bird bite make them sick?"

"The same way those who come into contact with plague victims might contract the disease. Granted, it is a mystery. I don't presume to know how the contagion is spread, only that it does. And you increase your chances of becoming infected if you come into contact with a victim. Some believe the contagion is in the air surrounding the sick and the dead and that you inhale the disease. But the contagion could be on the skin. The contagion could be in the saliva. We can't see it. But I can certainly speculate that it is there."

"In this case, you believe the contagion was carried in the saliva?"

"I believe so." Bianca turned her back against a sudden gust of wind. "Who knows from where this bird came? It is not of our native land. Likely, some sailor brought it back from the new world. And perhaps the bird could not adapt to our clime."

"I have heard descriptions of strange-shaped trees and heat that would make this sweltering summer feel cool by comparison."

"An environ different from ours," said Bianca.

Meddybemps held on to the railing and got to his feet. He continued to be unsteady, weaving and gripping the rail for support. He began to cough again and Bianca went over to him and patted his back.

"It appears Hughes was unaware the bird would create such havoc." Meddybemps held up a finger and cleared his throat. He continued, "Unless he knew it would eventually spread contagion and kill whoever came into close contact with it. It seems the satchel was his first concern."

"Or what was in it," said Bianca.

Barnabas Hughes opened his eyes and stared up at the two of them. Confusion spread across his face. He looked about, trying to place himself.

"Should we bind his hands?" suggested Meddybemps. "I should rather not wrestle him again."

"He is still dazed. Truth be told, I enlisted Constable Patch's help. He should be along."

Meddybemps groaned as much from the thought of dealing with the vainglorious Patch as from his overall soreness. Still, he continued their discussion. "Why would a physician give his patient too much sleeping draught?"

"More to the point, why would he give Goodwife Tenbrook

too much draught? I don't believe he had much sympathy for the widow, but is that reason enough to kill her?" Bianca pressed down her skirt, which was trying to billow in a gust of wind. "We don't know if Hughes suspected she had the contagion from the parrot. I doubt he purposely gave her enough to put her out of her misery. I suspect this may have had something to do with Stannum's journal. Why else was he following me?"

"So, perhaps the journal was in her possession?"

"The journal was missing the day Ferris Stannum was found dead. She could have taken the journal, thinking she could sell it."

Bianca looked over her shoulder in the direction of London. "I hear someone approach."

Constable Patch and a night watchman appeared from the dark overhang and stepped onto the open span. They were an odd pair, Patch with the buttons on his uniform shining in the moonlight, the watchman dressed in a doublet of rough cloth with only a sash of finer taffeta to trumpet his marginal authority.

"Well nows," said Patch, looking about. "This is most unexpected." He strode over to Barnabas Hughes and gazed down at him. "I would not have predicted finding him here."

Hughes did not respond. He slowly got to his knees. But even that seemed too much for him. He sat back on his heels, his head lolling to one side.

"Is this who was following you?" Patch asked Bianca.

"I admit I am surprised." Bianca gestured toward Meddybemps. "Hughes was trying to strangle him when I arrived."

Patch noted Meddybemps working his neck and rubbing it. "Not so pleasant. And why was he being strangled, besides the obvious."

Meddybemps shot a look at Patch. "Sirrah, I shall not suffer an insult slung by the likes of you. Speak what you mean!"

Constable Patch snickered.

"Where is it?" asked Hughes blearily. He looked about, searching the open span of bridge. Not finding what he sought, his eyes grew wide with distress. "Where is the satchel?"

"It fell into the river," said Bianca.

For a moment, Barnabas Hughes stared in disbelief. Then, like a crab seeking water, he scrambled to the edge of the draw-bridge. He peered down at the river through a gap in the supporting members, pressing his head against the railing. A sudden, desperate wail rose from the depths of his core. "Nooo!" His plea echoed off the stolid walls of wealthy residences on the bridge, but no one bothered to watch from their lofty vantages. He sat back and covered his face in his hands.

Constable Patch raised an eyebrow and exchanged glances with his watchman. "Methinks the man is sorry to see the satchel go."

The indigo hues of moonlight could not hide the flush of anger coloring Hughes's skin. He turned his face to the heavens. "Take her. I can do no more." The physician stared at the sky as if waiting for an answer. "Do not judge her soul by my false acts. Forgive me." He took a shuddering breath. "I pray, be merciful. She deserves Your loving embrace . . . while I do not."

Patch nodded at his minion, who bound Hughes's wrists behind his back and roughly pulled the physician to his feet.

"I believe answers will be forthcoming," said Constable Patch to Bianca. "But perhaps not tonight."

Patch and his minion led Barnabas Hughes to the edge of the open span. At the shadowed entry of crowded buildings, Constable Patch stopped walking. He abandoned the watchman and his prisoner and returned to Bianca and Meddybemps.

"I believe this is yours," he said, glancing over his shoulder at Hughes. The physician had his back to them, his head hung in despair. Patch reached under his uniform and pulled out a parcel wrapped in linen. "See that this doesn't fall into the wrong hands."

Astonished, Meddybemps gaped at the bundle. Patch turned on his heel and returned to Hughes, escorting him from the bridge. "And what is that?" asked Meddybemps.

"It is Ferris Stannum's journal." Bianca removed the cloth from the book.

Meddybemps chafed with annoyance. "So, what was I carrying in the satchel?"

"A box."

"A box?"

Bianca nodded.

"Was anything in that box?"

"Some rocks to give it weight."

Meddybemps blinked. "I carried a box of rocks and was nearly strangled trying to prevent them from being taken."

"Aye," said Bianca, shrugging. "You did."

It took a moment for Meddybemps to collect his thoughts, and once he did, he unleashed a torrent of expletives that bounced off Bianca with no perceivable effect.

"I am not apologizing," she said.

"Nay, I don't suppose you would." Meddybemps shook out his cap, glad it was not lost. He looked at his young prodigy, who was clearly unconcerned about their friendship. She continued to thumb through the pages of the journal, ignoring his tirade.

At last, his ire vented, Meddybemps sighed. "Well, at least you saved the journal from being destroyed. Now I suppose you can go back to your room of Medicinals and Physickes and conjure the elixir of life for John."

Bianca said nothing. She continued to flip through the pages, stopping at the process for the elixir of life.

"You cannot read in the dark," said Meddybemps.

Bianca fondly ran a hand over the page, as though savoring this particular one. She snapped the book shut and looked up. "Nay, I cannot." The side of her mouth turned up in a faint smile. Without another word, she walked to the side of the bridge and stepped on the lowest railing.

For a moment, Meddybemps feared she might throw herself off. One never knew what morose thoughts ran through that mind of hers. He started forward, ready to tackle her if that was her intent. Instead, she teetered on the railing, the flats of her feet balancing on the wood. The wind caught her skirts and they rose in front of her. She leaned out over the river.

"Bianca!"

Holding the alchemy journal against her chest, she ignored his alarmed cry. She cocked her arm and released the book, spinning it over the water like skipping a stone. It whirled and the cover opened. The pages fanned like the feathers of an exotical bird and the wind held it suspended, just for a second.

Meddybemps ran to the railing. The covers folded back like a gannet diving. The journal fell, landing on the surface of the water. For a second it rested, as if deciding its next venture. Then, as if its decision had been made, the book disappeared beneath the choppy waves.

Bianca hopped off the railing.

"I am stunned," said Meddybemps. "Pray tell me—why?" He caught Bianca's arm, forcing her to face him. "All of this effort. I was nearly killed. And you throw it in the river?"

"I realized something when Barnabas Hughes broke down."

"What conceivable revelation has suddenly enlightened you?" Meddybemps could not keep from voicing his frustration. Instead of wasting his evening on London Bridge and being strangled, he could have enjoyed an evening of entertainment at a certain boozing ken in London where men willing to gamble away their money were in plentiful supply and agreeable women even more so.

"Hughes tried to interfere with the natural order of life. I remember he once mentioned that his daughter was ill, but I didn't know she was dying. Apparently he believed God was calling his daughter and he did everything in his power to prevent His taking her. Hughes desperately wanted the means to make the elixir. How he was going to create it I do not know, but he nearly killed you because of his desire. And I expect we shall soon learn if he smothered Ferris Stannum and gave Goodwife Tenbrook a lethal dose of sleeping draught. Ultimately, Hughes valued his daughter's life above all others. We are not so supreme as to determine whose life is more valuable."

"And you believe God makes that determination?"

"I am not saying that it is God who decides. I am saying there is a natural order in all of life and death and we must not impose our will over that."

"What about your salves and medicinals? Does this mean you are finished creating them?"

"Nay, I still want to relieve people's suffering."

"But saving John with the elixir of life would not harm anyone. You aren't planning on murdering anyone to create the elixir, are you?"

"Of course not. I will do what I can to help John, short of granting him immortality."

Meddybemps looked askance at her. "You speak as if you have faith in God's decisions instead of being the heathen I know you are."

"You misunderstand me. If John fights his malady and survives this particular illness, then I believe he will live as long as his body serves his soul. But if his soul is finished with his body, should I concoct an elixir to prevent it from *ever* leaving?" Bianca fixed Meddybemps with her deep blue eyes. "Does it serve his soul to never part from his physical body?"

"So where do you expect his soul will go?" said Meddybemps. "Heaven or hell?" He gave her a sly look. "Because if he is bound for hell, you should do what you can to prevent such a journey."

"Who knows where souls wander off to," said Bianca. "I don't know why their destination has to be either heaven or hell."

"There is always purgatory."

"There is always nothing and nowhere."

"I don't fancy any of these choices," said Meddybemps, feeling petulant. "I prefer heaven. As long as it is my own version."

Bianca refrained from telling Meddybemps she had lost the kerotakis when she saved him from Hughes. Without the piece of equipment, the book was useless to her. "Besides," she said, "what if everyone lived forever?"

"I suppose believing in heaven is as good as living forever."

"I think I should graciously accept whatever happens."

"So you do believe in God."

"Faith in God is the ultimate superstition, is it not?" said Bianca. "We hedge our behavior in case He exists. And I'm not superstitious." Bianca glanced around. In a more contrite tone she added, "Well, not very."

Being the primero player that he was, Meddybemps said, "So, you are hedging your stake?"

"Nay, I'm placing it and calling."

"Come what may?"

"Come what may." Bianca took a deep breath and gazed over the Thames at Southwark beyond. Her words sounded bolder than she felt. She scattered them like seeds, hoping to grow some courage.

The two parted ways and Bianca headed home to Gull Hole. The breeze brought a welcome relief from the sweltering heat of the past week, reminding her that summer would end. The season would change. Impermanence was a certainty in life, and for the moment, she preferred not to be reminded of it. Such thoughts had an effect on her, as she had an abundance of black bile in her veins, always nudging her toward melancholia and introspection. She knew the perils of her somber thinking.

When contentment was abundant, why dwell on its ephemeral nature? Why consider for longer than a moment that this joy would not, and could not, last? Even when she was happy, morose thoughts lurked in her subconscious, waiting to dance unfettered.

Aware of what she might find once she reached her room of Medicinals and Physickes, Bianca trudged down Tooley Street. With her head down and hands plunged deep in her apron pocket, she gave no thought to her safe passage. Instead, her mind pondered her mother's advice—"Imagine the worst possible outcome, and work backward from there."

The worst possible outcome was one she mulled over as she neared her rent. What would she do if John had died while she was gone?

Regret pooled in the pit of her stomach. John might not be dead, so why even consider it? Days moved one second at a time.

She would survive each second and so would he, until she, or he, did not.

A few candles and lanterns winked in Gull Hole. She continued to wrestle her fears until she faced the door that separated her from reality. She could stand on its threshold with her hand on the latch or face her future. Staring straight ahead, Bianca banished her conjured misgivings and pushed open the door.

Moonlight squeezed past and lit the interior. The black tiger dropped to the floor, and as she looked in the direction of the bed, it leaned against her legs. The cat offered a quick greeting and began to purr. She did not move, but stared across the room at John. It was impossible to tell if he was breathing. She listened for his breath—for the sound of soft sleeping.

Bianca took a step and the black tiger ran ahead of her. It gracefully leapt onto the bed and walked across John's chest. Bianca softly gasped. Such weight would have stirred anyone in the deepest of sleep. The black tiger rubbed its chin against John's cheek. There was no response.

The cat sat on the other side of him, staring up at her. Bianca lowered herself next to John and laid her hand upon his chest. The rhythmic rise and fall of breath lifted her hand. Beneath her fingertips his heart beat slow and steady.

Bianca leaned over his ear and whispered his name. "John."

But he showed no sign of hearing her.

Weary from all that had come before, Bianca crawled into bed beside him. She curled against his body, finding comfort in just touching him.

CHAPTER 31

She could have slept a day. Bianca woke to a crash and heard the frenzied scurry and terrified squeak of a mouse. She heaved herself up on one elbow, rubbing her eyes. Particles of dust danced in a sunbeam streaming through the window. Another crash sent Bianca leaping out of bed to shoo the black tiger and its quarry outside.

"Eat it out there," she said, slamming the door.

She looked over at John, who lay oblivious to the commotion. He had not moved once in the night, though she might not have noticed, she was so tired. All trace of his worrisome rasp gone, John's breathing sounded unfettered and remained even. Bianca went back over and sat beside him.

She touched her hand to his cheek, rough with stubble. "Forgive me for not telling you of my love," she said. "I never said it often enough. I hope you never doubted. If you can hear me, know that I love you, John. I always will."

Her breath caught from the crushing pain of loss and she looked away. Her room was as before. Herbs dangled overhead. The table was strewn with bowls. The abandoned attempt to create the elixir of life. She smiled ruefully.

She realized he might not improve. He might never return to her. Slowly, silently, John would step into death. She could either watch helplessly as he did so, or she could commit the ultimate sin in the name of mercy. In the name of love. She bent and kissed his lips. Her tears dropped on his skin.

The clatter of street noise filtered through the window and she sat up. It was later than she'd thought. She rose from John's side to gaze down at him. He was not so unlike himself. She dipped her fingers into a bowl of water and dribbled it over his lips. Ending his suffering would change the feel of her own. It was still murder. She would have robbed him of the chance to live. The decision would no longer be his. She did not know if she could shoulder that burden. And ultimately, she lacked the courage to say good-bye.

Apparently finished with its midday meal, the black tiger observed Bianca from its perch on the windowsill. It dared not bring the remains of its meal to share with the people and left the hind legs and tail outside the door in case they got hungry later.

"Hello, my tiger," said Bianca, offering the top of her head so the cat could bump it. She ran her hand down its back. "Soon, it may be just you and me." It rubbed its chin against her cheek, appreciating the affection. "At least I shall have your heartbeat to keep me company. My little house spirit." She smiled and stroked its back. "I have never given you a name." She gazed earnestly into its green eyes. After a minute of thought, Bianca remembered a tale she once heard as a child, a story about house spirits. A hob was a magical, helpful creature but could become a nuisance if offended. "Of course," she exclaimed. "Hobs. I shall call you Hobs."

Pleased to have given him a suitable name, she lifted Hobs from the sill to feed him shaved cheese. It would not do for her to sit by John's side, waiting. Waiting for him to improve, or not. Perhaps she was a coward, but she could not bear it. She could not sit idly by. Seizing her ewer of washing water, she cleaned her face and went to pay Barnabas Hughes and Constable Patch a visit.

A hint of autumn replaced the heat of the past week. The air had lost its heaviness and the sky had lost its pewter cast, returning to a vivid blue. At the parish ward, Bianca was met by one of the minions Constable Patch paid in ale.

"By what business have ye come?" he asked, his eyes ranging over her. This took some concentration, as his eyes had a glazed appearance from too much drink. Instead of one Bianca, he saw two.

"I have come about Barnabas Hughes. I summoned the constable to help me last night."

This met with his interest. "Ah," he said. "Ye be the alchemist's daughter." He ignored her narrowing eyes and allowed her entry, closing the door behind her.

"Expect a visitor," she told him. She placed a groat in his palm. "For your trouble."

The underling pocketed the inducement and became chatty. "The physician refuses to speak until he has garnered certain assurances." He led her down a short hallway. "But miscreants are in no position to bargain," he said over his shoulder, punctuating his remark with a belch. He opened another door and held it for her, simpering with satisfaction as she passed.

The room was suitably austere, a holding cell. Once the accused had been interrogated to the satisfaction of the attending constable, he would be hauled off to one of the city's prisons. A narrow barred window allowed a shaft of light to fall on a patch of floor, insufficient to see by. Making its own contribution to the dim interior, a tallow burned in a wall sconce, reeking and spewing smoke.

Barnabas Hughes slumped on a stool, an ankle chained to an iron staple driven into the stone wall. His formal overcoat gone, he sat in his hose and shirt, soaked in perspiration. A thick wad of rope bound his wrists in a zealous attempt at restraint. Hughes looked up at Bianca's entrance, his face bruised and swollen. She wondered if he had received lacerations beyond those bestowed on him by Meddybemps.

A safe distance apart, Constable Patch sat at a table eating meat pie and sipping ale. His face brightened at the sight of her. "Bianca Goddard. How suspicious. Perhaps we shall make some progress now that ye have arrived."

Bianca hesitated at his odd choice of words, but his smile appeared genuine.

Patch continued, "Unfortunately, our prisoner is not cooperating. His confession is contingent on our agreeing to minister to his sick child." The constable stuck a finger in his mouth, dislodging a piece of meat caught between his teeth, and spat the offending morsel on his plate. "I, however, am not in the business of nursing ailing children. Nor do I care to find someone to do it." He patted his mouth with the end of a napkin tucked in his collar. "He has the misguided notion that there is money in this king's realm to provide care for the sick." Patch looked directly at his prisoner. "I assure you, sir, there is no such account."

"I shall look after her," said Bianca without hesitation. It was not the child's fault her father had erred. Meddybemps could bring her to Southwark and Gull Hole on his cart. Bianca sympathized with Hughes's overwhelming urge to save his loved one. She might not have murdered, but she understood how obsessive love could surmount moral judgment and prudence.

Barnabas Hughes responded to her offer. "She is not well. I do not see how she will recover. Promise me she is given a proper burial in consecrated soil. I fear she will be condemned to an orphan's grave because of me."

"Sir, I understand your desire to save your child. It is not for me to condemn her on your account. I shall do my best."

Hughes's eyes softened with gratitude. He drew his spine straight and looked pointedly at Patch. "I do not fear my punishment. Without Verity, my life is meaningless. I will see her again in the other realm."

Constable Patch exchanged glances with Bianca. He finished off his ale and dropped his wadded napkin on the plate. "I regret to remind you, sir, there is no place but eternal damnation for murderers." He rose from the table and came around to lean against it. "We should proceed with questioning now that your daughter's welfare is settled." He adjusted his sword so it did not jab him. "Let us start at the beginning," he said. "Why did you try to strangle that"—Patch glimpsed at Bianca and graciously replaced the word "scoundrel"—"streetseller . . . Meddybemps?"

"Constable, that is not the beginning," said Bianca. "Perhaps the physician might tell us of his connection to Ferris Stannum. That is where I first met him."

Constable Patch lifted an eyebrow at Bianca's interruption. From the look on her face he could tell she had come for some answers. He relented. If she wanted to pursue a direction in questioning, perhaps he should let her. She had a curious, if unconventional, mind, and her revelations had benefited him before. Indeed, he would not have made it out of Southwark without her. For the moment, he did not mind allowing her to ask questions, as long as she did not try to usurp his authority.

Barnabas Hughes dropped his gaze to the floor. "I had known Ferris Stannum for years. He often asked me for ingredients that he could not acquire elsewhere. I first met him ten years ago when I was summoned by his wife to treat him for a stye on his eyelid. Later, he asked me to attend his wife in her final hour. He was a man of extraordinary inquisitiveness.

"Our friendship developed over time. I believe Ferris enjoyed my company, but perhaps he enjoyed my interest in his work more. Alchemists rarely share their findings with each other, but I believe Ferris appreciated discussing his science with a learned confidant. His last discovery, the elixir of life, was years in the making. Of course I was skeptical and thought nothing would come of his dalliance. At the same time, I grew intrigued with its possibilities. Such a powerful antidote could have far-reaching import. I admit I was conflicted. I questioned whether he should even pursue such an objective. The implications reached far beyond what we mortals should be given the power for. But when I saw the miraculous recovery of a cat that was nearly dead, I could not deny my astonishment and fascination."

"Was it you who gave him the cat?" asked Bianca.

"His daughter, Amice, had left her father to be with Gilley. She and her husband pestered Ferris for a dowry. But there isn't an alchemist alive that has the ability to provide for a daughter's marriage. There simply *is* no family wealth."

Bianca knew well the lack of funds in an alchemist's home. Her marriage to John had been her decision and one not influenced by a dowry or her parents' wishes.

"His estrangement from Amice devastated Ferris. Since his wife died, he relied on her to cook for him, to run his errands. But most of all, he relied on her for companionship. If he had had the money for a dowry I believe he would have gladly given it—for the right man. Stannum profoundly disliked Gilley. And he made known to Amice his concerns with her choice.

"But Amice would not be swayed. I could see the effect this had on Ferris. Over time, he became doleful and withdrawn. I would find him staring at his alembics, refusing to eat. His love of the noble art vanished."

Hughes licked his lips, eyeing the mug of ale on the table. Bianca saw he was parched. She took the mug from the table and put it to the physician's lips.

"We do not indulge prisoners," blurted Constable Patch. He moved to take the cup away from Bianca, but she snatched it out of his reach.

Bianca put her palm against Patch's chest. "His voice is strained. How can he speak with his lips cracked and bleeding?"

Constable Patch sniffed. He clamped his jaws together and allowed her to continue, though he found her methods irritating.

Hughes tucked his chin in thanks. "There was a man whom I had been summoned to attend. Even by bleeding him, I could not ease his suffering. Not a soul in the world cared that he died. His only companions were a cat and a macaw. I could offer him nothing. My failure to even assure him peace of mind gnawed at me. Leaving the bird and cat to fend for themselves seemed a final injustice. I took them into my care and offered them to Ferris, hoping they would rouse him from his melancholy. He had once had a monkey that had delighted him with its antics, until it ran off."

"You had no misgivings offering an aged alchemist two creatures to care for?" asked Bianca.

Hughes looked at her sharply. "Why should he not enjoy companionship since his daughter had abandoned him?"

"The parrot was ill. It carried a deadly contagion."

"The parrot was healthy when I gave it as a gift."

"Amice and Gilley took the bird after Ferris Stannum's death. They have all died of similar symptoms."

"Of what symptoms do you speak?" asked Hughes.

Bianca did not immediately answer his question. She wondered if he feigned ignorance or whether he truly did not know. "Ferris Stannum gave his dying cat the elixir of life. Do you believe the elixir saved its life?"

"Initially, I had my doubts. I thought perhaps the creature had simply survived its illness. But Ferris swore of its miraculous recovery once he had given the animal his elixir. When my daughter grew weak and my efforts to heal her failed, I looked to the elixir with renewed hope. I began to believe in its powers. What father would not try everything he could to save his child?"

Constable Patch sniffed with disrespect. He hoped he would not have to listen to Hughes voice his penitence again.

"So you sought the elixir of life to save your daughter," said Bianca.

"There was no elixir of life," said Barnabas Hughes, shaking his head. "Ferris used the entire serum on his cat." The physician closed his eyes. "I begged Ferris to make more, but he was keen to have his methods verified by Madu Salib in Cairo. His journal was the only copy of the procedure and he was going to send it across the sea. I told him it was folly to risk the journal to an uncertain voyage. But Ferris was unmoved. He refused to take the time to write a second copy of his method." Hughes's voice was grave and flat. "He said it was unnecessary.

"Ferris Stannum was a fool to think the book would arrive at its destination. The chances are it would have been lost forever." Hughes fixed his eyes on a point far away. "I believed in the elixir. Think on its possibilities. Such a liquor could have changed the course of the world. A man possessing such knowledge could play God." Hughes searched their faces, looking for some hint of mutual awe that he himself felt. "A man could be God."

But there was no empathy in their passive stares. They lacked his appreciation of the elixir's significance. He hung his head. "It could have ended human suffering for all time."

Constable Patch gave Bianca a sidelong glance. She avoided his eyes and ignored a sharp stab of regret at having thrown the journal in the river. But she pressed on. "Ferris Stannum refused to surrender the journal to you."

Barnabas Hughes neither confirmed nor denied it.

"He was adamant to send off the journal," said Bianca. "To prevent him from doing so, you went to Ferris Stannum's and smothered him with a pillow."

Barnabas Hughes's eyes flashed. "Nay, you do not know this."

"But I do," said Bianca. She walked out the door and left Constable Patch and Barnabas Hughes wondering where she had gone.

A few moments later Bianca returned with a scruffy-looking boy in tow. The gamin followed her, cap in hand, his eyes as alert as a tawny owl's. He surveyed the room and its occupants, his attention settling on the accoutrements of the chamber, the chain and shackles that ended in Barnabas Hughes, the physician.

Patch, unaccustomed to entertaining children in his workplace, balked at the boy's unexpected entrance. "What do you mean bringing a street waif to gawk at a murderer? How scrumptious. A child has no worth."

"Unless you plan to have him for dinner, I believe the word is 'presumptuous'," said Bianca. "I agree that a child has not accumulated the years that give him influence. But he has two eyes with which to see. A child's words are the truest spoken. They haven't the guile of a man's."

Constable Patch puffed out his chest. "A child's word is impermissible in a court of law."

Bianca looked around. "Sir, I see no barrister here."

Constable Patch glared at Bianca, stewing with indignation. She was overstepping her bounds. He resented her trying to expose his incompetence. Still, thought Constable Patch irritably, he did not have an angle by which to question Hughes. He stalked to the door and called for his deputy to bring him more ale. Turning back to Bianca and the physician, he contrived a deferential smile. "Proceed."

Bianca waited for him to settle in his chair.

"This is Fisk. He lives across the lane from Goodwife Tenbrook's building. He spends most of his time outside his mother's rent sitting on the stoop. He sees the comings and goings in the neighborhood."

Bianca saw a muscle jump in Barnabas Hughes's neck. "He prefers the cooler air to the oppressive heat of his family's home these days. At night, Fisk sleeps on the threshold rather than toss in an airless room with his sisters. He is privy to everything that happens on the street."

Fisk was at the right height for studying the physician's face, though Hughes stared at the floor, avoiding the boy's scrutiny.

"Have you seen this man before, Fisk?"

The boy nodded.

"When have you seen him?"

"I have seen him a few times at the old man's."

"Do you remember the first time you saw me?" asked Bianca.

"Aye," said Fisk. "You first arrived last Wednesday. And I saw him visit the alchemist that day, too."

"Then let us begin there. When did you see this man next?"

"It was well in the wee hours of the morn. There was no one

about. It was hot like you said, and I slept outside on the stone stoop. A dog started barking across the way and I woke. I saw the man pet the dog to quiet him. Everyone had their doors open a crack for air. He stood by Goodwife Tenbrook's, and seeing no one about, slipped inside."

Constable Patch grumbled. "It was dark; how can ye be sure it was this man?" He was irritated just enough to try to make it difficult for Bianca.

"Because it was the day's first light," said Fisk, addressing Constable Patch. "And I could see his face clear as I see it now."

Bianca spoke. "So, he slipped inside. What did you do?"

"I got to wondering what he was up to. I thought maybe if I saw him thieving I might get him to give me a coin for not telling." Fisk turned his cap around in his hands and his eyes darted at Hughes and up at Bianca.

"Go on, Fisk," she said.

The boy swallowed and ran his eyes over the physician. His stare ended at the shackle and chain. He took a step back, distancing himself from the prisoner. "I crept along the wall outside the old man's rent and peeked through the open window."

"What did you see?" prompted Bianca.

"It was dark inside, but I saw the old man on his pallet—just his legs, though. I couldn't see his face."

"His face was obstructed," said Bianca.

"What do ye mean?" said the boy, puzzled.

"You could not see his face."

"Nay, I could not." Fisk looked at Hughes. "He was next to him, leaning over the old man."

"His back was to you?" asked Bianca.

The boy nodded. He looked longingly at the ale Constable Patch sipped. "Can I have a drink?" he asked Bianca.

Bianca held her hand out for the cup. Patch made to protest, but realizing his complaining only made for a longer inquiry, acquiesced, muttering as he passed it over. "Only to wet your tongue, boy."

Fisk gulped, wetting more than just his tongue. He polished off the cup and handed it back.

"At first I thought maybe they was talking," said Fisk. The boy's initial apprehension disappeared and his voice grew animated. "I heard some noise, and heard the man talk softly. I couldn't hear what he was saying. The alchemist brought up his knees. And the man kept leaning over him." Fisk shook his head. "It did not look right." He glanced at Bianca for reassurance. "Then the old man's legs went slack."

Patch interjected. "Ye say ye heard some noise. Explain yeself, boy."

Fisk hesitated a moment, then spoke. "It was a muffled sound. It wasn't a scream but was soft."

Barnabas Hughes brought his bound hands to his face and leaned his forehead into them. Fisk paused, wondering if he should continue.

Bianca watched Hughes's shoulders start to shake as he pressed his head into his hands. Constable Patch raised his eyebrows and sat up.

"Ye say, 'It did not look right,'" said Constable Patch. "What did ye see that did not 'look right'?"

Fisk was unashamed to explain. The urchin grew cocky from the attention. "I seen men doing it to each other. The thought crossed my mind." He flashed an insolent look at Constable Patch. "But that was not it." He shook his head. "Nay. When he stood up, I saw the old man." He directed his words pointedly to Constable Patch. "And a pillow covered his face."

Barnabas Hughes squeezed his eyes shut and rocked back and forth where he sat. He pressed his hands against his face but was unable to hide his torment.

Unaffected, Fisk kept on. "I heard terrible squawking. Loud shrieks. It was that bird the old man kept. It was bobbing its head and flapping its wings." Fisk wiped his nose with his hand. He shrugged.

Constable Patch rose from the table and came around. "Did you see Ferris Stannum move after Hughes stood?"

"He was stone silent. He did not move."

Fisk would have explained further, but his words were drowned by a sudden wail. The physician dropped his hands to his lap and threw back his head. All self-composure vanished and his face twisted with remorse. Barnabas Hughes wept.

CHAPTER 32

"God forgives those who confess their sins without omission," said Bianca, repeating the familiar words of a priest during confession.

Constable Patch scratched his goatee. He had to admit, the girl was cunning. Appealing to a man's conscience would not have occurred to him. It was faster to just beat a confession out of a man. He scuttled to the door and motioned in his deputy to witness.

The tipsy assistant sauntered through the door and with difficulty stood beside it.

Barnabas Hughes looked round at Constable Patch, Bianca, and Fisk. "It is true," he said. "I smothered Ferris Stannum. I murdered my friend."

He dropped his head and took a deep breath. "My daughter has not been well for months. I tried every remedy I could think of. The more Ferris told me about his elixir, the more hopeful I became. With every success, I grew eager to learn more. But when Amice left home, Ferris grew despondent. The man I had just attended, who left behind the cat and the parrot—his symptoms were quite ghoulish. He hemorrhaged from the ocular orbits, from the nose and the mouth. It did not occur to me to suspect the animals were carriers of a contagion." Hughes looked at Bianca. "I gave the animals to Ferris so he would not be alone."

Hughes sighed and shook his head. "And Ferris responded. Their antics cheered him. He became productive and interested in his work again. As Verity became increasingly ill, I grew anxious. I pushed Ferris to complete the elixir. I wanted it for my daughter.

"But his beloved cat became sick. About that time, Ferris complained of his own sensitivity to light. His eyes were intensely bloodshot. I wondered if he had the same disease that I had seen before. If that were true, it was only a matter of time before he, too, would succumb to the ghastly malady.

"But I said nothing of my suspicion. We had discussed testing the elixir of life on my daughter. Ferris had reservations. He feared giving a sick child the philter. I begged him—it was my only chance to save her."

"But he refused?" interjected Patch. The constable wanted to remind Bianca that he was still the official authority in the room.

"I thought I'd convinced him. I swore I would not hold him accountable if it failed. He said he had more to do but it was nearly ready." The physician's face darkened. "I returned later to collect the elixir. Instead, I learned he had given the entire mixture to his cat."

"The entire elixir?" said Patch, hardly believing it.

"You can see how deceived I felt. How could he give the elixir to a cat instead of my child?" He looked round at them indignantly. "Who is guilty of the greater sin? Ferris Stannum condemned my child to die."

"Perhaps he could not bear feeling responsible for your daughter's life. What if it had killed her outright?" said Bianca.

"Refusing her was as grievous as condemning her to die. He committed murder as sure as I did," answered Hughes sharply.

Bianca and Constable Patch said nothing in response. To do so would have further provoked the man. Instead, they waited for Hughes's flare of resentment to die down.

"The fool." Hughes brought his hands to his face and wiped the perspiration from his brow. "Imagine how I felt." He looked up at Bianca and Patch, searching their faces for some indication of empathy. Finding none, he continued, "If that wasn't cruel enough, Stannum was sending the journal to Cairo for validation."

"And would not be making a second batch of elixir," said Bianca.

"Nay," said Hughes, bitterly. "His health was waning. The journal containing the process was my last hope. I sought to prevent him sending it to Madu Salib."

Hughes addressed Bianca. "The day you came to Stannum's alchemy room, I knew I needed to act. That evening I agonized over what had happened. My anger, my resentment, consumed me. I went to his room of alchemy to steal the journal. I would find another alchemist to perform the process. There isn't an alchemist alive who wouldn't want to know Ferris Stannum's recipe for the elixir of life.

"There was still a chance I might save my daughter. He was not going to take what little hope remained in my heart. When I got to his room I searched for the journal. He slept soundly from his earlier celebration and didn't know I was there. But my search revealed nothing. I could not believe he had succeeded in sending off the journal. The more I searched, the more disheartened, the angrier, I got. I could not find it. I was wild with frustration.

"Ferris began to stir. He turned in his sleep and I went over to him. He murmured in content. I thought, 'You foolish old man. You condemned my child to die.' I picked up the pillow on the floor." Hughes stared ahead, unblinking, reliving the moment. "He condemned my child to die," he repeated. "I placed the pillow over his face and leaned on top of him. He was old and weak."

The room went silent but for their breaths.

"Two days later I tended Goodwife Tenbrook. A neighbor summoned me and I saw that she, too, was suffering from symptoms similar to Stannum's. While there, I saw the journal under a pile of clothing. She had taken it! My hope returned. I gave her a sleeping draught and planned to visit later."

"So you poisoned her?" interjected Patch.

Hughes's face jerked up. "Regardless of what you say and think, I did not poison her."

"But you gave her a sleeping philter," said Bianca. "You gave her too much."

"I gave her a sufficient dose to aid her sleeping."

"The wine alone would have assured that."

"What are you insinuating?"

"Sir, I only suggest that perhaps the addition of sleeping draught was ill-conceived. You said yourself that she was showing symptoms of Ferris Stannum's illness. Mayhap she was not well enough to recover from drink and sleeping draught both."

"I have little control over my patients' actions. If the woman was fool enough to partake in drink with the philter, then how am I responsible for her recklessness?"

Constable Patch plucked at his wispy chin hair. "So, the tally rises," he said. "Luckily for you, sir, you can only hang once, as you only have one neck. It does not matter the additional number of bodies."

"I refuse to burden my conscience with that woman's death! I take responsibility for Ferris Stannum, but not for her. She was a shrew and London will miss her not."

"Who misses whom is not for you to say," said Patch, enjoying this outburst of emotion. Nothing interested him more than seeing a fellow of high esteem fall from his marble tower.

"Constable, let Hughes continue." Bianca abhorred Patch's attempts to antagonize the physician. It was a tendency familiar to Bianca and one that delighted the constable.

Patch glared at Bianca. He sought to put an end to her self-appointed charge in the matter. "I would appreciate it if you kept your commentary to a minimum, my lady." He turned a smug face to Barnabas Hughes. "Continue, sir."

"My intention was to secure Ferris Stannum's alchemy journal. When I returned I could not find it."

Patch glanced at Bianca and broke in before she had the chance to open her mouth. "You did not ask Goodwife Tenbrook why she had it?"

Hughes shook his head.

"So she was already dead by the time you got there," said Bianca.

Constable Patch shot an angry look at her. He had wanted to say that.

Barnabas Hughes said nothing.

"Sir, your silence is suspect." Patch waited for Hughes to speak. After a moment, Patch sighed. "So's, you went to her room and could not find the book."

"It was gone. The journal simply disappeared."

"Why did you not wait for her to fall asleep, then take it?" asked Bianca.

"Do you not remember? I could hardly take it while you were there," he said bitingly. "Besides, I needed to return to Verity. I had left her alone."

"When did you next learn of the journal's whereabouts?" Patch asked.

Hughes looked at Bianca. "When she summoned me to bleed her husband."

Two days ago, Bianca had sat at her table studying the book when Hughes arrived. In her exhaustion she had not bothered to conceal the journal or even consider that the physician could have wanted it. "So it was you who followed me to St. Benet's," she said.

Hughes nodded.

Bianca's belief that Tait had wanted the journal was ill founded. But why did she associate the smell of roses with the night she was attacked? She had remembered a rosebud tucked in a buttonhole on Tait's doublet and mistakenly directed her suspicions on the usurer. "You were not successful in taking the journal," she said. "Someone stopped you."

"Thomas Plumbum intervened on your behalf," said Hughes. "The idiot."

"But he did not take the journal," said Bianca. "He left it in the satchel."

"He did not want it. He had his chance to take it. Why else would he have left it? He wanted you to have it."

"He must have been the one who threw it into my rent. How else would he have known I had it?"

Hughes looked up. "Is that how you came into possession of the book?"

"I found it one morning on the floor of my rent."

Hughes sniffed. "It is becoming clear to me."

Fisk, having remained unusually attentive and respectfully quiet, spoke. "Goodwife Tenbrook had me deliver a note to Thomas Plumbum, the alchemist."

"Plumbum acquired the journal from Tenbrook," said Bianca.

"For a price, I am certain," said Hughes. "Goodwife Tenbrook was a shrewd woman."

"But why would Plumbum give it to me?"

"Plumbum was more accomplished in lying than alchemy. He was probably unable to decipher Stannum's method. I imagine he sensed you had more ability. Or assumed you had greater knowledge of the process since Ferris Stannum had taken you into his confidence. But make no mistake, if Plumbum had not met an unhappy end, he would have found a way to profit from your success."

"But why throw it through my window and hope for such an outcome? Why not approach me directly?"

Constable Patch believed Bianca was vying for control of the inquest again. "Perhaps he was unable to," he said, looking pointedly at Hughes.

"I never knew Plumbum had the journal," said the physician.

"If Plumbum feared being followed, he may have supposed it

was because he had the journal," said Bianca. She remembered her own skittish feelings and concern that the journal may have been cursed. "But we know Plumbum was being followed for reasons unrelated to the alchemy journal.

"You followed me and Meddybemps to the tavern last night."

"You gave him the satchel," said Hughes.

CHAPTER 33

It was altogether appropriate that he dwelled beneath a bridge spanning two cities, disparate worlds apart. Like the bridge, he, too, was caught in between.

He was wrought from those who had succumbed to plague. He was vulnerable to their tortured souls, and they poured into the vessel of his being, for he was neither living nor dead. The Rat Man was caught in a limbus of his own making.

A failed alchemist, a broken man, his quest for immortality had gotten him what he wished for—eternal existence. But this endless purgatory was not what he preferred.

His chance for salvation had twice passed over the trestles above him. He knew the smell of alchemy. The acrid stench of chemical on paper. And he knew the journal had passed hands. He eagerly wished, indeed willed, a chance to obtain the journal. Possession of the journal, possession of its knowledge, was all that he needed.

But the physical world and his did not perfectly mesh. In the small hours of night he poled the shallows near Romeland, which was lined with warehouses and an abundance of rats. He hunted the creatures, fare for his unearthly appetite, and tossed them in a pile to be savored later. That night, the prey had been plentiful and his skiff rode low in the water from his industry. In his focused pursuit he missed the tang of alchemy wafting from the bridge. Only when he stopped hunting did he notice its smell.

He turned his nose in its direction and flicked his tongue.

Abandoning his rodent hunt, he pointed his boat toward the bridge. He rode the river's swells and valleys, his black cape billowing in the wind.

The wraith saw a struggle. He willed his skiff faster and a man appeared against the railing, leaning dangerously out over it. An arm dangled over the water. A satchel fell. The bag tumbled through the air, caught by the wind. For a hopeful moment he wished it to stay suspended. He would be there to catch it. But he had no power over nature's pull. The rucksack fell into the water. The satchel descended to the river's depths.

Yet he still smelled alchemy.

Wind blew through the Rat Man, being of no consequence to his skeletal frame, but his wherry slowed from its force. The gale succeeded in keeping him just far enough away. When Bianca Goddard stood at the railing, the Rat Man could do nothing but watch. She hurled the journal with its secret for the elixir of life out over the water. The book spun and its covers opened. A silent scream rose from the depths of his being. Helplessly, the wraith watched the journal land on the surface of the Thames, then sink under its waters.

When he had reached the bridge with its twenty starlings, Bianca had gone. He searched the supports, hoping by chance that the book had landed on a wooden structure instead of the water. But his search was futile.

In his disappointment, he waited beneath the span for the tides to change twice before he ventured out from the darkest cavern, in the blackest hour of the night. The air had changed and with it came the small hint of chemistry. His nose twitched. His skiff darted out from an archway and disappeared under the drawbridge.

No one approached. No one passed overhead.

The Rat Man sniffed the air.

He listened.

The souls that dwelled within, the restless souls who sought their refuge while hounding his outcast state, rejoiced.

His work was not yet done.

There, against a wooden structure that had supported the bridge for three hundred years, lay a book. Half-submerged, its leather covers were spread like a cormorant drying its wings. The wraith moved close. He extended his pole, fishing the book into his boat. Some of the pages were sodden with water, but all was not ruined. He placed it upon his mound of dead rats.

Ferris Stannum's journal of alchemy.

CHAPTER 34

The sharp sliver of light through the window had softened with the day's end. Their questioning of Barnabas Hughes came to an end. Bianca, now satisfied she understood what had happened to her mentor, Ferris Stannum, thought of home and John.

She and Fisk left Barnabas Hughes with Constable Patch. No doubt the constable would smugly commend himself for solving yet another murder. Patch would have the justice of the peace draw up the necessary indictment and writ of arrest. Barnabas Hughes would face his end at the gallows at Tyburn.

Bianca and Fisk walked together as far as the Little Conduit on Cheapside.

"Ye be going to see about his daughter?" he asked.

"I promised I would," said Bianca, digging around in her pocket. She withdrew a groat. "This is for your trouble."

Fisk brightened, snatching the coin and tucking it inside the band of his cap.

"Someday you might undertake such duties of conscience without asking for money in return."

The boy shrugged in reply, set his cap on his head. With a sly smile, he took off running, as if late for his next misadventure.

Bianca turned in the direction of Barnabas Hughes's home. After a short walk, she discovered the lane, less traveled than most. A pair of oaks grew in side gardens, their limbs arching heavily over the road. From Hughes's description, Bianca found the stone building with ivy clinging to the front. He had said his neighbor, Goodwife Malcott, was caring for his daughter, though he expected she had probably taken her back to her rent, which was next door above their bakery.

After trying the door of the physician's home and finding it locked, Bianca knocked at the bakery shop door. In a moment a muffled footfall grew louder and the door creaked open. The plump face of a man peered out at her, his thick eyebrows holding a dusting of flour.

"The shop is closed for the night," he said wearily.

"Is this where Goodwife Malcott lives?"

"It is."

"I have been sent by Barnabas Hughes. He has asked me to see after Verity."

The man's expression was inscrutable, puzzling Bianca. She shifted uncomfortably under his steady gaze.

He asked, "Might I ask why the good physician sent you?"

"Unfortunately, sir, he is no longer able to care for her." Bianca felt a prickling guilt, having pressed Hughes into admitting murder. For a moment she was stricken with shame, realizing the consequence of her desire to know what had happened. She had, in effect, orphaned a child. And an ailing one, at that.

"Can you tell me why, all of a sudden, can he not care for her?"

Bianca swallowed. Her conscience screamed at her. She was no better than the physician who had murdered a man to save his child. London was rife with neglected children, cast from their homes due to loss or abuse. She saw them every day, wandering the streets, sleeping beneath empty food carts, their eyes vacant and scared. She thought of the two children with whom she had shared a wherry. She hoped they had found a loving home with their aunt. But so many children were not so fortunate. Was not John once among them? And her friend Jolyn?

Bianca stared past the baker into the dim light of his shop. She sought to care for a child who was already loved. Desperately loved. What could she offer the girl that her father could not? And now she had succeeded in denying the girl the one person who cared for her beyond all others. One day, the girl would ask about her father, and what would she say?

The baker's expression changed to disdain, and Bianca, in her sensitive state of mind, could not help but think his enmity was directed at her. And why not? Didn't she deserve the man's scorn?

He snorted. "Well, it is no matter now, I suppose. The child has passed."

Bianca started from her thoughts. "She has died?" Her voice sounded far away.

"You look as pale as milk," said the baker, seeing her blanch. He took hold of her elbow. "Here, come and sit." He guided her inside to a stool.

Unblinking, she lowered herself and sat. Her only chance to make good on her promise and she was too late.

The baker poured her a cup of ale and she dutifully drank. The ale wet her mouth and warmed her throat, but she did not taste it. He could have given her bilge water and she would not have noticed.

Was this God's grace? Was Verity's soul so inexplicably bound with her father's that neither of them could survive without the other?

"May I see her?" Bianca asked.

The baker led her up a stairwell to his quarters above the shop.

Inside, his two boys and a girl sipped boiled stew. They raised their heads at Bianca's arrival. Their spoons paused long enough so they could watch as she walked past. Near the front of the room facing the street, Goodwife Malcott stood beside a priest.

His susurrations were punctuated with the sound of slurping, but the children were mindful to keep from conversation until he finished his prayers. He glanced over his shoulder as Bianca neared, made no acknowledgment of her presence, and returned his attention to Verity. His murmurs and gesticulating continued without falter.

Bianca was struck by the child's angelic face. Her delicate nose and mouth resembled the physician's. Over her pillow, her fair hair spread like white ivy. Bianca wondered if its color had reminded Hughes of his wife's. Death had not stolen the child's innocent beauty or the gentle quality of her life.

It would have been easier for Bianca to have left when Malcott told her of Verity's passing. She could have let the baker and his wife tend to her final needs. After all, the child had been familiar with them and Bianca was nothing more than a stranger. But she wanted to see Verity. Bianca wanted her face emblazoned in her memory.

She waited for the priest's final "amen" and crossed herself. The smell of incense traveled the inroads of her memory to a time when she had obediently attended mass. When had she stopped going? When had she become so cynical?

Had her interest in chemical process and her desire to understand sickness replaced what tenuous belief she had in faith? Faith, with its demand to believe in the intangible, the impalpable, the abstruse. When had she decided that if God's existence could not be proven empirically, then there was no reason to believe?

She might not be any closer to deciding if she believed in God, but at least she believed in love. And was that not proof of the divine? The divine inherent in each of us?

Yet she could not deny a certain underlying steadfast certainty (or was it simply a wish?) that people's souls *were* immortal. A soul could not be seen. It could not be bottled. Did it even exist? But Bianca needed to believe that it did. If believing offered nothing more than comfort as one contemplated mortality, was that so wrong? There was nothing to lose by believing it so.

Bianca handed Goodwife Malcott the coins in her purse, saving enough for a fare home. She would later return with more.

Goodwife Malcott looked at her questioningly. The children stopped eating.

"For a resting place in consecrated soil."

With night falling, Bianca opted to take a wherry rather than cross the bridge on foot. To satisfy a question that had been troubling her since Hughes's confession, she strode past St. Benet's on her way to Burley House and Paul's Wharf. She slowed as she neared the spot where she'd been attacked two nights earlier. Bianca closed her eyes and, lifting her chin, sniffed. A heavy whiff of river and mudflat masked any underlying odors. She moved away from the bustling pedestrians and street traffic to the side of the lane and stood still. Turning her back to the river, she concentrated on the area's subtle undertones. As she sorted them out in her mind, cataloguing the foul from the less offensive, she caught the faint scent she'd been seeking. The sweet perfume of roses.

With eyes slit barely open, she followed its bouquet until it was strong. When a stone wall stopped her, she opened her eyes. It had not been her imagination that night. She had smelled roses. But the fragrance had not come from Tait's buttonhole. A rosebush twined with careless abandon in the rectory garden.

At Paul's Wharf, she shared a boat with a gentleman, too well dressed to be a resident of Southwark. He was probably out for an evening of recreation. She paid no heed to his appraising ogle, knowing it was typical, the disagreeable habit of men anticipating their visit with London's wanton sister.

The previous evening's wind had lingered, leaving a drier feel to the air. Even the rank odor that permeated London had been chased away. Or at least beaten down and momentarily forgotten.

Autumn's cool breath reminded her of winter's creeping imposition. Seasons didn't remain the same. Nothing remained forever. Time changed life, but she saw in winter's quiet attendance the opportunity for study and contemplation.

As she passed the neighbor's chicken coop in Gull Hole, Bianca's steps slowed as she neared her room of Medicinals and Physickes. Her life had been better for loving John, and she would follow that love through to its conclusion. Whether his end had already come or whether it would be ten years in the future, she knew that inevitably, it *would* come.

Instead of hesitating on the threshold, she took a breath and pushed open the door.

The room was dark. It kept its secrets. Hobs jumped from a height and padded over. She stroked his back, lit a candle, and raised it in the direction of the bed.

No movement or reaction issued in the light. John lay as she had left him. Her heart in her throat, Bianca went to him and touched his face.

He did not startle. His skin was still warm against her fingers. She sat and laid her ear on his chest. His heart beat softly. John was alive.

She watched him for a long while. She watched his chest rise and fall as if he were sleeping, wishing he were merely asleep but knowing he was not.

Bianca reached across and picked up her pillow. She held it in her lap. If she ended his suffering, her suffering, it would be easier to do it now rather than in the morning. Night mutes what would be harsh reality by day. Yet she could not place the pillow over his face.

Her mind churned. Rational thoughts tangled with her emotions until she was utterly confused from trying to sort it out.

Sleep would elude her. The only way to calm herself would be to begin another experiment. Chemistry would clear her head and eventually sleep would come.

Bianca placed the pillow beside John on the other side of the bed. With the knowledge she had gleaned from Ferris Stannum, she vowed to start anew. She would not let her mentor's accomplishments fade with his memory. The kerotakis for creating the elixir of life sat at the bottom of the Thames, but she knew what to try to get her sublimations to work.

Hobs watched with interest as she unhooked sprigs of silverweed from the rafters and ground the leaves in a mortar. Batting herbs off the table and chewing dried stems failed to engage her. Eventually, the black tiger tired of her single-minded focus and escaped through the window for greater adventures elsewhere.

She would start with a decoction, boiling the herb and mulberry root bark to extract their valuable properties. Starting a new remedy for the sweating sickness would give her time to think on what additional ingredients she might add. The process comforted her. She found solace in her methods, having practiced the steps so many times before.

The hours passed and Bianca's mind settled. Liquid bubbled in a glass cucurbit; the flame licked its round bottom while a vaporous cloud collected near the top of the alembic. The weight of the past week pulled her head to the table and she laid her cheek upon her arm. The familiar sound of flame and boiling liquid soothed her troubled heart. Bianca's eyelids closed.

Sleep spared her from thinking about John. Murder may have simmered in her subconscious, but at least for now she escaped its sad exigency. Any thoughts or dreams would escape her when next she stirred.

In this void, death was. If Bianca suddenly died without the pain and transformation that forced her soul from her body, this empty silence was what death would be. Emptiness and void were descriptive, but neither measured the essence of death.

Death cannot be defined with words or description. It was simply *not life*. But Bianca gave no thought to this, because in her exhausted sleep, she had no thoughts at all.

It was with dawn's first light that she felt a weight upon her shoulder. A touch so sure and familiar that it brought her sailing back through layers of consciousness. She blinked, remembering where she was, then jolted upright. In her haste to turn, she fell off the bench.

And John caught her.

GLOSSARY

Bawcock—a fine fellow

Boozing ken—a drinking establishment

Codpiece—a covering flap or pouch attached to men's hose to accentuate a man's genitals

Cozen—cheat

Cucurbit—a gourd-shaped flask

Cuffin—fellow

Div—a fool

Flicks—thieves

Footpad—robber or thief preying on pedestrians

Gates—stages of a chemical projection

Jackdaw—common bird

Jordan—chamber pot

Kirtle—dress worn by women

Ordinary—an eating establishment

Pizzle—penis

Pottle pot—a two-quart tankard

Puffer—a derogatory term for alchemist

Rakehell—scoundrel, libertine

Rampallian—a mean wretch

Sack—fortified wine from Spain

Starlings—bridge supports

Stew—brothel

Stibium—antimony, a silvery-white crystalline metal

Trug—slut, whore

Wodebroun blue—the blue color of the flower of bugleweed or *Ajuga reptans*

Zedoary—white turmeric, a perennial herb

AUTHOR'S NOTE

I began writing *Death of an Alchemist* during the 2014 Ebola outbreak in West Africa and epidemic scare in the United States. Hemorrhagic fevers are nothing new. Dengue and yellow fever are familiar hemorrhagic diseases, if only in name. The illnesses are usually viral and vector borne.

As a berry farmer I've seen alien pests and diseases introduced to our country that cause widespread impact on our ability to manage crops and our food supply. As a former health-care worker, I've also watched our country panic over epidemics that are feared could rage out of control.

Is there a hemorrhagic virus carried by parrots and transferred by a bite? Not that I found. But the reader will forgive my taking license with the concept. In Tudor England there were plenty of diseases that were mysterious and unexplained.

Sweating sickness is now believed to have been a variant of the modern hantavirus, perhaps carried by rodents. It was not a hemorrhagic fever, but I threw it into the mix to show how diseases can overlap and confuse, especially in a time when science was not around to distinguish them. Like the bubonic plague, the sweat was much feared and little understood.

While researching this book, I watched *Parrot Confidential*, a documentary that aired on PBS in 2013. The film brings attention to the problems of abandonment resulting from the overbreeding and importing of exotic birds. It is an incredible documentary. Please consider supporting the organizations struggling with this problem. Check the PBS *Nature* Web site for more information.

One last topic I wanted to mention. Homosexuality in the modern sense was not defined as such in the 1540s. It was considered an inclination and was believed to be part of human nature, though essentially it was thought of as a masculine sin. To the Tudor mindset, it could surface when judgment was dulled (perhaps from drink). Thus sodomy was a political and religious crime in Tudor England. It was a sin committed against the king: both celestial and terrestrial. One could be accused of treason and duly punished for it.

Many of the alchemy "phrases" were adapted from *Liber Secretisimus* by Sir George Ripley.

Again, I apologize for anachronisms and inaccuracies regarding language and syntax. My aim is to capture the "flavor" of the period without alienating modern readers. Some phrases are modernized on purpose.

Another liberty I took was with smoking tobacco; my characters exhibit attitudes more common to the 1580s. I imagine a few folks got hold of the weed before then, but I enjoy using it as a "particular" to Meddybemps's personality. The Bianca Goddard Mysteries hope to entertain and are not meant to be referenced as fact. It is my intention to accurately depict attitudes and history to the best of my ability, but I do not presume to get it perfect.

ACKNOWLEDGMENTS

I am writing this a few days before the release of my first book, *The Alchemist's Daughter*. It is strange wondering how the series will be received. I am grateful to the people who have contributed their help and expertise. . . .

My thanks to Fred and Susan Tribuzzo for their wonderful suggestions. Chatting with Fred gets the wheels moving, and the series is so much stronger for his insight and guidance.

Andrea Jones, what can I say? Thank you for your enthusiasm and love. To have a writer-friend who understands this insanity and truly supports from the heart is a precious find.

Thank you to Liliane Yacoub and Don Ross, pathologists extraordinaire, who steer me in the right direction in all things medical. If there are issues with how I present disease and mortality, it is completely my fault. They enthusiastically offer their opinions and are marvelous resources for me.

This book would have suffered immeasurably without Tracey Stewart's critical reading and editing. I am extremely fortunate to have found her. She kept Bianca from "grabbing" everything in sight.

Thank you to Megan Beattie, Jeff Umbro, and the PR/Marketing team at Kensington. It isn't easy getting attention in this noisy field.

Thanks to John Scognamiglio, my editor. I continue to be awed by his ability to remember small details about my stories and characters when he has to do it for hundreds of other books. Not only that, I can send him an email and get an answer in a few minutes. Amazing guy.

Thank you to the team at Kensington, from the art department to production. . . . I am lucky to be in such capable hands.

Thank you to coffee growers and distributors the world over. This book would not have happened without your fine product.

Dave, you are my anchor, my bosun, and the smile that keeps me sailing.

And finally, thanks and love to my family and friends who stand by me. Your support and reassurance means the world to me.